LUSH
LIFE

•

Books by Dallas Murphy

Apparent Wind

Artie Deemer novels:

Lush Life
Lover Man

Published by POCKET BOOKS

LUSH LIFE

•

DALLAS MURPHY

POCKET BOOKS
New York   London   Toronto   Sydney   Tokyo   Singapore

This book is a work of fiction. Names, characters, places, and incidents are either products of the author's imagination or are used fictitiously. Any resemblance to actual events or locales or persons, living or dead, is entirely coincidental.

 POCKET BOOKS, a division of Simon & Schuster Inc.
1230 Avenue of the Americas, New York, NY 10020

Murphy, Dallas.
  Lush life / Dallas Murphy.
    p.   cm.
  ISBN 0-671-68555-4 : $20.00
  I. Title.
  PS3563.U7283L87   1992
  813'.54—dc20   92-18546
                                                              CIP

First Pocket Books hardcover printing October 1992

10   9   8   7   6   5   4   3   2   1

POCKET and colophon are registered trademarks of Simon & Schuster Inc.

Printed in the U.S.A.

For my folks

My thanks to Norman Bloch, Damien Bona, Jane Chelius, Fran Crimi, James Griffith, Douglas Grover, David Konigsberg, Ken Kurtenbach, Wade Leftwich, Myron Schulman, John Thackray, Pat Thackray, the folks at Amsterdam Billiards—Greg Hunt, Ethan Hunt, and David Brenner—my friends at Paperback Discounter Video 83, and as always to Eugenia Leftwich.

A Note on Nine Ball

THE OBJECT OF THE POOL GAME called nine ball is simple—pocket the nine ball, and you win. The balls must be played in numerical order, one through nine. To make a legal shot (as opposed to a "foul") all you must do is cause the cue ball to hit the lowest-numbered ball on the table. This is referred to as a "good hit." Thus, you can win the game at any time by hitting the lowest-numbered ball in such a way as to cause it to sink the nine. This is called a "combination shot." Since there are so few balls in the game, good players can often "run out," in other words, sink every ball in numerical order up to and including the nine. But let's say your opponent runs balls one through eight, playing brilliantly, but he/she misses the nine. If you then make the nine, you win. Sinking that ball is all that matters.

These are the general rules. There are some subtleties. There is, for instance, the "one-foul, ball-in-hand" rule. A foul results when a player scratches or fails to make a good hit. The penalty for a foul is serious, often decisive: the other player gets to place the cue ball *anywhere* on the table before he starts shooting. From that start, even medio-cre players often run out.

A NOTE ON NINE BALL

You can try to cause your opponent to foul by driving the lowest-numbered ball into a strategically disadvantageous position, say, behind a cluster of higher-numbered balls. Since now he cannot hit the lowest ball directly, your opponent must bank the cue ball off one or more rails to make a good hit. Even if he succeeds, you have forced him to make a purely defensive shot.

Nine ball is all about cue-ball control. The point isn't just to pocket that lowest ball, because doing so means nothing. The point is to pocket it and move the cue ball around the table in such a way as to leave yourself a good shot on the next lowest, and the next, and so on up to the nine or to an easy combination on the nine. It takes several years of experience to learn how to "play position" and many more to execute it consistently.

Finally, a word about the handicapping system in nine ball: in order to give a lesser player a chance against a better player, the lesser is given a "spot." The spot comes in the form of a second "pay ball." The spot is agreed upon before the match begins. Say the lesser player gets the seven ball as his spot. He now has two ways of winning, either by sinking the seven ball or the nine ball. From the better player's perspective, this is called "giving weight." If no spot is involved—if the players' ability, or "speed," is equal—the game is said to be played "head up."

LUSH
LIFE

.

OWNING A WEALTHY DOG frees up one's schedule. While other poor sods who don't own wealthy dogs must work for the man, I can devote my days to any endeavor that takes my interest.

That was my trouble. None did. I remained uncommitted. I felt guilty about that. I listened to hours of jazz and played a lot of pool. While jazz uplifts the spirit, listening can't be called *doing* in the participatory sense, and playing pool can't be called productive, even if one wins a lot of money. I don't. I was languid, torpid, depressed.

I had retreated inside my head. That had always been my way. As a child, I had thought of that solipsistic retreat as "going into the tree house." My father got killed in an airplane crash when I was still an infant, and my mother, as I look back on it, launched herself on a quest to marry, then divorce, as many fighter pilots as possible. They were a swaggering lot, full of certainty and self-confidence. The absence of a shooting war was the most vexing problem in their young lives.

One high-ranking type with whom we shared a year in a sultry southern climate before he got transferred to Goose Bay, Labrador, was called Spider. Spider had brush-cut hair and boozy breath. He lived off base in a decaying mansion surrounded by live oaks already mature when Sherman's army passed. In one of these, dripping Spanish moss, was a duplex tree house with a rope ladder and complete privacy. Up there, I fashioned my own reality. I've been doing that ever since.

But now solitude had degenerated into discontent, an itchy longing for something I didn't have. What did I long for? I spent many an evening listening to bebop and musing on that question. Did I long for a job of my own?

Job . . .

The very sound of the word, its hard monosyllabic poke, filled me with dread. Besides, who would hire me? *I* wouldn't hire me.

As he lay at my feet dreaming (paws flexing, tail thumping) I wondered whether Jellyroll would miss his career if I decided to retire him. Say I decided to chuck it in and move us to the rural regions, there to take up organic farming, or to the coast of Maine, say, to experiment in mariculture, would he grow dull and dispirited? (Would I?) The limelight's hard to kick over, even for dogs. Yet lately his career had been making me feel absurd. Take, for example, the day the Space Traveler broke his tibia:

Intergalactic music swelled from out of the cosmic darkness. A pinpoint of light appeared, approaching, enlarging as it spanned imponderable distance at unearthly speed. What could it be? A spaceship, of course. It whooshed overhead.

Saucer-shaped, a stupid-looking dome in the center, the spaceship wheeled, turned, and reappeared, hovering. The engines didn't roar or whine like you would expect spaceship engines to; they went, "R-r-ruff, r-r-ruff." Steam and smoke swirled. The intergalactic music built to a cre-

2

scendo. Red, green, and blue spotlights probed the ground before they converged—on a big yellow bowl of dog food.

Then a disembodied voice reverberated from the spaceship: "Contact. We have contact-tact-tact. We're beginning our approach-approach-approach."

The music was intolerable, of course, the engine noise ludicrous, but the landing effect worked okay, and the lighting disguised the spaceship's cheesy, cut-corners construction as it appeared to settle beside the bowl of dog food. "NEW & IMPROVED R-r-ruff" was painted in glossy red letters on the bowl.

The hatch creaked open. A gangplank emerged, but then it wedged in its track and stuck fast. It retracted and tried again. Nope. Again it stuck in the same place, poking out like a vandalized diving board.

"Cut, for chrissake!" Brian Thornbough, our director, bellowed from the control room. "What town is this? Hickberg, Indiana? No? New York City? Oh. You'd think in New York City, the capital of the stinking world, I wouldn't have to be saddled with a rickety pile of pus for a spaceship!" His words reverberated around the soundstage like the Space Traveler's.

Work lights came on. Sullen technicians—it wasn't their fault, it was the budget cutbacks—scurried from the shadows. They braced their boots against the hull of the spaceship and, on three, heaved at the gangplank, but it was no use. The gangplank was stuck.

"It's stuck," somebody said.

"No shit?" boomed Brian from the booth.

"The whole frame has shifted," said the floor manager, glowering up at the booth, "so the gangplank's pinched."

"Grease the slut!"

Chips flew as the floor manager took a hammer and chisel to the gangplank, pretending it was Brian's brainpan. His crew waited to grease the slut.

3

"Are we *about* ready?" Brian wanted to know. Brian had tried to make a go of it in Hollywood, but he was pegged as a dog food commercial director, and nobody would give him a smell. That had made Brian bitter.

Work lights went off. Landing lights came back on. "Stand by, steam," said the floor manager. "Go, steam." The steam went. Music recrescendoed. They cued the plank. The plank worked perfectly. Its foot settled onto the floor right beside the bowl of New & Improved R-r-ruff.

Then Jellyroll, a cute brown-and-white mutt, ran happily down the gangplank toward the bowl of dog food exactly as rehearsed. (He doesn't need rehearsal for a move that simple. In fact, I think it bores him.) Jellyroll enjoys everything, except baths and vacuum cleaners, and his delight with life is apparent on his face. That smile has made him a star and me financially, if in no other way, untroubled.

The Space Traveler wore a transparent bubble helmet, like an inverted goldfish bowl, over his head. His gleaming white suit was so bulbous and heavy he had to bounce stiff-legged down the gangplank. He stopped halfway and pretended to look around the landing zone. His helmet fogged up. The techies had drilled holes in the back to alleviate that problem, but apparently they were too small. He tried to do a double take when he spotted the dog food, but the move got lost in the costume. It just looked like someone had goosed him—

"Look, Ruff!" he said. "After all these intergalactic light-years we've found a planet that serves *New and Improved R-r-ruff*. This must be earth!"

But something was wrong with Jellyroll. . . .

He slunk up to the bowl and wrinkled his muzzle in repulsion. That pause, the silence, was terrible. We held our breaths. I thought for a moment he was going to puke. . . . Jellyroll hated the New & Improved formula! He searched for me with confusion and alarm in his soft brown eyes. Why was I doing this to him, putting this shit in his face after years of loyalty?

It seemed days before Brian bellowed, "Cut!"

The technical folks tried to quell their giggles. A couple of them had to leave the set. Strangled titters bounced around the studio as Brian marched onto the floor. Christ, the spokesdog hated the New & Improved formula!

"Uh, since we've stopped, Brian," said the Space Traveler, further fogging his helmet, "let me ask you this—" I had seen the Space Traveler do Robespierre in *Danton's Death* off-Broadway, and he seemed to be a real actor. I felt sad for him up there in that helmet. "I don't exactly understand the line, 'After all these intergalactic light-years—' Isn't a light-year a measure of speed, not—"

The gangplank snapped. The Space Traveler plunged from sight like a hanged man.

"Deemer!" shouted Brian. Brian always shouted. "Get me Artie Deemer!"

"Right here," I said.

"Did my eyes deceive me, or does that dog hate the New and Improved formula?"

"He didn't seem to relish it, did he?"

"Relish? Are you kidding, relish? He about barfed at the stink of it!"

The Space Traveler began to keen in agony beneath the gangplank's remains.

"I think he's injured, Brian," I pointed out.

"Space Travelers come a dime a dozen. He liked the other shit—the regular formula, right? Somebody get me a bag of the regular shit."

"No," said a somber voice from the rear of the studio, "we can't do that." It was Mr. Fleckton, the poor sod who had conceived and spearheaded the introduction of New & Improved R-r-ruff.

"Christ! She's gonna go!" screamed a technician.

The spaceship was wavering on its landing pad, creaking and groaning, its structural members cracking. The Space Traveler cried out in terror. Techies scurried in all directions, but they knew exactly what to do. They ran back onto the set with wood and heavy hammers, shoved two-by-four bracing beneath the ship, pounded and kicked it into place.

"Why not?" Brian wanted to know.

"My leg!" wailed the Space Traveler. "I can see my leg bone!"

"Because I'd be a laughingstock, that's why," said Mr. Fleckton. He shuffled up beside Brian and me. He held his hands in a strange prayerlike posture under his chin. Beads of sweat sprouted from his upper lip. The man was watching his standard of living diminish to homelessness before his very eyes. He looked at me pleadingly and said, "Does he really hate it, Artie?"

"He hates it," said Brian. "What can I tell you, he hates it."

Mr. Fleckton kept removing his glasses, blowing on the lenses, and replacing them. "Our own spokesdog . . . hates it. Is there nothing you can do, Artie?"

The Space Traveler whimpered from out of sight beneath the spacecraft. "I can *see* my leg . . . bone!"

"I'll try to hand-feed him," I said.

"Food! Get me fresh food!" demanded Mr. Fleckton. One of his assistants hurried over with a twenty-pound bag of it.

"Come here, pal," I said gently.

"God help us," said Fleckton.

I scooped a few pieces of kibble from the bag and petted Jellyroll with the other hand so he'd know I wasn't mad at him. I held a single kibble under his nose. He turned his head. He blew out his lips as if to expunge the stink of the thing. "He hates it, all right."

Mr. Fleckton wavered like the spaceship. His assistants supported him. The R-r-ruff honchos would probably have him executed gangland style and dump his body in the Meadowlands beside that of the guy who invented New Coke.

"I think I'm gonna . . . pass out," said the Space Traveler weakly.

"Fuck it, let's just stick a steak under it," said Brian.

As I mused subsequently in my morris chair, Brian's words, *"Stick a steak under it,"* struck a metaphorical chord with me. That's what I should do with my life, I decided. But what was the real-world equivalent of this metaphorical meat I'd stick under my life? I pondered that question, Jellyroll at my feet, listening to Ben Webster's assertively erotic version of "Love Is Here to Stay," when the answer struck me like an epiphany.

I needed to fall in love.

I had been in love before, and I remembered how love took the edge off the hideous, how it brightened the world and made one feel all warm and runny inside. . . . But whom would I love? Where might I meet my new lover? I had read in a magazine that the two best places to meet a lover were at work or at recreation. I didn't work, and for recreation I hung around a pool hall. I wondered what the third best place was.

Shortly thereafter, I met Crystal Spivey—in the poolroom.

2.

MY DISBARRED ATTORNEY, Bruce Munger,
introduced us.

"Don't call me Bruce," said Bruce.

"Who are you today?"

"Viscount Pitt." He also went by the names Mr. DeSoto,
Special Agent Rock, Captain Jacoby, and Samuel Beckett.
There were others. "Never mind that now, just back me
for fifty bucks. I can beat this guy. This guy is a no-talent
bum. Besides, what's fifty bucks to you?" My attorney was
talking about Too Louis, who stood, cue in hand, grinning
greedily, hoisting his seeds from between crushing thighs.

"Wha' chu wan' do, Bruce?" cooed Too Louis.

"Don't call me Bruce."

Bruce was partly right. Too Louis was a bum. He lived
with his mother, and together they sold cheap stolen goods
on St. Mark's Place. Too Louis was ugly enough to break
your heart. He took the aesthetics right out of the game.
But he had talent. It was my attorney, already down $150,
who lacked talent. Thus far the games had only seemed
close.

"Come on, Artie, I got this fish right where I want him,"
my attorney whispered. "He's overconfident. He's ready to

give me the seven ball. The seven! I can *stomp* him with the seven ball."

"Not if you continue to dog the six," I pointed out.

"Look, I'll tell you what. If you place Jellyroll's financial might behind me to the tune of fifty bucks, I'll introduce you to Crystal Spivey. Don't think I don't notice how you moon over Crystal Spivey."

"I don't moon."

My attorney called to Outta-Town Brown, who sat on the bench in the corner with a group of regulars: "Hey, Brown, does Artie moon over Crystal Spivey or what?"

"Moooon River, wider than a mile," sang Outta-Town Brown. Ted Bundy and Chinese Gordon giggled. "I'm crossing you in style sommmmeday."

I ignored that.

I had tried to meet Crystal on my own. Once, when she was practicing alone, I strolled by her table with Jellyroll. He is so cute, friendly, and famous that most women fall all over themselves to pet him, thus leaving me an entrée to introduce myself. Crystal was no different. She had just stroked the cue ball with that lovely, languid follow-through of hers. It was a tricky sharp-angle shot, but the object ball split the pocket and the cue ball softly caressed three rails with running English, then stopped precisely where she wanted it to. "Isn't that the R-r-ruff Dog?" she asked.

I smiled. "Yes, he's—"

Crystal knelt and ruffled his ears. I admired her stately neck below boyishly bobbed black hair. Jellyroll smiled at her and began to lick her cheek.

I envied him that. "I'm Artie Deemer. I—"

"Oh, you are *wonderful!*"

For a giddy instant I had thought she meant me.

She presented her other cheek to Jellyroll and mewed over him. They carried on like that for a while. I stood shifting my weight from one leg to the other. She nuzzled his muzzle; he kissed and kissed.

"I'm Artie Deemer."

"Uh-huh," she said without looking up. Then she straightened, picked up her cue, and resumed sinking balls as if she could do it in her sleep, with me mooning around or off visiting business associates on Baffin Island. Only recently have women pool players come into their own as professionals, but most still maintain a guarded pose, because there's always somebody waiting to hit on them in poolrooms.

"You don't know Crystal Spivey," I said to my attorney.

"I do indeed. In fact, we were an item once."

"You were not."

"Well, we almost were. She wanted me, but I had to demur in the interests of my practice. She hung around poolrooms with those of questionable character. That would have given the appearance of infelicity. Felicity is bad enough. *Infelicity* is out of the question. C'mon, Artie, fifty bluchers. I can beat this cretin, after which I'll take you and Crystal out for an eau de vie."

I gave my attorney fifty bucks. Jellyroll looked up at me. His eyes seemed to say, "You are a true chump." Then I sat down on the regulars' bench to wait for Crystal to come in. Outta-Town Brown, Ted Bundy, and Chinese Gordon sat with me. I tried not to watch my attorney lose, but fifty bucks isn't such a high price to pay to meet the woman you moon over, if you don't have to watch.

"Hey, Artie," said Ted Bundy out of the side of his mouth. Ted's real name was Albert Bundy. Naturally, everybody called him Ted. "You ain't backing that fish of a viscount, are you?"

"Do you think I'm a chump?"

Ted didn't reply.

Pool has changed. The game is enjoying a prosperity and

wide interest it hasn't known since the twenties. With that, there has arisen something entirely new—the upscale poolroom. Now, instead of in grotty dives where your shoes stick to the floor, you can play in refined rooms with attendants who empty the ashtrays. Now respectable contributors to the GNP, real citizens who have checking accounts and pay income tax, play pool on double dates. In some poolrooms today, you can order herbal tea and veal sandwiches with Mornay sauce, and no one will question your sanity or sexuality.

I had spent many years in grotty, preboom poolrooms. I could hear my mother's voice from out of the murk of the past: "Arthur, where are you going? You're going out to play pool with bums, aren't you?"

"Oh, no, Mom. I'm going over to work on the homecoming float." I envisioned myself sticking multicolored tissue paper up a chicken-wire badger's ass and turned left to the poolroom. I should be a better player than I am. Maybe I lack talent. Or drive. Or what my mother used to call "gumption."

Ted Bundy said, "I'm worried about our nation. Take this fuckhead President, for example. Here's a guy can't run four balls in a row, yet he's boss over a major country."

Thumper, an aging amputee, swayed over and sat down on the regulars' bench. He stretched out his existing leg painfully. "Artie, you wouldn't be interested in a top of the line Toro Snowblower, would you?"

"No. I don't blow much snow."

"Your Toro never loses its resale value. You don't need to use it. Toro's a solid investment."

"Hey, Brown," said Ted Bundy.

"What?"

"I'll play you one game for a t'ousand."

"Let's go," said Outta-Town Brown.

"Of course, I'll need weight," said Ted.

In poolrooms talk is incessant, talk is a way of life.

"Here it comes," said Brown, rolling his eyes. "What weight do you need?"

"The seven and the eight."

"Are you nuts? Are you twisted? The seven and the eight? This guy can beat me head up, and he wants me to give him the seven and the eight. Charity. He expects charity. Charity belongs in the home. Besides which, I don't give weight to no serial killers."

"I also need the break."

"I'm speechless."

"We should be so lucky," said Chinese Gordon, who'd heard it all before.

"One game for a t'ousand. Right now, rack 'em up. Oh, I forgot to mention—you got to bank the nine at least six rails."

"You're deeply full of shit, Ted," said Brown. "You ain't even ever seen a grand in one location before. If I was gonna give weight to somebody in a big-money game, I'd give it to somebody with money, somebody, say, with a rich dog."

The regulars thought Jellyroll's existence behooved me to lose enough to each of them to put their loved ones through the colleges of their choice. "Okay, Brown," I said just to hear him say it, "I'll play you some straight pool next week."

"I'll be outta town."

"Hey, Brown," said Ted Bundy right on cue, "just what is it you *do* outta town?"

"I travel."

Jellyroll sprawled on my feet. I scratched between his ears the way he likes.

"One game for a t'ousand. Rack 'em up."

Nobody moved.

The PA system emitted piercing squeals of feedback,

then Davey, the deskman, announced, "Phone call for Thumper. Thumper, you gotta call." Thumper made his tortured way toward the desk.

By this time my attorney was down three games to none. Too Louis wasn't even trying to make it look good.

Never-Miss Monroe came in. He did so each and every day. He'd carefully rack all fifteen balls, place the cue ball on the head spot, screw together his custom-made, mother-of-pearl-inlaid, ebony four-point cue, lean it against the side pocket, and then he'd sit down on the bench. Never-Miss would light a great stinking stogie, cheeks puffing like Diz soloing on the cigar—and sit. He never played, he never hit a single ball. Ever. As a result of this routine, Never-Miss Monroe had attained legendary stature.

"Hey, Monroe, how you hittin' 'em?"

"I'm playing like God."

"Can't miss, huh?"

"Not without I try."

Legend had grown up around Never-Miss. It held that he was a hustler/gambler of the old school, the sort who'd travel the nation pretending to be a bumpkin in shitty coveralls with a sprig of straw in his mouth. The locals would fight over who'd get to skin him. Then he'd take them for every cent in the room and beat it out the window in the john.

Never-Miss, it was said, used to bet on absolutely anything, and that's how he arrived at his current pathetic state. Caught on the golf course in an electrical storm, he bet his partner two grand that the partner would get struck by lightning before he did. They went out on the fairway and held sand-trap rakes over their heads like Benjamin Franklin. Never-Miss won. A bolt fried his partner's footprints into the grass. Ironically, the bolt leapt across to Monroe's rake. It didn't injure him physically, but it turned him weird.

The legend further held that Monroe, who found only eight charred bucks in his dead partner's pockets, hit the widow up for the winnings right after the funeral. He is said to have pointed to the gaping grave and announced, "I knew this guy like a brother. He wouldn'ta wanted to go down a welsher."

"Hey, Monroe, I'll play you one game for a t'ousand," said Ted Bundy.

"What game, Ted?"

"Nine ball. One game for a t'ousand."

"I don't play nine ball, Ted. Nine ball is a game for riffraff. Sheep fuckers play nine ball. I play straight pool, Ted. Only straight pool."

"Okay, straight pool for a t'ousand."

"You're on, Ted."

Nobody moved. Chinese Gordon sighed deeply and said, "Anybody wanna order out?"

Thumper hobbled back and took his place on the regulars' bench.

"Hey, Thumper, I'll play you one game for a t'ousand."

"One game of what, Ted?"

"Hopscotch."

Too Louis made the nine on the break and chortled, setting several layers of blubber twitching and pulsing.

"Hey, Too Louis," said Viscount Pitt, "when's the last time you saw your prick without a mirror?"

Time was running short for my fifty dollars, but Crystal hadn't come in yet. Too Louis scuttled around the table, thighs chafing, sinking balls, and when he lacked reasonable run-out opportunities, he played smart, demoralizing safeties. My attorney seemed to be growing visibly smaller each time he stepped to the table.

Crystal Spivey walked in carrying her hand-tooled leather cue case. She wore tight jeans and an attractive fuchsia tank top with no bra. I mooned as subtly as possible. Outta-Town Brown elbowed me in the ribs and giggled.

My attorney didn't get a shot in game five.

Savage feedback, followed by Davey: "Phone call for Ernie's wife. Ernie's wife, you gotta call." Ernie's wife had gotten good enough to beat Ernie's brains out, so Ernie never came in anymore.

Crystal took a table by herself and began to assemble her break cue and her playing cue.

My attorney got a shot in game six, actually made two balls, the two and the three, and the rest of the table up to his seven-ball spot looked easy. He missed the four. Too Louis ran out.

Crystal was practicing by shooting the same long-rail shot time after time. With some shame, I tried to look down her top, but she was too far away.

In the next game, Too Louis made the one on the break, and the nine rolled to a stop in front of the end pocket, four inches behind the two ball. My attorney whimpered. Too Louis pounded in the two-nine combination. "Double or nothin'?" Greed seemed to make Louis lighter on his feet, almost balletic.

My attorney would actually have done it. He looked to me and made that money sign by rubbing his thumb and forefinger together.

I motioned him over. "If you don't introduce me to Crystal Spivey right now, you'll never get another red cent."

"Okay, okay. But first a word." He grasped my elbow and glanced around furtively as if somebody might be listening. He always did that as a way to enhance the significance of the bullshit he was about to shovel on the listener. "There's something I should tell you about Crystal."

"What?"

"She's married."

My heart sank.

15

"You'll never imagine who to. To Trammell Weems."

"No—!"

"God's own. As a matter of fact, I introduced them. Trammell, of course, paid me handsomely for that service, but I wouldn't expect the same from you. At least not until something comes of the relationship."

I had ambivalently attended law school about a hundred years ago at a second-rate southern institution which should remain nameless. Among my fellow students, using that word loosely, were Bruce Munger and Trammell Weems. There were Weemses on the *Mayflower*. A Weems had signed the Declaration of Independence and served as secretary of the treasury in the Adams administration. Another from the naval side of the family fought under Farragut at Mobile Bay, charted a major chunk of Antarctica, and invented some kind of celestial-navigation wrinkle for determining longitude. And there was Thaddeus Weems, the powerful publisher of a New York abolitionist newspaper who is supposed to have carried on a lifelong affair with Harriet Beecher Stowe.

While we were in law school, Trammell's uncle was the senior senator from Virginia. There was also a famous Doctor Weems, who did something big in the battle against tropical disease, but I forgot just what. Then there was the famous psychologist after whom a syndrome or two were named. And, of course, the world of finance and international banking was aswarm with Weemses.

Plus Trammell himself had been a child star. He played Timmy in "The Mayhews," a sickening comedy series about family life that the entire nation watched in the early sixties. He had contacts everywhere. And he had the brains and charm to do anything he wanted, even without the heavy family connections. But Trammell wanted only to be a professional black sheep. He referred to his kin as "the inbreds." He wanted mainly to climb up on some high place and flash obscene gestures at them, anything at all to offend, embarrass, and outrage them.

In school, he seldom bathed. His hair, tied in a ponytail with fat rubber bands, was always matted and greasy. The drunken old coach who ran the gym where we played handball insisted Trammell take showers *before* he played or go find another gym to stink up, fucking hippies. This pleased Trammell. Also, being at the bottom of the class pleased him. Only Bruce scored lower, until Trammell bribed someone to falsify Bruce's records, moving him up out of the place Trammell viewed as his birthright.

Trammell Weems was also a doper. One of the reasons I discontinued my study of the law was that I didn't want to be a lawyer, but another was that law school became a threat to my physical and mental health. I had a brush with dangerous drugs. So did Bruce. Trammell led the way. We lacked the character to resist. In fact, we flocked along.

"Look, students, at what I got from my cousin at the San Diego Zoo—*rhino* tranks. These soothe the savage beasts."

There was medicinal-strength acid from the uncle-with-the-syndrome's office, ether from the Boston School of Medicine, pure THC, Vietnamese pot, Campuchian opium mailed to us by Ambassador Weems's assistant, Apache peyote, and a lot of pills from vets at the San Diego Zoo. The ingestion of these interfered with my understanding of jurisprudence. The law school agreed.

"Wait," said Bruce. "Did I say Crystal was married to Trammell? I meant to say Crystal *was* married to Trammell."

"You mean they are no longer?"

"Exactly."

"Bruce, is this bullshit?"

"Absolutely not. Crystal Spivey and Trammell Weems were husband and wife in the sight of God. But He blinked. However, if I were you, I wouldn't mention you knew Trammell. It's a sore subject with her."

Coincidences no longer surprise me. I think that at about the age when one recognizes that all governments lie, one has seen enough coincidences not to be knocked out by the next.

"Hi, Crystal—" said my attorney.

"Beat it," said Crystal without looking up from her stance.

"Come on, Crystal, don't be like that. I want you to meet an old friend of mine. We attended divinity school together."

"If he's a friend of yours, why would I want to know him?"

"I'm no friend of his," I said. "I picked him up hitchhiking."

Crystal peered at me. "You're the guy who owns the R-r-ruff Dog."

"Right. Absolutely."

"Where is he?"

"Jellyroll," I called. He had been lying on Ted's shoes, but he leapt up and trotted over for me to take advantage of his household name.

Crystal knelt down to fuss over him, and he kissed her cheek. She said, "Since you're no friend of this bum's, maybe you want to play some. I need to beat someone for practice."

At first I didn't realize she was talking to me. "Sure." Did she like me, or was she just after my dog?

Bruce hung around kibitzing for a while as Crystal and I played, but, ignored, he finally wandered off. "Excuse me," he said, "I think I'll just go into the john and open a vein."

"Make sure you use the men's john," Crystal said.

"You play pretty good," she said to me after she'd won the first set. I had made her work hard for it, however, and she seemed to enjoy that. I enjoyed watching her move around the table, deep in concentration, planning her

18

moves, improvising when necessary, a lithe feline predator on the scent. Her long, fluid stroke seemed to me to be the most exciting thing I'd seen in a woman. She made the game beautiful.

I, too, was concentrating with an intensity unfamiliar to me. I had to. Whenever I made a mistake, Crystal would run the game out. We didn't talk much, and I tried to keep her braless fuchsia tank top separate from the business at hand. Pool is not a social game when played seriously, but we were communicating. We were speaking to each other across the great green gulf.

Once while I was racking the balls after Crystal had run out from the break with textbook control over the cue ball, she knelt down to pet Jellyroll, who was lounging happily under the table. "So do you work or do you live off your dog?"

"Oh no, I'm a hard worker."

"Yeah? At what?"

"I'm a test pilot."

She nodded.

"Spaceships, mostly. Very dangerous work."

Crystal broke the balls with that ferocious full-bodied snap of hers, and the nine rolled directly into the corner pocket like it had eyes and intent. She glanced up at me almost coquettishly from under her bangs as if to say, "There, that's what men get when they bullshit me, even in fun." I was utterly captivated by that break of hers. I felt as I watched her break that something wonderful had come into my life, and for the moment I forgot about Trammell Weems.

She missed finally, and I got a shot. I proceeded to run out the game, cleanly, never losing control of the cue ball, machine-precise, as if I did that every day. I was out of my head.

Ted Bundy's voice, from behind, said, "Anybody seen Artie Deemer? Glasses, geeky sort of fellow. Got a dog."

A crowd of regulars had gathered to watch. Here and there side bets were being settled. I hadn't even noticed their presence. The intimacy was blown.

"Are you free for dinner tonight?" I asked Crystal.

"No, but I am tomorrow night."

"Fine, I'll pick you up about eight. Oh, where do you live?"

"Sheepshead Bay."

"Brooklyn?"

"Yeah, it's one of the boroughs, south of here." Her eyes twinkled.

"How about coming over to my place for dinner?"

"Where do you live?"

"One hundred and fourth and Riverside Drive."

"Okay."

How quickly life changes.

3

I FELL INTO AN ANXIOUS SNIT. Too intimate, dinner at my place. I was getting ahead of myself, inflicting my private life on her, a virtual stranger. Besides, I wasn't that hot a cook. The entire evening would make her nervous. We'd stare glassy-eyed at each other. She'd leave early.

Wait. Why was I being so juvenile? Weren't we both reasonably cosmopolitan adult New Yorkers capable of at least one dinner and conversation? How hard was that? . . . However, I had been alone for a long time. Maybe I didn't even know how to act around available women anymore. Maybe I'd become an eccentric hermit.

Jellyroll recognized that something big was afoot, because I cleaned house from stem to stern. He sat watching with a smile on his face, thumping his tail on the floor every time I glanced his way. He barked and snarled at the vacuum cleaner, lips curled, teeth bared, tail wagging at the same time—I unintentionally traumatized him with the vacuum cleaner when he was a tiny puppy, and now he attacks its hoses and attachments. It's part of the routine of our lives. Cleaning accomplished, I went out to buy groceries.

One difference between New York and most other places is that in most other places you can go out to buy groceries without seeing the fabric of society unravel before your eyes. It's one reason why New Yorkers move so quickly. The walking dead wandered Broadway shoeless. The visibly insane, with no other place to piss, pissed on the hubcaps of parked cars. Because of the budget cutbacks, cardboard refrigerator crates had taken the place of public housing. The cruelty of class overwhelms the grocery shopper. I gave a woman with no teeth and dried shit stains on her insteps a five.

Remembering the effect Crystal's top had on me, I bought a bouquet of fuchsia-colored anemones. Emerging from the florist's, I ran into Seth, an embittered playwright, towing his bent shopping cart and his pale of funk. Everybody tries to duck Seth because he's so depressing, but I kind of like him. "How's it going, Seth?"

He stopped, rolled his eyes and sighed. "Had this staged reading last night. Broken Ass Rep. Way the fuck and gone out Queens Boulevard."

"How'd it go?"

"Things don't loosen up, I'm gonna have to get a job." The very thought seemed to bring up hot bile. He grimaced.

From the island in the center of Broadway, where winos repose, Crazy Rodney jumped out in front of a northbound car with Massachusetts plates. The driver stomped the brakes, skidded to a neck-snapping halt, and Crazy Rodney, who wears a pair of found golf shoes, leapt back onto the island, cleats clattering, where he lay on his back and clutched his stomach against peals of deranged laughter. The family of faces in the Massachusetts car had turned ashen. I could see them all jabbering at once.

"Goddamnsonofabitch!" the father probably bellowed.

"Don't say anything, Harvey! Roll up the window! That person's obviously insane."

"So's this whole stinking town! Fuck you, New York!"

"Fuck you, New York," the little towheads in the backseat began to chant, "fuck you, New York, fuck you—"

Crazy Rodney hadn't been doing his traffic-jumping routine for a while. About a year ago, he had disappeared from the neighborhood. The life expectancy of the Rodneys in New York is below the national average, so I figured somebody had killed him for no reason. Then Rodney returned—with a savage limp. For months, he hadn't jumped in front of a car. He was still limping when he leapt in front of the Massachusetts car. I guess traffic-jumping is a hard habit to kick.

"That'll be me in a few years," muttered Seth, "things don't loosen up. Hey, Artie, I hate to ask, but could you spot me a twenty?"

Heading home, I saw Mrs. Fishbein halfway down the block. She was going my way, lugging a bag of groceries, little shuffling strides on bunioned feet. "Hello, Mrs. Fish—"

"Ach! Ach! . . . Oh, Artie! *Mein Gott,* you scare me! I thought you vas a mugger!" She reached inside her coat, clutched her heart and squeezed to get it going again. The temperature approached eighty-five degrees, but Mrs. Fishbein wore a heavy wool ankle-length coat and fur earmuffs that looked like twin road kills clamped around her head.

"Want me to carry your packages?" I picked them up and about ruptured myself. What the hell was in the bags? New anvils?

"Za neighborhood, ach, it rots. All zis foreigners—zay make za neighborhood lousy. Some foreign mugger, he hit you on za head—boof, you're a vegytable."

I didn't say anything one way or the other. Mrs. Fishbein never listens anyway.

"And you know who iz za vurst mugger? Za verst iz

your homosessual mugger. Of course you—you're one of za good vuns."

"Good one what, Mrs. F.?"

"Homosessual."

"God knows I try."

All the way to our door, she kept slapping the palm of her hand and saying, "Boof, you're a vegytable."

Back at the ranch, I puttered and fussed and worried about my living room. I put Johnny Hartman's "Lush Life," John Coltrane's quartet in brilliant support, on the box, stoked up the volume, and let that glorious voice wash over me. By 7:30, I was as ready as I'd ever be. . . .

A vision in my hallway! She wore a dress! I had never seen her in a dress. This one was yellow. It left her shoulders bare. (I admit that I coveted the hollow place between her collarbones and the upward turn of her neck.) The hem fell to a delightful spot just above her knees, and the airy fabric clung fetchingly to her breasts and hips. She wore sheer nude stockings and low-heeled shoes with open toes.

I felt flattered that she had taken our evening seriously. I too had dressed for it, in an Italian sport coat and slacks from Barney's, the ensemble I haul out for animal-performer award ceremonies, but tonight I was rakishly tieless, at least I hoped for some rakishness. I even wore my black dress shoes, also Italian, that devastate my spinal column. I felt all runny inside. Crystal seemed girlishly shy at the door, but that probably had something to do with the way I was mooning over her.

I accepted the red roses she offered. I had been momentarily struck speechless by the contrast of their red and that of her lipstick against the black of her hair and eyes. Crystal always wore bright red lipstick, even in the Upscale Poolroom when she was mercilessly skinning a fish who thought women couldn't play pool because their tits got in the way.

Then Jellyroll got into the act, and I was grateful for another chance to collect myself. Wagging his whole body, Jellyroll spun with excitement, his greeting mode. "No," I said to him quietly.

"What'd he do?" Crystal asked.

"Nothing yet. But he was about to jump up on you."

"How do you know?"

"He had that look in his eyes. Tell him to sit, and he'll collect himself."

Crystal told him to sit. He did, and she knelt to let him lap at her face. We finally got out of the foyer and into the living room, at which Crystal did a quick double take.

My living room always warrants explanation or visitors think I'm an eccentric hermit. The living room contains no furniture except my morris chair and Jellyroll's Adirondack Spruce Bough Dog Bed, if that can be called furniture. This is our listening room. That's about all we do in here. I like to keep the acoustics clean. If I lived in Montana or another sparsely populated western state, I could have a listening room without losing my living room, but I live in a three-room Manhattan apartment. I like to give my four big speakers, facing inward from the corners, an unimpeded shot at my centrally placed morris chair. I've had no complaints from neighbors, mainly because the widows who live above and below are as deaf as socket wrenches, a condition for which I'm not responsible. But if someone wanted to live with me, I'd gladly remake my listening room into a living room. I was open to change.

"Jazz," said Crystal. Charlie Parker was playing "Bird of Paradise" (Miles Davis, trumpet; Duke Jordan, piano; Tommy Potter, bass; Max Roach, drums).

"Yes. Charlie Parker."

"They called him Bird, didn't they?"

"Yes."

I excused myself and went into the kitchen to pour us a glass of gewürztraminer. My hands trembled. Grow up, I told myself.

When I returned, Crystal was sitting in my morris chair with her head bowed. Jellyroll had sprawled against her shoes. "Gee," she said softly, "I didn't know he was so, you know, so spiritual."

That made my heart go pitter-pat. She liked Bird.

We listened to "Yardbird Suite," "Max Making Wax," "Ornithology," "Scrapple from the Apple," and "Carvin' the Bird" without speaking. I sat on the windowsill. Occasionally I refilled our glasses. Jellyroll stretched languorously, circled in his Adirondack Spruce Bough Dog Bed, and flopped. He sighed with contentment. Things looked fine to him. Me, too.

She wanted to hear more. "I've heard of these people before, but I've never really listened to them. I mean, when listening was the whole point."

We tried some Monk. She dug it. When we got to "Pannonica," Crystal said, "What's that mean?"

"Oh, that's the Baroness Pannonica de Konigswater."

"Who?"

"She was an early patroness of bebop. She used to live at the Stanhope Hotel until they kicked her out because she held jam sessions until dawn. All of the greats were there at one time or another. Charlie Parker died in her apartment. Before that, she was a pilot and member of the French Resistance. I think she got captured by the Nazis."

"The Baroness, huh? What else do you know about her?"

"I have a book that talks about her. Would you like to borrow it?"

"Yes. I'm always looking for heroes."

"Women heroes?"

"Yes."

I got Crystal the book. "I like Amelia Earhart."

"Yeah, me too. I did her about three years ago."

"So this is an organized search?"

"Absolutely."

I needed to start cooking the crabs.

"Do you want any help?"

"No, but your presence would be nice." I caught her looking at me in a kind of scrutinizing way. Jellyroll followed us into the kitchen.

The softshell crabs were all set to go, according to Julia Child. I popped them into the appropriate preheated pan.

"So did you grow up in Sheepshead Bay?" I asked.

"Yeah. Over a poolroom. What about you?"

"I'm not really from anywhere particular. My mother married a lot of pilots, and we moved around. I never finished one year of school in the same place I began it."

"A rolling stone, huh?"

"Yep, a man on the periphery."

She grinned and leaned against the sink. Jellyroll sat at her feet and peered up at her, his "don't-you-want-to-pet-me?" look. She scrunched down to do so. She didn't seem uncomfortable with the long lovely line of stockinged thigh that came visible.

"Did your family own the poolroom?"

"My father did."

"What was it called?"

"The Golden Hours. It's still there. I still live in a little apartment upstairs."

"Did you start playing pool when you were an infant?"

"Just about." A dark look came into her eyes.

"A sore subject?"

"No. My father died recently. When I was about six, he gave me a sawed-off cue and stood me up on a box. I loved his attention, but as I got older the whole thing became a drag."

"You mean he pressured you to play?"

27

"Yeah, well, I felt a little freakish. When I was eleven or twelve, I was playing pretty good—for a twelve-year-old kid. And he'd put me on display. It was okay to be a kid who played good, but not a young woman. Like when I was in college, somebody would suggest we go over to the student union and play some eight ball. I'd shoot left-handed so I didn't look good. Poke at the ball. Then he died. He just dropped dead over a rack of straight pool. He'd given me this skill, but I was ashamed of it. Luckily for me, that was about the time women's professional pool was just getting started. Now I'm a sportswoman. Before I'd have been a bum. A bummess."

I tried to picture the little girl standing, maybe in a stiff little organdy dress, on the stool, a crowd of men watching, the old man gloating.

"What about your mother?"

"What about her?"

"Is she alive?"

"I don't know."

"She left?"

"Yeah, she ran off with a West Coast road hustler. I found out about twenty years later that they called him Jesuit Johnny, because that was his dodge. Pretending to be a priest. You know, play a little friendly nine ball before his audience with the Pope. I have a tacky past."

"No, full of character."

"Yeah, right." She thought I was kidding. She rose from her crouch and took a seat at the dining-room table. Jelly-roll went with her.

So did I. The crabs were sizzling in the pan, nearly ready. I was reasonably well in control of my meal. I no longer felt like a stumbling prom-night geek.

"I rented Jellyroll's first movie last night," said Crystal, as she removed her right shoe to rub his spine with her stockinged foot. She wore a gold chain around her ankle.

"The one where he plays the Seeing Eye dog to the blind detective?"

"Yeah, pretty stupid, all right. But he was wonderful. He has so many expressions. How did you teach him how to do all that stuff?"

"He just does it. One of these days he's going to catch on to my irrelevance. I don't have much to fall back on."

Crystal giggled. "Maybe he'll keep you around to hail cabs, pick up the laundry, like that. I also saw *The Big Top Caper*."

"A classic." In it, Jellyroll plays a performing dog who investigates suspicious circus accidents.

"It must be tough to be a human in a Jellyroll movie."

That was true. Most had some kind of substance-abuse problem.

"Could I ask you a favor? You can feel free to say no. Could I go with you once when he's working?"

"Oh, sure. Anytime. He just finished another of the blind detective movies, but I have a feeling there's still more to shoot. You could go to that."

"I'd love to. I suppose every woman tells you this, but I'm a big fan of his." Maybe with time she'd become a big fan of mine.

My crabs were successful. We ate them all. We drank a lot of wine. We talked without pause through dinner and laughed at each other's jokes. We discussed the city's general decline, the differences in day-to-day life between Manhattan and Brooklyn, the right-wing Supreme Court, the urban riots, and we talked about leaving New York, a topic that comes up often these days. In the eighties, you couldn't go to any sort of gathering without having to listen to real estate talk. Now the talk is of departure before it's too late.

"Yeah, but where would you go?" Crystal asked.

And that was always the question that ended the conversation.

"Doesn't Jellyroll need to be here?"

"Or L.A. But I think about retiring him sometimes."

"No!"

"No, probably not."

"Think of all the people who'd be disappointed, me included."

"You can see him anytime you want."

"I meant on the silver screen . . . but thanks."

We discussed The Hustler, Jackie Gleason's pool skill, the real Minnesota Fats, Weenie Beanie, Wimpy Lassiter, Willie Mosconi, and whether or not pool's new fashionableness had taken color from the game. Somewhere in there, in a largely spontaneous gesture, I touched her hand. She turned it over and squeezed mine.

Then I told her that I happened to have known her ex-husband. It seemed dishonest to pretend I didn't.

She stiffened, but she didn't withdraw her hand.

"I mean, I used to know him. Not well. We weren't close or anything like that. We were classmates. In law school."

"You're a lawyer?"

"No, I—"

"He was a crook. You're not a crook, are you?"

"No, no, I didn't even finish law school."

"Good. 'Cause Trammell was a crook who tried to ruin my life."

"I'm sorry. I won't mention him again."

"It's all right. Sorry I reacted like that."

"Sure—"

"That's what he does for a living—ruin people's lives."

I said, "Are you free tomorrow night?"

"Yes, but I have to go to a tournament in Philadelphia day after tomorrow." (She pronounced it "torn-ament.") "You

30

seem civilized. . . . Evolved. Most men aren't. Especially those you meet in poolrooms."

"Or law school . . . Would you like to stay? Tonight, I mean."

She peered at me with those black eyes.

Was that a crude question? I hadn't thought about it. I just blurted it out. It was spontaneous. Spontaneity can kill.

"Do you have furniture in the bedroom?"

"Huh? Oh. Yes indeed, and I can prove it."

"We need to talk first. I've never used needles. Have you?"

"I smoke a little dope, but only on special occasions. The Olympics, like that."

"What about condoms? Do you object to condoms?"

"Some of my best friends are—"

"Come on, Artie. This is serious."

"I know. That was nervous humor. I have no objections to condoms."

"I have a tattoo."

"You *do?*"

"I thought I'd tell you."

"Fascinating. Where?"

She pointed to a spot on her right hip, about four inches below her waist.

"What is it? I mean what does it depict?"

"A parrot, about a half inch high."

"A half inch? Oh. The way you said you had a tattoo, I thought you meant something like a road map of Florida running down your leg."

"I used to be a doper, Artie. I'm recovering. I just wanted to tell you."

"Really? What kind of dope?"

"Pills. I woke up one morning about dusk and found myself with a tattoo on my hip, but I had no idea where

I got it. I went straight into treatment. I've been sober for three years."

Gee, I didn't have a tattoo or an ex-drug problem or anything interesting. I did have a dog.

We sat side by side on the bed, shyly, silently, fully clothed. Jellyroll peered at us from the floor, making Crystal edgy, I thought, so I told him to go get in his place. He gave me the stink eye, but he curled into his Adirondack Spruce Bough Dog Bed. (He has two.)

"Uh, could I see your tattoo?"

Crystal and I were breathing audibly as she stepped out of her yellow dress. Maybe we *both* had been alone too long. She wore black lingerie, a tiny lace bra, and silk tap pants. The stocking tops clung to her thighs of their own accord. She turned sideways and elevated her left hip— and there it was, in full color. She had said it was a parrot; it looked to me like a macaw, but this was no time for ornithology. I knelt for a closer look. Rolling her stockings slowly down her legs filled me with inexpressible delight. I kissed the bird. She released the clasp of her bra and shed it with a shrug. I stood up. She clasped her breasts in both hands and said, "No fair, you're still dressed."

That made my heart go pitter-pat. With trembling hands, I removed my Italian ensemble, and for a moment I stood naked before her. From the living room, Johnny Hartman was singing, and that voice ran right through me like a sexual shudder. She sat on the bed, slipped out of her tap pants, but they remained hooked on her left foot as we made love. . . .

Simultaneous orgasms can change the world, at least on an individual level. Still, the world could change two orgasms at a time, and it would be a better place for all concerned. Love can turn cynics into sonneteers.

4.

"**L**OOK HOW SAD," said Crystal before I knew she was awake.

"Huh? Who?"

She leaned up on one elbow. "Jellyroll. Is he sick?"

"No, he's theatrical." When he's ready to go, he sits peering at me with forlorn eyes, ears adroop, betrayed loyalty itself. The bed is low, so in the mornings he sits breathing on me—dog breath smells vaguely of fish. This morning he was doing his number on Crystal. I rolled over and kissed her. Her body felt sweet. Life felt sweet. Maybe this relationship had legs.

She hugged and kissed Jellyroll. He looked across Crystal at me as if to say, "Watch, now she's going to ask you what I want."

"What does he want? Breakfast?"

"He wants to go to the park."

"Park" was one of the first words in what has grown over the years into a huge vocabulary. At the sound of it, he began to wag his tail and whine. Pretty soon he'd begin to puff out his cheeks with suppressed barking sounds. His lips would flap soon, and he'd begin to make long, sustained moaning sounds. Dogs are ego cases. I could have lain there naked with Crystal for a decade or two.

"Let's take him out," she said.

"You mean you want to go with us?"

"Sure. We're going, Jellyroll."

"No barking," I reminded him. He has several barks, depending on the matter at hand, but the hot-damn-we're-all-going-to-the-park is the worst, high-pitched, brain piercing. I discourage it. But I shared his joy that Crystal was going with us. While we watched, she got up and put last night's clothes on, minus the stockings.

"Does this look ridiculous for the park?"

"Absolutely not."

"Sure it does," she said, checking herself in the mirror. "I can't go to the park in a dress at nine A.M."

"I see what you mean." I considered the problem. The next step in our romantic development would occur when Crystal began to leave clothes in my closet. I longed for the day when I'd see her cue case leaning against the closet door. That would bespeak commitment.

"You have to put on your clothes from last night. It'll look like we're going to brunch, or something."

"Okay. Do you want to go to brunch?"

"No, I hate brunch."

It was another hot day, and by noon, when the bricks and concrete heated up like a tandoori oven, the city would slow to a lethargic, dispirited pace. But now, before the day's assault by 800,000 automobiles, the air was still cool and thin enough to breathe. I felt wonderful strolling arm in arm with Crystal. On the way to brunch.

Jellyroll and his collie friend Barney played tug of war with a stick while a half dozen other dogs frolicked and gamboled and milled about sniffing. Atavistic juices flowing, Jellyroll and Barney snarled and growled as they dug in and yanked at the stick as if it were a caribou tibia.

Groggy looks on their faces, the human contingent stood around watching their dogs' delight. The contrast was striking. Dogs have been blessed with life in the moment, humans cursed with expectancy. The humans expected to go to work, most by subway. I know how the other dog walkers talk about Jellyroll in the light of their own tedious employment.

"Hell, Freddie's as cute as Jellyroll."

"Sure he is, so's Sascha."

"So how come Jellyroll's pulling down the big bucks, while I'm working for a living?"

"Aw, it'd be a drag. You got to be real pushy. You got to be a stage mother. Mama Rose for your dog."

"Yeah."

"I'd rather stay with the firm."

"Yeah."

The dog walkers looked Crystal up and down covertly. I introduced her to the Chinese lady who owned Barney, to Phil and Les, the gay couple who jointly owned two overweight golden retrievers, and to Amy and Phyllis, actresses with their first dog, an ex-stray they'd named Uta. And I introduced Crystal to Seth. Even Seth's dog, an overweight Lhasa apso, seemed bitter. Seth grinned at Crystal in a way he probably thought was sexy.

"You're all dressed up," noted Seth.

"Brunch," I said.

"On Wednesday?"

There were other dog walkers with whom I had nodding acquaintance, but they didn't seem to want to be introduced. I didn't know their names anyway, only their dogs' names.

"Did you hear?" Seth asked.

"No, what?"

"Somebody took a shot at me yesterday afternoon."

"No!"

"Look at this." He led Crystal and me to a nearby English plane tree, and a few dog walkers followed. Their faces were grim. Seth pointed at the tree trunk.

A thumb-sized hole went deep into the heart of the tree. I seemed to be the only dog walker who hadn't heard. The others, standing around the tree, nodded gravely at the hole. One of the goldens peed on the tree trunk.

"When I moved here, the last thing my father said to me was, 'Don't get hit by any stray bullets,' " Phil remarked.

"You?" said Seth. "It was me they shot at."

"Stray bullets aren't shot *at* anyone," Phil countered. "That's what makes them stray."

"Yeah, but what if it *wasn't* a stray bullet?" said Seth gravely. Then he looked from face to face around the tree, cuing each of us to ask, "What do you mean, Seth?"

No one did.

"What do I mean?" said Seth. "I mean there's a lot of people who would like to see me dead. Producers, directors, hell, *costume* designers, for that matter, Equity. This was an assassination attempt, pure and simple." Seth would rather have been assassinated than ignored.

"Did you call the cops?" Crystal asked.

"Sure. You know what they said? They said, 'Probably just a stray bullet.' They don't want to entertain any conspiracy theories. Just call it a stray bullet, that way you can forget it. Another stray bullet."

"Where was it fired from?" I asked.

Seth pointed to the wall that separated us from the northbound lanes of the West Side Highway, cars whizzing past, any number of them driven by crazies toting automatic weapons.

A tall, gawky stranger approached. He carried a guitar case festooned with travel stickers from places like Busch Gardens and the Kennedy Space Center. Exuberant Barney ran in front of the stranger. He had to stop abruptly. "Hey," he snarled, "those goddamned dogs are supposed to be *leashed!*"

"Don't take it out on dogs just because you got no talent," said Seth.

"It was probably him," said Phyllis after the stranger had moved on. "He probably hates dog owners because he stepped in dog shit once when he was a child. Now he goes around the city parks killing dog owners. There's probably been dozens killed, only the cops never made the dog-shit connection, so it doesn't get reported for what it is: another *dog-walker* killing."

"Now, don't get yourself all upset, Phyllis," said Amy. "You don't have any proof of that. Without proof, it's paranoia. Besides, it was probably just one of Seth's ex-collaborators come back for revenge."

"Yeah," said Seth gravely.

The dogs continued to frolic, but we took little pleasure in it now. No dog has ever discharged firearms in a densely populated urban area.

I put my arm around Crystal's shoulder to shield her from mass murderers and New Jersey drivers as we re-crossed Riverside Drive. Commuter traffic had clotted, and the drivers honked at each other mindlessly. The car commuters always seem surprised and thus outraged to find *traffic* in New York City at rush hour. Day after day, the same inevitability seems to befuddle them and turn them dangerous: "Why *can't* we go sixty miles an hour up West End Avenue, goddamnit?"

Crystal said, "I have to go."

"Go?"

"I'm running a tournament for my uncle at the Golden Hours. The Golden Hours is the reason I don't have to have a part-time job. Look, how about coming with me?"

"Sure. But I don't play in tournaments."

"No? How come?"

"Too challenging."

"Nerves? After a while you get over that. Would you bring Jellyroll?"

"Jellyroll, you want to go to Brooklyn?"

He wants to go anywhere.

"I told my uncle I was going out with the guy who owns the R-r-ruff Dog. He loves the R-r-ruff Dog."

Deeper and deeper into Brooklyn we drove, and with each mile my nerves tightened further. Out of the Brooklyn-Battery Tunnel, Crystal picked up the Gowanus Expressway, southbound past the derelict piers rotting on their pins and listing into the slate-gray waters of the upper bay.

"Crystal—"

"Yes?"

"Maybe I'll play."

"Oh, good. You'll enjoy it. It's just a friendly local tournament."

"Nine ball?"

"Yeah. Don't worry, you play good. You just need to concentrate." She turned onto Shore Road, the scenic route that looped along the water's edge around incongruously luxurious homes in Bay Ridge, where a lot of mafiosi live. We passed beneath the foot of the Verrazano Bridge onto the Belt Parkway.

Why was my mouth so dry and my palms so wet if this was just a friendly local tournament, nothing at stake? I tried to hide my nerves from Crystal, a seasoned pro.

"Are you the tournament director?" I asked.

"Yes."

"Do I get a spot?"

"No."

"Nothing?"

"What'd you expect?"

"The seven."

"Forget it. You're too good for that. I can't show up with a ringer and give him a spot. Especially a ringer I just slept with."

"Did you hear that, Jellyroll? No ringer Crystal sleeps with gets a spot."

"At least not the first time," she grinned.

I *needed* a spot. It would make me look better. But I didn't want to whine.

We were close now. The defunct parachute drop that still looms over Coney Island like a headstone hove into view.

"I can't pass Coney Island without thinking of Topsy," I said before I could stop myself, which I probably would have done, but the Topsy story had always troubled me. I never went to Coney Island because of Topsy.

"Topsy? Who's Topsy?"

"Topsy was a performing elephant at Coney Island about 1910. They treated her like shit and made her mean. She killed three men, the last of whom had just fed her a lighted cigarette. They decided Topsy would have to be put down. They tried cyanide-laced carrots, but it didn't take. Then they decided to hire Thomas Edison's people from New Jersey to come over and electrocute Topsy. They chained her up, put electrodes on her ears and legs, and flipped the switch. They filmed the whole thing and then marketed the film. I somehow saw it as a kid. It took several minutes for Topsy to die, twitching and shaking and screaming."

She took her eyes off the road and peered at me. "That's a terrible story. Fuck you, Coney Island." She gave it the finger as we passed. "You're a sad guy, aren't you? I mean, sort of in general, all things being equal."

"Oh, no, not me. I'm a laugh a minute. You'll see when I play in this tournament."

39

We drove in silence for a while, then Crystal said, "My uncle Billy's not all there. I just thought I'd tell you so you wouldn't be surprised."

"What do you mean?"

"He's sort of like a child."

"Was he born that way?"

"When he was a kid, he almost drowned. He and his father were fishing from a boat off the Rockaways. Somehow Billy fell in. Billy's father jumped in to save him. Nobody's sure what happened exactly, but Billy's father drowned. So did Billy. He actually drowned. He was clinically dead, I guess. They brought him back to life, but the lack of oxygen had ruined his brain. Before my father died, he asked my permission to leave the Golden Hours to Billy and me jointly. He said I could make it in the world on my own, but Billy couldn't. I just wanted you to know ahead of time."

I thought about that for a while, dying and then being brought back to life. Maybe it wasn't the lack of oxygen that blew Billy's mind but the sights he saw on the other side.

She took the Sheepshead Bay exit. A sign pointed toward Emmons Avenue. "Funny," she said to the rearview mirror.

"What?"

"Probably nothing."

"What?"

"Can you see out of the side mirror? You can adjust it with that little knob there—"

I turned the mirror so I could see behind us.

"That blue Buick with four guys in it—they've been behind us since upper Broadway."

"Following us?"

"I don't know. Hell, maybe they're playing in the tournament. Let's make a couple turns." First onto Neptune Avenue and then into a maze of short residential streets lined with single-family red-brick houses, left, right—the Buick was no longer behind us. "I guess it's just my imagination," she said without conviction. "The last few days, not quite a week—I felt like I've been followed, like somebody's back there."

"Those same guys?"

"No, never the same. It's hard to know in New York whether you're being followed or not. Whenever I do something to be sure, like make a lot of turns, they disappear, so it's probably nothing. But I'm getting sick of making all those turns."

I didn't think any more about that because after one more turn, we had arrived at Golden Hours Billiards. It was situated on the ground floor in a block-long strip of two-story shops all sharing the same mansard roof. There was a Chinese restaurant called Wu Fat's on one side and an H&R Block on the other.

Two little old ladies built like fire hydrants and dressed in black from top to toe, despite the heat, greeted Crystal in heavy Italian accents as we entered the Golden Hours.

I stood in a short line with other cue-toting competitors to pay my $20 entry fee, collected by a bleachy teenager whose jaw dropped when she got a load of the celebrated dog at my heels. There were thirty or so tables, all occupied. The players warming up and the spectators standing around waved or called to Crystal. She called some by name, returned a few quick quips, and I realized how at home she was here. Most everybody gave me the once-over.

Then things changed, as I've seen them do so often when folks spot Jellyroll. First a thin ripple of recognition passed through the room. It began at the nearest tables and quickly crested in the center. People nudged each other and pointed. Play stopped.

"Naww," I heard someone say, "couldn't be."

"No, it *is*," another insisted. "Look at him smile."

I motioned for Jellyroll to sit in a naked demonstration that he belonged with me as I forked over my twenty. I had brought my own ringer. He'd blow their concentration entirely.

The room was dim, even in broad daylight, except for hot puddles of light over the tables. I liked that. That's how poolrooms should be. The Jellyroll stir was bolstering my confidence. Even if I didn't play well, I was still the guy with Jellyroll *and* Crystal.

What I feared was humiliation. Pool can, in my case often does, humiliate. At a certain level—after you learn how to stroke, not hit, the cue ball, after you learn how to control the ball in order to get position for the next shot, and the next, after you learn the moves—the game steps up onto a mental plane, and that's where my problem lies. Mentally, I'm lemonade. I think like a loser. But now Jellyroll was helping. While he brought the room to a standstill, I wasn't thinking like a loser, not a winner yet, but at least not like a fall-down loser.

"Come and meet Uncle Billy," said Crystal. "Then I've got to go change before the neighbors start whispering about promiscuity in Manhattan." She took my hand and held it while she introduced me to her uncle.

Billy was sitting on a stool near a glass case displaying pool paraphernalia, boxes of balls, tip tampers, a row of cues, and novelty items like nine balls on key chains. He was a long, gangly man with a prominent Adam's apple that seemed to bob up and down of its own free will. Though he appeared about seventy, he was spry, sporting a full head of wild black hair. He stood up and took my hand in both of his.

"Maybe you'd tell me something, Mr. Deemer?"

"Artie."

"Artie. What's it like, Artie, to be around the R-r-ruff Dog all day long?"

"It's happy. He's like a clown in a dog suit."

"Wow. A dog like that could break your heart."

"I know what you mean." I did, too. I whistled for him, and he trotted over. He had been off working the room. "Jellyroll, meet Uncle Billy."

Billy's knees cracked about four separate times as he knelt to Jellyroll's level. They nuzzled each other for a while. Then Billy said, "This is about my favorite dog in the world."

Crystal squeezed my hand and said excuse me. On her way up the stairs, she gave Billy a peck on the forehead.

Billy looked left, then right as if for eavesdroppers, then said, "Listen, I don't mean to be a buttinski, but let me give you a piece of advice—don't play her for money."

I said that sounded like good advice to me.

Crystal made a fast change. Ten minutes later, wearing jeans with a frilly blouse, she stood on a chair and asked for the players' attention. "Billy and I are glad to see you here. We have a big turnout today, so the winner will get $300, second $100, and third $75. We'll play five-game matches, single elimination. Tournament rules apply: one foul—you get ball-in-hand. You're allowed one push-out after the break, but you must call it. Those players with a spot—remember, you don't get it wild. You must call it. And if you make your spot on the break, it comes back up immediately. If you play it off a combination, you have to call it before you shoot. And today we're starting a new rule the pros are using: if an object ball leaves the table, that's a foul. The ball spots, and the other player gets cue ball in hand. What else? Oh, if your opponent faces a questionable hit, call me over before he shoots, and I'll act as referee. Any questions? . . . No? Well, thanks for coming, it's nice to see you all here. Have fun and good luck."

We drew numbers from a bowl to determine who would play whom in the first match. I drew a heavy fellow with a face that had been around the block a time or two.

"Hello, I'm Greek," he said. I had to give Greek the eight ball. He flipped a quarter for the break. I lost. He broke— and made three balls. Great, it was going to be one of those sessions.

Greek was the kind of player who didn't aim, didn't really get into position. He just leaned down and shot fast, but he knew what he was doing. Balls kept going in. He pocketed everything up to the six, and I was already counting myself out, the way losers do.

But then he screwed up his position on the seven ball. Stroking it too hard, he parked the cue ball directly behind the eight, no chance for a shot. He turned red as he glared at the offending white ball. Without pausing to line up the angle, he kicked the cue off the side rail, but he missed the seven by a foot.

That was a foul. I could place the cue ball anywhere I wanted, and I had to make only three balls to win the game. With ball in hand, a child could get out from here. If I only had a child . . . I made the seven, eight, and then the nine, to win game one.

I broke solidly. The nine went directly into the corner pocket. I'd won again. I was up two games already. There is nothing like making the nine on the break to bolster confidence. I noticed that Greek had started to wilt. I won game three off the break as well. I didn't pocket the nine, but I left it, through sheer luck, two inches from the far corner pocket. I made the two and the three and left myself an easy combination off the four. I made the combination to go up three games to none. Gee, this was fun.

We seesawed back and forth in game four—the balls were lying hard, frozen against their friends or against rails. We both played good safeties, and we both escaped cleverly from them. But then Greek played a bad safety, leaving me an easy shot on the five. I ran out from there. I needed one game to win the set and eliminate Greek. I won it. Greek looked sad, but he shook my hand like a gentleman.

Jellyroll and I waited by the desk for our next match, and Uncle Billy walked over to join us.

"Win?" he asked.

"Yes. I played Greek."

Billy nodded. "Poor old Greek, he's a shortstop. First time he misses, he folds up and goes home."

"Who's tough?" I asked.

"Anthony. That Latin kid on table two." He nodded at Anthony, who had eyes like an underfed predator. "And Bird. It'll be Anthony and Bird battling it out in the finals. That is unless Mr. Artie Deemer slips right in there. I'm rootin' for you."

"Thank you, Billy."

"I just want you to be good to Crystal. She's like a daughter to me."

"Don't worry about that, Billy."

Crystal called me for the second match, and Jellyroll and I strode toward the table she indicated. My heart sank. My opponent was Bird. Tall and slim with piercing black eyes, this bird was a raptor. We shook hands. His was bony. . . .

Well, I beat Bird five games to four. It was close all the way; he'd win one, I'd win the next. A crowd gathered to watch. He was a better player than I. That was clear from his stroke and by the way his cue ball took English. He did things with the cue ball I couldn't do, but I was playing well, making the hard shots, and I got two lucky rolls, which, I admit, made the difference. Bird knew he was the better player, and he didn't like those lucky rolls one bit. After it was over, he shook my hand and walked away without looking me in the eye. Crystal had been watching. She made a small nod my way.

I felt high, flushed with victory. I was moving up in this tournament. My next opponent, named Vic, was about seventeen years old. He was a veritable beginner. He had the six for a spot. I cautioned myself against overconfidence, but I was counting on a win. I played well. They were going in like they had eyes. I didn't try to do anything fancy with the cue ball, just play the natural angles and use speed of stroke to put me where I wanted to be. And then I happened to glance into the faces standing around the table. Thus far I had avoided doing that. I don't know if unconsciously my mind's eye had taken him in or whether I chanced to look up right into his face.

It was Trammell Weems. The jaunty bastard stood with his hands in his chinos pockets and grinned at me. I tried not to see him, but what could I do? There he was. I missed the nine by a half a foot. The stroke was so bad, I was lucky I didn't hurt myself. Vic, reprieved, leapt to his feet, his eyes shining like an eight-year-old's on Christmas morning. He pounded it in.

Trammell strolled up in his floppy boat shoes. "What say, counselor?"

I was speechless.

"It would have been best if you'd made that nine ball. I think this kid has heart. Actually, I'm a little surprised to see you're still at this vulgar game, a man of your standing in the legal community."

"Hello, Trammell."

"I hear you're brazenly escorting my wife about town."

"Yeah, I figured it was all right, because she's not your wife anymore and because she doesn't like you very much."

"How about putting in a good word for me? She'll listen to you."

I didn't see Crystal until she was upon us. Her jaw was fixed, and her eyes were hard. "What are you doing here, Trammell?"

"I'm watching my old schoolmate dog the pay ball." He leaned over as if to give her a peck on the cheek.

She bobbed away like a boxer. "Get out, Trammell. And leave my uncle alone. He doesn't need your shit."

"He's the only one in the Spivey family who'll give me the time of day."

"I'll give you this cue in the head, I'm not kidding."

"Okay, okay." Still grinning his charming grin, he headed for the door.

He looked good, I thought with some regret. I tried to get Crystal to see me, but she just glared at the back of his head.

I was finished in this tournament.

I should have conceded, walked out. Vic stomped me five to two. I couldn't shoot the cue ball in the hole. The kid couldn't believe his luck.

After I absorbed that dreadful drubbing, put my cue back in its case, I wandered over near the desk. Crystal was giving Billy hell. "Did you give him his money back?" she asked.

"I couldn't, Crystal. We already made a deal. That would be welshing. I couldn't welsh." His voice cracked. I thought for a moment he was going to cry.

Crystal softened her voice. "He hurts people, Billy. That's his career in life. He'll hurt you."

"I'm sorry, Crystal."

"Okay."

"But I couldn't welsh."

"Okay, but let this be it. Stay away from Trammell."

"I understand."

Crystal went away to referee a hit, and I walked over to Billy, calling Jellyroll with me. He has a knack for making humans feel better. He sat and peered up at Billy, whose knees cracked as he lowered himself to my dog's level.

"Crystal's mad at me."

"She probably won't stay mad."

"No . . . Are you out?"

"Yep."

"Well, you probably lost concentration."

"I sure did."

Crystal returned. She kissed Billy on the cheek. "I think we're gonna go, Uncle Billy."

"Sure, you go on. I can handle things from here."

"It was nice meeting you, Billy."

He said he hoped we wouldn't be strangers, and I assured him we wouldn't, though I was very glad to get out of there. Trammell's presence had always changed the complexion of a room.

Crystal and I were passing Coney Island before she spoke. "I saw how you were playing before he showed up."

"Pretty good, huh? What did he want from Uncle Billy?"

"His boat."

"His boat?"

"Yeah, Billy has an old fishing boat. He and Trammell, and sometimes Bruce, go fishing in it. They're pals, Billy and Trammell. He paid Billy seven hundred dollars to use the boat."

"Seven hundred dollars seems like a lot."

"Yeah, but it probably isn't."

I didn't want to talk about Trammell Weems anymore.

5.

I TOOK HER TO DINNER at an Alsatian restaurant I like on West Nineteenth, and before we'd finished a light first course, we weren't thinking much about Trammell. At least, I wasn't, and since the glimmer had returned to her black eyes when she smiled, I assumed Crystal wasn't either. It felt, in fact, as though Crystal and I had weathered a small piece of adversity together and were stronger for it. Hell, this was *real relationship* stuff.

We made love with Thelonious Sphere Monk doing his work, but gently, in the background. I felt like a teenager who'd never felt sex and love together before. Maybe I hadn't. Damp, we lay together listening. I watched her breasts rise and fall with her breathing.

"Artie—"

"Humm?" I had orally occupied myself with the nearest nipple.

"Artie, I have to go."

"Noooo."

"I have that tournament."

"Could you mail it in?"

"That would be unprofessional."

"What's first place pay?"

49

"Eight grand."

"Jellyroll will pay you ten to stay."

"Do you want to go with me?"

"Oh . . . Sure." The idea excited me—Crystal running balls in a floor-length, low-cut evening gown, say, of basic black, with shoes and stockings to match. In a crudely male way, I added a garter belt gripping the turn of her hips, perhaps even a black lace merry widow, but of course no pool player could wear that kind of gear, all those wonderful snaps and stays to chafe against the table. Pool players probably wore sensible shoes and panty hose with their evening dresses. I wanted to ask but suppressed the impulse. "Where is it? The tournament, I mean."

"Philadelphia."

I noticed a wave of misgiving wash over her face. I asked why.

". . . Can I take the invitation back?"

"You couldn't concentrate?"

"I wouldn't care. So I dogged the nine? I'd be thinking of you in the stands. And in the room. Those women would have me for breakfast."

"You need solitude."

"And celibacy."

She couldn't spend the night. She had to go home and pack. "Will you be here? I'll call you. I'll be back by Monday. Unless I get eliminated early."

That was four days, almost a week. I could always hope for early elimination. "I have to do a Jellyroll shoot tomorrow," I said, "but I'll be here tomorrow night waiting for your call." I would pine for the sound of her voice by then.

I had given no thought at all to the shoot or to any other Jellyroll business, but what difference did it make? These things just happen. I merely attend to protect him from assholes:

"Trust me, Artie. There is *no danger* here. Do you think I'd endanger our star? Of course I would not," pronounced Dirk Black, the director, in his sincere voice, brow furrowed with real caring. "Why, he's the only reason we're here."

The first two Seeing Eye–dog movies had been directed by a friend of mine, a talented man who had moved on to bigger things, leaving us with Dirk Black, headed in the other direction.

We stood, Dirk, Jellyroll, and I, amid the ruins of the South Bronx. Production vehicles were parked nose to tail on the shattered street. Most of the cast members were taking a break in their individual trailers, where they figured they wouldn't get mugged, while the crew fiddled with gear, struck their lights and reflectors from the "set," one of the few buildings still standing—it was roofless, floorless, void. This was the bad guys' hideout, and Dirk had just finished the Bad Guys' Hideout Scene. Now he was ready to bullshit Jellyroll and me—

"It's a piece of cake, Artie." He flipped an arm around my shoulder. "Nat rides from that block right up there to this block right down here where we're standing. Two blocks, that's *it*, two blocks only. What's two blocks? What could go wrong in two blocks?" He led me across the street, and we stopped at the edge of a watery pit where the sidewalk used to be. "Artie, I happen to be aware of how much weight you place on artistic integrity, so I know you'll appreciate my problem. I tried it with the dummy, but it didn't work, artistically. It didn't have that artistic credibility. I can't put a thing up there on the big screen that lacks artistic credibility. TV Movie of the Week, that's one thing, sure, but this is the big screen, Artie. You can't-bullshit-the-big-screen. So that's where we are today, Artie."

"Where's that, Dirk?" I knew what Dirk wanted. He wanted to strap Jellyroll to the back of a Harley-Davidson while some idiot pretending to be blind drove him at high speed.

In this edition, Nat Penn, blind PI, and Jellyroll retrieve some Dutch masters paintings stolen by swarthy, effeminate villains, but that really didn't matter because audiences don't go to Jellyroll movies for the plot. They go to see Jellyroll be cute. But Dirk Black had stuck in this motorcycle chase, because he thought chases were "intrinsically cinematic." Strapped to the back of the motorcycle, Jellyroll was supposed to scratch Nat's back once for a right-hand turn, twice for a left, or maybe it was the other way around.

Absurdly, the traffic lights still worked. Dirk waited at the corner until the walk sign came on, then led us across the dead street. "Artie, I know you're going to be a team player on this thing. Just this morning I was telling Victor Castaway, I said, 'Vic, I know Artie's going to get with the program on this thing.' My words. I happen to know the dummy approach offends Victor, too."

I happened to know Vic Castaway (Nat Penn) didn't give a shit about anything. Vic smoked a lot of northern California homegrown in his van. I knew because the swarthy effeminate villains and I often joined him.

"I mean, come on," Dirk continued, "a dog dummy on the big screen? It isn't tenable. It's untenable." Jellyroll sniffed Dirk's shoes. "And that's why I called you out here today. I want you to meet someone, in case you imagined just any old butthole biker would be driving our star around. This guy will set your mind at ease on the motorcycle trick—"

Dirk turned me around and led me back across the

street—for a moment I thought he was going to wait for the walk sign again—down the line of shiny trailers to a long white RV parked in front of a dead bakery, its entrance cemented shut forever with cinder blocks. Two toothless derelicts sat on the bakery steps gumming pint bottles of Night Train Express and wondering who you had to know to get a piece of this intrinsically cinematic action. Dirk knocked on the white door.

A big stubbly-faced man with ancient acne pits on his cheeks flung it open. "Ready for me, Blackie?" He was clearly the sort of man's man a man could trust the life of his dog to.

"Won't be long now, Pud, boy, but first I'd like you to meet the star of the show, ta-da: Jellyroll—" Jellyroll sniffed Pud's boots. "And this is his handler, Mr. Artie Deemer. Artie, meet Pud Atwell."

"Put 'er there, Artie Deemer," said Pud, offering me his left hand. Shaking it, I noticed his right hand. It had only one finger and a thumb. A purple scar wended a jagged path from the corner of Pud's left eye to the point of his chin. Perhaps a chain-saw trick had gone awry.

"Pud is known as the King of the Stunts," announced Dirk. Then he pretended to punch Pud in the gut, and the two of them did a boxing routine, forehead to forehead, pummeling each other, man to man. Jellyroll cocked his head from side to side, trying to understand what it meant.

"Yeah, but hell, on the Coast I'm known as king. We're in the Big Apple now. All bets are off once you're in the Big Apple. Ain't that right, Artie? Is that where you live, Artie? Right in the Apple?" He said it with pity in his voice, as if we were talking about my brain tumor. "Must be hard on a dog right in the city." Pud leaned down to pet Jellyroll. "Shake," he said. Jellyroll doesn't shake. "Shake," Pud insisted. Jellyroll's tail drooped. Pud straightened, paused, said, "So you're the trainer of our star, huh,

53

Artie? . . . You wanna know something interesting? I had a dog looked just like him. Back in Lubbock. I was a half-pint then. I called him Bubba. Yep, I'll never forget Bubba. Bubba kinda brings up a lump in the throat. Who'd have thought old Bubba mighta been worth the big bucks? But then, this is the Big Apple, that was Lubbock. Come on in, sit a spell."

Pud limped jerkily into the dark, air-conditioned depths of the trailer, which was set up like a little house, complete with kitchen. His right leg didn't seem to work at all. He basically dragged it along as if he had a log in his pant leg. I thought of walk-this-way gags. He offered us our choice of a dozen different mineral waters. The Formica surface on which we poured our water was stacked with prescription vials. I saw Percocet, Darvon, extra-strength this and that. The labels all said, "As needed for pain."

"Artie's a little concerned about his meal ticket, Pud." Dirk playfully elbowed me in the ribs as I sat down with my water. "He thinks Jellyroll might meet with a mishap in the motorcycle trick."

Pud grimaced as he folded himself onto the couch. He interlocked what remained of his fingers behind his head, sighed theatrically, paused, adjusted his log leg, smiled, and said, "Nev-er happen."

"There! See, Artie, what did I tell you?"

"Well, I'm much relieved."

Dirk put his arm back around my shoulder as we finished our waters and left our audience with the King of the Stunts. "You know what?" said Dirk. "I'm going to tell you something. Remember, when you see him on the TV special you heard it here first: that guy Pud, he's going to get himself inducted into the Stuntman Hall of Fame."

"Piecemeal?"

"What? Oh! Piecemeal! Ha! Good one, Artie!"

"Hey, Dirk—"

"Yeah, pal?"

"Forget it."

Dirk jerked his arm away. Artistically offended, he stomped off.

Two hours later, after much standing around and many calls to the Coast, where Pud was king, we were ready to shoot the motorcycle trick—with the dummy. Jellyroll sat between Vic and me on the curb to watch Pud, dressed exactly like Vic in the Nat Penn costume, saddle up the big Harley. With both hands, Pud hefted his ossified leg over the bike and settled into the seat. It looked to me like Pud was rubbing his nuts on the gas tank. Stoned, Vic giggled like a naughty boy in study hall as Pud put on his dark glasses, adjusted them, and gave the throttle an ear-wrenching twist. "How do I look?" he asked after another rev. "Do I look blind or what?"

"Blind as a hoe, Pud boy," said Dirk.

Then the grips and assistants made a big production out of clearing the street, even though there was no one on the street. They called on electric bullhorns for quiet, jabbered with high seriousness on walkie-talkies. Pud loved the focus, you could tell, and that was probably why Dirk had the grips make a big production of it. Pud revved the motorcycle a few more times. Then he tested the strings that controlled the Jellyroll dummy's scratching legs. "Now wait a minute, I forget. Is it one scratch for a left turn or what?"

"Whichever grabs you, Pud boy. Improvise. You can be spontaneous on this thing."

Pud glided into position a block and a half to the north. When everybody was ready, Dirk called for action.

The big engine whined and screeched as Pud cracked through the gears. Dust and litter flew up behind the roaring bike. Pud must have been going fifty miles an hour, accelerating, when the front wheel buried itself to the axle in a pothole. Pud continued on over the handlebars at only a slightly diminished velocity.

I averted my eyes. Jesus, the impact would be hideous. Poor Pud. Pud had had his last Percocet. The EMS guys would be collecting Pud with paint scrapers. Long after we'd gone, dry and crusty pieces of Pud would drop off the sides of the buildings onto the winos' heads. When I looked up, the motorcycle was still cartwheeling, shedding parts. And when it came to rest, barely recognizable as a motorcycle, silence filled the set. . . .

"Look at *that!*" Vic gasped, pointing with both hands—

It was Pud. Pud was climbing to his feet, shakily, to be sure, but he was actually *standing up!*

People were sprinting toward him. Vic, Jellyroll, and I found ourselves swept along. A crowd gathered around Pud. Here and there, people reached out for him tentatively, then stopped, as though he'd fall to gory pieces if touched. His forehead was skinned raw; blood and asphalt mixed in the wound, but there seemed to be no further damage. He shook the dust out of his clothes. Everybody was asking him how he was.

"Well, lemme just check an' see," he said with a grin, patting his parts.

"Break it up, spread out, give the man some air." It was Dirk, elbowing his way through the astonished crowd.

"Christ, Dirk," said Dirk's assistant, "I think he's all right!"

"Of course he's all right. What do you think? This is Pud Atwell." Dirk stepped up beside Pud, put an arm around his shoulder, and said to the crowd, "This is the King of the Stunts." He milked that for about five minutes, then said, "Where's my stills person? Where's Greta? Greta, get a shot of Pud beside the smashed bike. Come on, right over here." He moved pudgy little Greta around by the shoulders until he found the most artistic angle. Pud assumed a heroically masculine pose.

Dirk leaned down to examine the Jellyroll dummy still strapped to the mangled fender. The dummy was decapitated.

"See, right there," said Dirk, pointing at the torso, "that's why I decided to go with the dummy."

"Let's burn one, Artie," said Victor Castaway when he'd stopped giggling.

I missed Crystal. I pined for her. Lovers-who-had-to-part songs spun in my head as the car service drove Jellyroll and me home. We were still on the Cross Bronx Expressway surrounded by tractor-trailer trucks when, idly, I picked up the *New York Times* a previous passenger had left on the seat. A fourteen-year-old had been shot dead by a twelve-year-old in a squabble over a basketball. Another tourist had been killed in Macy's. . . . At least I was keeping up with current events.

I was about to put the paper back on the seat when I saw the article. I must have gasped audibly, because the driver glanced at me in the rearview mirror with alarm on his face.

Trammel Weems, 36, was declared missing and presumed drowned yesterday after a boating accident off Coney Island. Weems' companion, Bruce Munger, 35, called the Coast Guard when Weems fell overboard while trying to remove a rope which had become fouled in the boat's propeller. Munger reported that he had gone below to search for a sharp knife, and when he came back on deck, Weems was gone. A spokesman for the Coast Guard, Captain Stephen Schwartz, said the search, a combined effort by the Coast Guard and units from the New York Police Harbor Patrol, had been discontinued at dusk. "There are strong currents in that area," he said. "It's possible we'll never recover the body." Mr. Weems was CEO of VisionClear Bank and Trust, a New York bank.

Trammell was dead. . . . How did I feel about that? I couldn't tell precisely. It seemed vaguely ironic, but I didn't have any deep feelings about it. I wondered if Crystal knew. How would she feel about it?

6.

THERE WAS A MESSAGE from Crystal waiting on my phone machine. She had lost her first match to Gracie Cobb. She said she missed me, and she left her number. I called it.

"Liberty Bell Hotel, your gateway to freedom. Marcia speaking. How can I help you?"

"Crystal Spivey, please. Room Three thirty-eight."

No answer. I explained to Marcia that Crystal was playing in the pool tournament held in the hotel ballroom. "Could you send a message to her?"

"Well, sir, my records show that she checked out at noon."

"I see. Thank you."

"Thank you for calling Liberty Bell, your gateway—"

The phone rang soon after. I snapped it up.

"Is he eating it?" Mr. Fleckton. I had forgotten entirely about the New & Improved problem. His voice had a panicky edge. "Don't hold anything back, Artie. I can take it."

"Well, actually, he showed considerable interest this morning," I lied.

"You mean he ate it?"

"No, but he sniffed it. I took that as a hopeful sign."

"Jesus, that's wonderful. He sniffed it. Yes, that is a hopeful sign. Call me anytime day or night if he eats it. We can shoot at a moment's notice."

"Okay."

Now what? I tuned in WBGO, the area jazz station, and listened nervously to a special on early Louis Armstrong. I heard "Azalea" and "Weatherbird," and they still seemed fresh and modern, but I wasn't really concentrating. I was thinking about Trammell Weems. In law school, I had found his utter contempt for sacred cows attractive. Even though I had had an inkling back then that rebellion wouldn't sustain one forever, I dug the stance of the out-sider with a sense of the ridiculous. Now I began to feel sad, but not exactly for Trammell. Somehow, sitting there in my morris chair listening to Mr. Armstrong, I linked Trammell and my youth. Both were dead. Nothing is sad-der in life than the tendency of time to pass. Let alone of humans to sink in deep water.

The phone rang.

"Hello, Artie. Did you hear? Can I come up?"

"Of course! Where are you?"

"Around the corner."

She carried a plastic garment bag over her shoulder and her cue case in the other hand. Her eyes were red-rimmed, but whether from crying or driving, I couldn't tell. We waited to speak until Jellyroll finished his effusive greet-ing. Meanwhile, I took her stuff, hung the garments in the hall closet and leaned the cue case against the wall.

Then we embraced.

"Who told you?" I asked.

"Uncle Billy called. He's very upset. He loved Trammell."

She sat at the dining-room table. I made her a BLT. She didn't speak as I did so, just sat sadly petting Jellyroll. I wanted to know what exactly she felt.

"Something's wrong, Artie," she said finally.

"What do you mean?"

"I don't know exactly. . . . It doesn't feel right."

"What doesn't?"

"Trammell's death. I feel scared."

"Scared? Why?"

"Artie, people are following me. I know they are. Sometimes I think they want me to know they're back there, like they're making it obvious."

"Who?"

"I don't know. Do you believe me?"

"Sure, if you say so."

"I hoped you would."

"I didn't know he was a banker. Did you?"

"Yeah. He got indicted in Miami for fraud. We lived together then. Trammell and two other guys owned a bank. They loaned money to each other and skimmed off the interest."

"What happened?"

"Nothing. All charges got dropped. Trammell knew they would. He was never worried. That was the first time I left him."

"Because you didn't want to be married to a white-collar criminal?"

"That, and other things I don't feel like talking about right now. I've tried to feel sad that he's dead, but I can't. I feel sad for myself. I was just a girl when I married him." She began to cry. She said something else, but it got lost. "You know what I was to him? I was a fuck-you gesture. Trammell Weems—of the great Weems family—married a pool player from Sheepshead Bay. That was a laugh. Even her name was a laugh! Crystal Spivey. Let's take our clothes off and get into bed."

"Sure."

And so we did. But we didn't make love, we just held each other. "Can he come up?"

"Sure."

Jellyroll floated up onto the bed and began licking her face. I told her he'd keep doing that until her cheeks were gone, so she should call him off when she'd had enough. "Crystal—"

"Hmm?"

"Do you want to get out of town for a couple days?"

"What did you have in mind?"

"I have a neighbor upstairs who owns a place in Fire Island."

"I went there once. A bunch of us rented a share in Kismet one summer."

"Jerry's place is in Lonelyville."

"Sounds wonderful. Can I stop and see Uncle Billy on the way?"

"Sure."

I phoned upstairs. A woman answered.

"Hello," I said, "I'm with the Sierra Club."

"Just a minute."

"Hi, Artie, what's up?"

"Can I rent your Fire Island place for a few days?"

"Cash?"

"Cash."

"Come on up. But if you see any strangers on the stairs, don't stop." Jerry was holed up in his apartment to skip the process servers. He was wanted by the SEC to testify in the matter of something or other. I never ask. Nobody was lurking on the stairs.

Jerry answered my coded knock in a terry-cloth bath-robe. He was barefoot, tousled, and his eyes looked like burnt holes in a smallpox-infested Army blanket. The guy couldn't have passed for fifty. He was twenty-six years old. He opened the door wide enough for me to sidle in. Two years ago, he was pulling down two hundred grand a year. I used to feed his cat while he jetted off to merger acquisitions and subordinate debentures. There were summer homes and boats, cars and fancy women in short black dresses, but then the bottom dropped out, and the Jerrys of the financial community plunged into a narrow pit.

His apartment was identical to mine, a one-bedroom in a prewar building undistinguished except for the view. From the western windows, Jerry and I could see all the way north to the George Washington Bridge and the bend in the river beyond. Looking south, we could see to the World Trade Center. But Jerry had the shades drawn tightly against the view. Except for bars of daylight beneath the shades, the only light in his living room came from a flickering, muted TV. Until my eyes adjusted, I didn't even see the young woman sprawling on the leather sofa. She, too, wore a frumpy robe and no shoes.

"Artie, this is Fritzi Kellior."

She waved unenthusiastically. She was even more unkempt than Jerry, but gradually, in the TV light, I could see that her features were long and patrician. Her short, unwashed hair was expensively cut. Humphrey Bogart caught my eye. *The Treasure of the Sierra Madre.*

Jerry and I quickly settled on a price for three days. Jerry asked me if I wanted to buy the place. I said no. "That's right. You don't own anything, do you? Except a dog."

I just let that slide by. "Have you ever heard of Trammell Weems?" I asked.

"Yeah. Glub-glub," Jerry said.

"What about before the glub-glub?"

"What about it?"

"What did he do? The paper said he was a banker."

"Yeah, right," said Fritzi.

"Ponzi banks. There probably used to be an honest man at VisionClear Bank and Trust, but he died in the last cholera epidemic. The interesting question is, who pulled the strings? How high did it go? You know?"

"No. How high did what go?"

"The cover-up."

The intercom buzzed. Jerry went off to answer. Fritzi stared blank-eyed at the TV. Bogart staggered through the purgatorial thicket blabbering about gold. Jerry hustled back. "We gotta split. That was the super. I paid him a hundred bucks to tell me when they're on the way up. Well, they're on the way up."

"Shit!" said Fritzi Kellior.

"Use my apartment." I tossed him the keys. "I've got a friend staying there. I'll try to deflect them."

"You will?" said Jerry. "Jesus, thanks, Artie."

"I'm sick of this," muttered Fritzi as they beat it out the door. "I'm real sick of this as a way of life."

I gathered up vodka bottles, glasses, and an empty orange-juice carton, dumped them in the sink, and hurried back to the living room to see what I'd missed—Fritzi's panty hose and pumps. I had had a brief affair with a woman who had once worked for Salomon Brothers, long before they got busted. She told me that exposing toe cleavage was bad form for a woman on the fast track. It was simply not done. I tossed Fritzi's shoes into the dark, cluttered bedroom. The banditos were slithering down the banks of the ravine after Bogart. He was finished.

The doorbell rang.

I peeped out the view hole. A little guy in a rumpled blue seersucker suit, no tie, stood in the hall. "Mr. Gerald Thwactman. I have a subpoena from Federal Court for the Southern District in the case of—"

I opened the door. "He's not here."

"When will he be back?"

I wondered how official this guy was. He didn't look like he carried much clout, but you can't always tell in

New York. However, if he were a cop, he'd already be inside, and I'd have footprints on my face. He looked like an out-of-work actor, and I felt sorry for him standing there, snapping a manila envelope against his thigh. "I'm house-sitting for Jerry. He left this morning for Hawaii. His father had a stroke. Paralytic, apparently."

He didn't even pretend to believe me. He just sighed. "Tell him sooner or later they'll send the cops."

I told him.

7.

"THEY WERE A CUTE COUPLE," said Crystal as we crossed the Brooklyn Bridge. "Jerry and Fritzi."

"The blush of youth . . . If you want to invite Billy to go with us, that would be fine with me."

She stroked the back of my neck with one hand and drove with the other, and I felt intense desire for her. I wondered if we'd be able to make love with Billy there. Jerry's walls were summer-house thin. But she didn't say any more about it until we stopped in front of a two-family house somewhere on Avenue X, near the Golden Hours. Crystal said it was her aunt Louise's place. Billy was staying there.

I waited in the car. It seemed simpler that way, and besides, I didn't want to see Billy sad. As I sat there I began to feel that I was being watched. I decided to forget it. This was a quiet street in south Brooklyn. What happens in Sheepshead Bay? Once a year an elderly lady slips on the ice and breaks her hip, but this was midsummer. . . . The feeling didn't abate. It intensified.

I slid into the driver's seat so I could use the mirrors. I watched an old gas guzzler, a Buick, I think, double-parked across the street and several car lengths behind. There

were two men in the front seat. The driver was black, and
the passenger was white. They didn't seem to be watching
me, but then that would be part of their job—to watch
without seeming to.

I started the engine. I waited to see what the Buick
would do. Nothing. I leaned out the window and pretended to wave good-bye to a nonexistent person standing
in Aunt Louise's vestibule. Then I pulled away, noting
landmarks as I went. It would have been ludicrous to get
lost.

I took the first right, drove two blocks toward the ocean,
then took another right. There was no one on my tail. I
made a few more random turns before I cruised slowly
back down Aunt Louise's block from the other direction.
The Buick hadn't moved, and its occupants paid no attention to me as I passed and parked in the spot I had vacated.
What did that prove? . . . It dawned on me that if they
were following Crystal, they would have remained right
where they were, regardless of what fool's errand I went
on. . . .

Crystal had tears in her eyes when she returned. I slid
back to my side. "How is he?"

"He loved the asshole."

"Did you invite him along?"

"No."

I was glad to hear that, but I didn't say so. I was busy
vainly adjusting the mirror on my side to see the Buick.

"What's the matter?"

"Check that big black car double-parked across the
street."

She looked in her mirror, pretending to straighten her
hair. "Which one?"

I described it further.

"There's no Buick."

I spun in my seat. The Buick was gone. Crystal and I looked at each other.

The ferry ride from Bayshore, crossing the Great South Bay to Fire Island, seemed a voyage to a fresh, foreign shore. We sat topside in the open, where the wind blew urban grit from our brains. About halfway across the bay, gulls and cormorants crossing our stern, I began to relax. My shoulders dropped to the horizontal. Easing tension, fresh air, ocean breezes, cormorants made me randy. I whispered a moderately lewd proposal in Crystal's ear. She giggled.

"Don't make any promises you can't keep."

I sat there anticipating, and by the time the captain slowed his boat to approach the dock at Ocean Beach, I had again forgotten about Trammell Weems. But Crystal hadn't—

"Maybe Trammell drowned accidentally, and that's too bad, I'm sorry for him, but that's the end of it."

"What do you mean, *maybe* he drowned accidentally? Didn't he?"

". . . A lot of people drown in boating accidents each year, right? A guy I know named Arnold towed Billy's boat in. I called him from Aunt Louise's. He said there was forty feet of rope tangled around the propeller. He said they were lucky it didn't pull the propeller shaft right out of the boat. It could have sunk. So that part checks."

"What are you thinking?"

"Naw, nothing. . . . Nothing really."

Fire Island is a long, narrow barrier beach, cars prohibited, an utterly different world from the city, but it lies only an hour and a half from the Triborough Bridge. The residents and renters are New Yorkers. They travel here with that New Yorker don't-hassle-me, self-involved mentality. It wears off after a day or two, but debarking the ferry at Ocean Beach still feels like changing trains at Times Square. Our fellow passengers didn't even notice Jellyroll. They were absorbed in lugging their bags, groceries, bicycles, boogie boards, cats in crates, plants in pots, rubber trees, sand chairs, volleyball nets, stereo equipment, laptop computers, electric bug zappers off the boat, hefting the stuff aboard little red wagons. Traveling light, we beat it off the dock.

Ocean Beach, a block-long stretch of shops, noisy nightclubs, and restaurants, is the island's major metropolis. I went with a woman briefly—the one who told me about toe cleavage—who owned a house there, so I knew the lay of the land. We bought our island-priced provisions and set off for Lonelyville, about a twenty-minute walk west.

"I forget how loud New York is until I leave," said Crystal, pausing to sniff a bright red flower drooping over someone's garden fence.

During the eighties, when people had absurd quantities of money coming in, they built houses too big for the scale of the island. But the older ones fit perfectly, little single-story cottages nearly enveloped by indigenous vegetation—beach plum, holly, other low-slung, gnarled trees I couldn't identify—and like most things that fit, they seemed full of peace and pleasure. I was definitely interested in some of the latter, even if the former was too much to hope for.

The best of the day was gone now, so deeply tanned bathers in French-cut suits passed us heading home. It seemed an island of burnished breasts and hams. Crystal glanced at me to see if I was ogling the bouncing flesh. I let my jaw fall slack and bugged out my eyes. She giggled. Had her shoulders dropped some, too? I thought they had. We were the only people on the island without a little red wagon to pull our stuff in, and I mentioned to Crystal, who suggested we hijack the next one that came along.

Paved walkways expired at the western edge of Ocean Beach. From here on it was sandy paths, tough going for little red wagons without balloon tires. I was feeling giddy in the salt air. Jellyroll took a shit in the sand. I picked it up in a plastic bag, but there was nothing to do with it, now I had it in hand. Fire Island government doesn't want the public around, so there were no public receptacles. I deposited the load in a private garbage can.

Nearby, three small deer picked at the bushes, impervious to our presence. Jellyroll stiffened. He was about to give chase. I told him no, and he looked up at me disgustedly. He loves to chase. I'd need to keep an eye on him or he'd turn feral.

On creosote logs, Jerry's house perched a full story above the natural rise at the top of the beach. We climbed the steps. Jellyroll took them two at a time, expecting to meet strangers interested in making a fuss over him at the top. There it was stretched out before us—the Atlantic Ocean. The house itself was simple, but the view from the porch was worth a million bucks, in a decent market.

Crystal dropped her packages, kicked off her shoes, and flopped in a weathered chaise longue. She moaned with contentment. "This is wonderful, Artie. Thank you. It's just what I needed and didn't even know it." The soft, warm wind pulled at the ends of her hair. "You wouldn't believe how I played in that tournament."

"Bad, huh?"

"And who'd I draw in the first round but Gracie Cobb. I was so bad, I think she began to feel sorry for me. Gracie Cobb doesn't feel sorry for anybody. She'd sacrifice her house pets for one lucky roll."

"Yeah, but you'd just heard Trammell had died."

"No, I heard that after Gracie stomped me."

"Oh."

"Maybe I should get a real job."

"Ugly word, job." I opened the sliding glass door and carried our groceries to the kitchen. Jerry's place was modest, but the single open room had that salt-damp feel of summer vacation when we were children, when the days seemed as endless as the ocean. Arranged seashells, pieces of driftwood in unusual shapes, and desiccated horseshoe crabs decorated the surfaces. Tracked-in sand felt wonderful crunching beneath my feet. As I opened all the windows and the other door, I wished I'd taken the place for a week. When I went back out on the porch, I couldn't help but notice that Crystal had removed her blouse and bra. That boded well.

She looked at me with theatrical coyness. "We can't be seen from here unless we stand up."

"Then let's not." I removed my shirt and squeezed in beside her. Her bra had left red lines under each breast.

"I could get sick of this in a couple decades."

I wondered if she meant the environment or my ministrations.

"Hello up there, anybody home?" called a man from the bottom of the steps.

Jellyroll barked. Crystal covered herself with her forearms and bolted into the house. I looked over the railing. It was a stocky guy with thick, hairy arms. He wore a silly-looking lime-green shorts and shirt set, with high-top Reeboks and white socks. Cop, I thought immediately. "Yes?"

"May I speak to Mrs. Crystal Weems?" His hair was dark and curly; so were his eyebrows. He squinted up at me.

"No, that's not my name," said Crystal, beside me now with her blouse back on. "Go away."

He pulled a gold shield from his shirt pocket. "Detective DiPietro, NYPD. We can talk here in this pleasing environment with birds and sea breezes, or I can jerk you off the streets of New York City."

"So talk."

"In private, please."

"No way. This is my attorney, Mr. Deemer. I want him present. That's what I pay him for."

"No need to get tough, Detective," I said. "We're always ready to cooperate with the police." A shiver of delight ran up and down my spine. I was her attorney.

"Can I come up?"

"Yes," said Crystal, "but don't call me Mrs. Weems."

"You're a little out of your jurisdiction, aren't you, Detective DiPietro?"

He sat in Crystal's chaise longue. Crystal sat in the aluminum lawn chair. I sat on the wooden railing.

"Nice place," said the cop. He folded his hands behind his head like a houseguest and breathed deeply. "Yours?" he asked Crystal.

"No."

"Don't you love that fresh salt air? I know I do. What is it about salt air? Hard to say. Maybe it's the freshness. This is my day off. I live over across the bay in Islip. Actually, this beach right here is part of the Town of Islip. Fancy Fire Island types don't like to admit that, but it's true. I came over with my family in my boat. It makes a nice day for the kids. A little waterskiing, little flounder fishing. Let's talk about VisionClear Bank and Trust—"

Crystal sagged.

"What's the matter, Crystal?" said the cop. "This ring bells for you? Cops questioning you about your husband's banking practices?"

"He's not my husband. I told you that."

"But he was your husband when they came to get you in Miami, right?"

"So what? I wasn't involved then, and I'm not now."

"As her attorney, I protest the smartass tone you're using on Ms. Spivey."

"As her attorney, did she tell you she got busted for bank fraud?"

"That's a lie!" said Crystal. "I never did."

"I've seen your mug shots, Crystal."

"I wasn't charged with anything." Her voice was flat, but her black eyes flashed. "Why are you harassing me?"

"I'm not harassing you. I just want to talk about VisionClear and Trammell Weems. VisionClear served the financial needs of criminals. Weems looted it, and then he drowned. Only we have reason to believe that he didn't really drown."

"What do you mean he didn't—?"

"I mean we think he faked his death to cover his tracks. You wouldn't put it past him, would you, Crystal? I mean, it's his style, wouldn't you say?"

"I don't know."

"Let's just say that's what happened. Hypothetically. In which case he'd need an accomplice, somebody to tell the world that Trammell drowned. This Bruce Munger person, for instance."

"So why don't you go talk to him?"

"I will. But since I was out here with the kids, I thought I'd start with you."

"Have you been following Crystal?"

"No."

"Then how did you know we were here?" I asked.

"Coincidence. I saw you getting off the ferry. Somebody's been following you? I'm not surprised."

"Why?" I asked.

"Because the bad guys want their money back. You think I'm a smartass, wait till you meet them. There's the Mafia, there's international arms merchants, drug smugglers, and some crooked politicians. A bunch of beauties. You won't like them or their methods."

"Goddamnit," snapped Crystal. "These people are going to come after us?"

"Look, I'm willing to believe you're nothing but an innocent bystander, but in my work, I try to see things from the bad guys' point of view. And from there, it doesn't look good for you. What do they see? They see the fact that you were married to Trammell. They see the boat off which he drowned belonging to your uncle. And they see the only eyewitness to the drowning—this Bruce Munger fellow—as a friend of yours. If I were in the bad guys' shoes, I'd start looking for Trammell and their money right here."

"So what do we do?" I asked, trying to ignore my rising fear.

"Well, I might be able to help. I'd like to help. But you're going to have to tell me everything, and you'll have to tell me if anybody approaches you about Trammell, VisionClear, and so forth. Anybody at all. Is that clear? When was the last time you saw Trammell?"

"Day before yesterday. He came into my uncle's poolroom to rent his boat."

"How common a thing was that, renting your uncle's boat?"

"I don't know. Trammell and my uncle used to go fishing a lot. I don't know if he ever rented the boat before."

"Did you speak to Trammell on that occasion day before yesterday?"

"I told him to get out."

"And why was that?"

"Because Trammell fucks people up—just like he's fucking me up right now."

"Did Trammell and your uncle ever have any business dealings? I mean besides boat rentals?"

74

"No. Look, my uncle is retarded. He doesn't have business deals."

"Retarded? What do you mean retarded?"

"He's like a child. He loved Trammell. I saw my uncle on the way out here. He's grieving for Trammell. If Trammell faked his death, my uncle doesn't know it."

"But it's still possible Trammell used your uncle in some way."

"How?"

"I don't know. You tell me."

"I can't. I don't know."

"But you wouldn't put that past Trammell either, would you?"

"I think Trammell really loved my uncle. . . . But that wouldn't stop Trammell from using him."

"Has anybody spoken to you before this?"

"No."

"Nobody at all?"

"No. I said no."

"Well, I want to help you, and I can. But you're going to have to come clean with me."

"I have! What do you want from me! Hell, I never heard of VisionClear Bank until I read about Trammell's death in the newspaper."

"Okay." He slipped a card from his shirt pocket and snapped it down on the wooden arm of the chaise.

I picked it up. There was nothing on the card but DiPietro's name and a phone number.

"That's in case you ever need a cop. Personally, I believe you. But it's very important for me to know if you are approached by any individual wanting to discuss this matter. Any individual at all."

"Why do you think Trammell is alive?" I asked.

"I can't go into that without jeopardizing my informant.

Call me any time of the day or night if you hear anything."
He stood up. "Thanks in advance for your cooperation."

We stood at the top of the steps and watched him descend. Then we sat silently, stared out at the horizon. Crystal was near tears.

"Maybe this isn't far enough, Fire Island," I said.

"I can't just pack up and leave because of something fucking Trammell did."

"True."

". . . Where would we go?"

"The Bahamas."

"The Bahamas?"

"A place called Poor Joe Cay."

"Who do you know there?"

"A man called Calabash."

"Calabash, huh?"

"He used to be my bodyguard. Now he's my friend."

"You had a bodyguard?"

"Yes."

She glanced at me, but she didn't ask any more about that. She said, "Thanks for being my lawyer."

"My pleasure."

"Artie, they arrested me in Miami, like that cop said. But I hadn't done anything, and they let me go. Do you believe I didn't have anything to do with Trammell's scams?"

"Of course."

Pause. "That cop wrecked the sexy feelings for me."

Two stern-draggers fished on the horizon. They seemed pinned there, unmoving. I have in the past found peace looking at the ocean, something about perspective and timelessness, but now that seemed like a lot of romantic twaddle. There was nothing out there but a couple of fishing boats. Whatever this Trammell business was about at bottom, I think we knew even then, grudgingly, that we wouldn't escape the toxic runoff. I felt completely exhausted.

Crystal was asleep in the chaise when the sun went down over our right shoulders. I could see the top of New York in the far distance, the architecture of reality. The ocean turned to teal in the dying light. Mosquitoes rose and drove us inside.

8.

CRYSTAL SLEPT IN THE NEXT MORNING. I watched for a while, kissed her forehead. I still hoped we could salvage the romantic component in this weekend. After all, what did we have to do with Trammell Weems? Nothing. That was past; this was now. Without opening her eyes she reached behind my neck and gently pulled me to her. I told her I was going to take Jellyroll for a walk on the beach while it was still early, the beach empty. When the beach is crowded, we get stopped every fifty feet by admirers, his, not mine. It's like walking with Madonna. I made coffee and took a mugful with me. The coffee, the deserted beach, Jellyroll's joy, and Crystal back at the house in bed combined into a feeling of contented bliss, a feeling striking in its unfamiliarity.

We walked west about a mile, almost to the community of Saltaire. On the way, I threw driftwood sticks for Jellyroll until he panted. Jellyroll is not a swimmer, only a wader. He wades in up to his chest and drinks great gulps of seawater. Then, after a while, he throws it back up. I used to carry a jug of fresh water on beach trips, but I gave up, because it wasn't thirst but some kind of compulsion that drove him to drink from the sea. Certain dog behavior will remain forever inexplicable to humans. So now I try to avoid that drink-hoop routine by engaging his attention with driftwood.

But both of us grew tired of it, and we sat down on the beach near the high-tide line. There I sifted absentmindedly through the flotsam and jetsam entangled in the snaking lines of seaweed. One summer a red tide of medical waste had washed up on New York beaches. Everyone knew its origin—illegal dumping by Mafia-owned garbage collectors—but no one seemed inclined or able to stop it. I saw no medical waste. I found a few black, leathery skate-egg cases, fish bones, and a large, dead horseshoe crab. I mused for a while on the simple creatures, on lives spent scuttling along the ocean floor. I saw the man approach from the upper beach, but I ignored him until his shadow fell across us.

"That's the R-r-ruff Dog, right?"

"No, but he looks like the R-r-ruff Dog," I said without looking up. "Lot of people mistake them."

"Come on, that's the R-r-ruff Dog. And you're Artie Deemer."

"Who are you?"

"I'm Chet Bream." Unbidden, he sat down beside us and began to pet Jellyroll. "I'm a journalist. It's my job to know people."

"Could you go do it somewhere else?"

He didn't move. He was a skinny-faced guy with freckles, a long lower lip, and close-set eyes that darted around my head, only seldom settling on mine. At first I thought this was another Jellyroll proposal. Somebody or other always wants a piece of him for self-serving purposes. Local TV idiots from all over the country want to "interview" him, make faces and cock their heads the way he does while they ask him stupid questions. They make him appear ridiculous, a clown, and his innocence in the face of that exploitation (not totally different from my own) depresses me. I always say no. I started to say no now—

"So how's Crystal taking it?" he said.

". . . What?"

"Weems's death."

"Beat it."

"I've been following a story on the CIA and the financial community. More precisely, the CIA *in* the financial community."

I didn't say anything.

"That joker from yesterday in the lime-green getup, he was a cop, right? He wasn't federal, right? He was a local cop, right? Only a cop would dress like that." Eyes darting east and west, he whipped a tube of ChapStick out of his shirt pocket and smeared his lips with jerky, birdlike motions. "Mind telling me what he's investigating?"

"Yeah."

"I can understand your reticence. Guy sits down with you and your dog at the beach—incidentally, I'm a big fan of his—and starts asking you questions. Besides, the press isn't held in the highest esteem of late. I can understand that. But I'm alternative press. I first came across Crystal down in Miami in the mid-eighties. You got to understand what Miami was like in those days. Your standing in certain social circles, your hipness quotient, was determined by how much dirty money you had around you. Narcoterrorists, savings and loan crooks, crazy spooks, deposed dictators, crooked developers with politicians in their pockets, gunrunners, stock manipulators—they were the cream of the social crop for a time. It was hip to have a hit man to dinner and talk about him behind his back. Cocaine was the lingua franca. It was Reaganomics strung out on one-hundred-percent–pure pixie dust. Coke, money, and bloated corpses in the canals." He spoke a mile a minute like a speed freak, but this guy wasn't stoned. He was just intense.

"Back in Miami there was this bank called Tropical Trust. Trammell Weems ran but did not own Tropical Trust. Everybody knew Tropical Trust was a laundry. What are you gonna do with six million bucks in twenties? Rent a U-Haul and take it to Trammell Weems at Tropical Trust. Dry-cleaning while you wait. As a result, Trammell was a local celebrity. Here was this charming, urbane cat, rich, socially connected. Rode cigarette boats and polo ponies. And how hip can you get?—he was married to a professional *pool player* from Sheepshead Bay, Brooklyn, New York!

"In addition to dope money, Miami was the nerve center for all the weird spook activity going down in Central America. And that's where my story begins. Take a Contra to lunch in Coconut Grove, sell him a Tow missile or two. There were riches for all in the anti-Communism dodge. The spooks were in bed with the narco-terrorists, and everybody had great bundles of illegal bread. The sides blurred. Only the money mattered. Hell, even the Sandinistas needed a bank like Tropical Trust. Through good old-fashioned journalistic digging, I learn that one Reggie Archibald is among the owners of Tropical Trust." He stopped to slather on another layer of ChapStick. He pursed his lips to spread it around. "That name ring a bell?"

"Reggie Archibald . . . from 'The Mayhews'?"

"Yep. Honest Milt Mayhew. Voted TV's finest citizen, represented all those traditional values that made this nation strong. How about that for irony? Milt Mayhew runs banks for criminals, drug dealers, spooks, and gunrunners. Don't you love irony? So fucking American. You can't make up better stuff than that. Especially when you add that Trammell Weems played his son, Timmy Mayhew!

That's the thing I love about this whole story. With these fuckheads, truth is stranger than fiction, if you don't blanch at the cliché. And I don't."

I was growing more depressed with each machine-gun sentence.

"Then it blows. Ka-boom! Tropical Trust goes bust. In 1985 it showed assets in excess of two billion dollars. In 1986 it's insolvent. Flat broke with one point five billion in bad loans. Where'd all the money go? And why didn't the Feds know what every cocktail party hanger-on knew for years?

"You wouldn't have liked to see Crystal Spivey when they hauled her away in handcuffs. She looked like death warmed over. Turns out she was a pill freak, totally strung. That was to be her defense. She doesn't know a thing. Too stoned.

"But defense was unnecessary, because the case suddenly got dropped. Why? Lack of evidence. I saw the evidence—I got friends in the DA's office—it was ironclad. So I recognize right there that we're dealing with more than crooked bankers and seamy depositors. We're dealing with the big fix. I mean bi-ig. I'm talking the halls of government! I'm talking Justice, State, what's quaintly called the intelligence community, maybe even the oval fucking office! I mean, nobody would kick up a fuss if Trammell Weems and his lovely wife Crystal went down, but if Trammell goes down, chances are Reggie Archibald's gonna go down, too. It's gonna come out that Tropical Trust is just one in a string of banks secretly run by old Reggie, and they're all as crooked as Tropical, and they're all connected to some very heavy folks. In short, Artie, this is the story of the fucking decade!"

I sifted morosely through the seaweed with a stick. "Then why don't you go write it? You'll probably get a job with Ted Koppel. What do you need me for? Or Crystal?"

"You want proof?"

"No, I don't want proof. I want peace."

"Well, proof is right at your fingertips. Trammell Weems gets busted for bank fraud, but all charges get dropped. What's he do? Fade away, fortunate to have gotten out with his ass intact? Not our Timmy Mayhew. He moves to New York and opens VisionClear Bank and Trust. See what I'm getting at? This is a federally insured bank. Artie, the same people who ordered the Tropical Trust charges dropped approved VisionClear."

"What did you say your name is?"

"Chet. Chet Bream."

"You're not listening to me, Chet."

Finally his eyes rested on mine. "You want to know what this has to do with you, right? Patience, I'm getting to that. What we got here is different from your average corruption conspiracy in several ways. One, it's bigger and juicier, but that's not its main distinction. Its main distinction is that there's a smoking gun. I admit that my story came to a dead end. It's very tough to follow covert money. That's why they make it covert. But then I get wind of the smoking gun." He paused, peered at me.

Clearly, it was my turn to ask, "What smoking gun?" but I didn't. I continued to sift seaweed.

Chet didn't let that stop him. "What smoking gun?" he said. "A smoking gun in the form of a videotape. Picture this scene: poolside, summer, the water shimmers in the sun. Several guys are sitting outdoors at a round table under a green canvas umbrella. There's a garden party going on around them, tight bodies in tiny bathing suits. However, the guys at the table aren't participating in the revelry.

"Since you're so busy, I'll get down to the dramatis personae in the tape without further ado. There's five men sitting under the green umbrella. There's Trammell

Weems, looking really slick in Bermuda shorts and an open-necked shirt. There's Reggie Archibald, who weighs in these days at about three hundred and fifty pounds. And then there's three other colorful fellows. Let's focus down on them—" But first he needed another hit of ChapStick.

"One, you got Handsome Danny Barcelona. Handsome Danny got busted back about 'eighty-five here in NYC along with Sammy 'The Neck' Randolucci and a half-dozen other overweight wiseguys. But the Feds couldn't make it stick.

"Two, you got a very shady figure, a man of many identities. He was identified to me in Miami, by a source I'm not at liberty to divulge, as one Anthony Bonaventure. My source offered compelling evidence that Bonaventure ran a cell of anti-Castro bankers trying to undermine the Cuban economy by shooting it full of counterfeit pesos. I did some research on Senor Bonaventure. You don't do that kind of research in the public library, so I had to depend on certain questionable sources for information. Under the name Captain Norman Armbrister, U.S. Navy, he served in a secret cadre that ran incursions into Cambodia as early as 1967. Well, they got caught out in the open one day and had the shit shot out of them. Only one man came back—Norman Armbrister. Seems he walked back across the border with the top of his head blown off. It took him two weeks. This made him a spook star. The man sitting at that table under the green umbrella is leaning forward. You can see the top of his head—there's the scar plain as day." Chet paused for a dose of ChapStick.

"Now let's look at the fifth man at the table. The camera's stationary, and the fifth man's sitting with his back to it. He's a distinguished gentleman in a pin-striped suit, with silvery gray hair. Who is he? Who's that fifth man? I haven't been able to identify him yet, but I'm working on it.

"There's an audio portion to the tape. The sound quality's not great, but it's good enough. They're talking about the means of security for deposits in Archibald's offshore banks. Tiny—oh, I forgot to tell you, speaking of irony, that they call him *Tiny* Archibald—Tiny's telling these hoods and spooks how to launder their cash and then how to get it overseas where no questions will be asked. It only runs about seven minutes, but it is ho-ot stuff! Tiny brags all about his connection to big shots on the federal level, he tells them his associate Trammell Weems will take care of all the details."

Was that it? I waited to hear. This guy had stopped talking. "I still don't see what that has to do with Crystal and me."

"You don't?"

"No, I don't."

"I'm disappointed, I took you for a beach-smart individual. Look at it this way. Trammell Weems was married to Crystal Spivey. Trammell drowns off Crystal's uncle's boat. No body was recovered. Whose word do we have to take? One Bruce Munger. I saw Crystal and Munger—not to mention you—together at a pool hall in Chelsea just the other day. You seemed to know each other."

"We do know each other. That's no secret."

"Right, that's my point. How would it look like to you if you were one of those five fuckers under the umbrella?"

My head was spinning.

"So you might be in danger just because you were in the wrong place at the wrong time. That depends on what you know."

"Nothing!"

"What about Trammell's so-called drowning? I was hoping you could shed some light on that."

"What do you mean so-called?"

"I'm saying his drowning was bullshit. I'm saying it had

something to do with that tape. What about this uncle? William Spivey?"

"What about him?"

"Could you set up an interview? I went looking for him, but he's not at his pool hall or at his home. Maybe you could set something up with him. Crystal probably knows where he is. Come on, strictly off the record. In the interests of justice."

"Yeah, right, justice."

Chet Bream paused. He began to cover his knees with handfuls of sand. "I'm interested in justice. These guys piss me off. They're running their own government, arrogant bastards. They rob federally insured deposits with impunity, and who pays? The poor average taxpayer pays. Ma and Pa Kettle, who can barely scrape together enough to make the monthlies on the Bronco, and everybody gets butt-fucked right on down the line. These guys think they're above the law, and that puts me right off, Artie. I'm a very patriotic fellow, when you get right down to it. I think this is a great nation if it weren't for the government and the banks and the secrecy. I want to expose it for the corrupt system it is. Of course, I want to be a media star for doing it, but that doesn't mean I'm not interested in justice. I've just cultivated this cynical attitude over the years. Basically, I'm a shocked innocent."

I watched him bury his knees. I believed him, but what difference did that make? "Where is this tape?"

"That's the question. Where is the tape?"

"Who made it?"

"That's an area I can't talk about."

"But you've seen it?"

"Yes."

"How?"

"I can't go into that, except to say that the man who

showed it to me had to be identified by his dental records."

"Terrific. That makes me want to get deeply involved."

His eyes settled again on mine. "I'm here to tell you you are involved."

I believed him there too, but I held out hope that he was wrong. "What are your plans? Are you going to continue following us around? We're not going to like that."

"Yeah, I wouldn't either. . . . Look, let me talk to Crystal. I didn't want to barge in on her. Women take a lot of shit these days—it doesn't work to just barge in on them. You introduce me to her. If she doesn't want to talk to me, I'll go away."

"And stay away?"

"Yes."

"Promise."

He gave the Cub Scout oath sign. Then he gave me a card with an address in Chelsea penciled on it.

Jellyroll's body began to twitch and heave as if he were trying to expel a hot anvil from his guts. Then he began to retch.

"What's wrong with him?" Chet Bream wanted to know.

We walked back toward Jerry's house. I wondered how Crystal would take it, me showing up with a ChapStick-junkie reporter to talk about the death of her ex-husband.

"You know, I spoke to this guy Bruce Munger," said Bream on the way. "He tried to hit me up for a hundred bucks to talk to him."

"Then you got the right Bruce Munger."

"When I didn't pay, he told me Trammell drowned."

"Maybe he did."

He gave me a sardonic sidelong glance.

"You know, for a reporter you're not very objective."

Crystal, small in the distance, watched us approach from

the porch. She waved like a sea captain's wife to his ship in the offing. Maybe she thought then that Bream was just a stranger who happened to be going our way, until we trudged through the soft sand at the head of the beach, Chet Bream on our asses.

We stopped beneath the porch where Crystal stood. She stared down at us. Jellyroll smiled at her. "Crystal, this is Chet Bream. He's a reporter who wants to talk to you about Trammell."

"Tell him to beat it."

9.

IT SEEMED TO TAKE TWO DAYS to tell it all.
Crystal just shook her head when I was done. Her shoulders hunched. She withdrew. I made us some coffee. It was only a little after eight, but I felt like I'd already put in a full day loading concrete blocks.

"Everything looked gray to me," she said when I returned to the living room.

"What?"

"Even the neon lights at the beach looked totally"—she pronounced it "tot'ly"—"gray."

"You mean back in Miami?"

"Yeah. Especially when they were taking me away in handcuffs."

"You were depressed."

"I was a doper."

"You told me our first night together."

"I'm sorry, Artie."

"You don't need to apologize for an unhappy past."

"No, for getting you into this."

"Maybe it's nothing. Maybe this guy Bream's just a conspiracy weirdo. He's a ChapStick junkie."

"He is? How do you know?"

"He kept slathering it on."

"You think he's just a goofball, and we don't need to worry about it?"

"Sure. But we can get out of town if you're worried about it." Flight is my best response to reality.

"We are out of town."

"Way out of town."

"Artie, I can't just leave. I have commitments. If you want to go I'd understand."

"As your attorney, I'm under retainer to stay."

"Do you mind if we go home?"

We returned in heavy traffic. The air was blue. A funk of effluvia hung over the city, and the backs of our necks felt gritty just driving through it. In these conditions the population moves more from memory than intent. Everywhere, fire hydrants gushed. Gutters flooded as litter-clogged drains backed up. People sat on their stoops with their arms and legs spread so flesh wouldn't touch flesh, a city full of prickly-heat sufferers. Rain clouds gathered over New Jersey, but they never developed into showers, dashing hopes for relief. Come nightfall, tempers would fray, and people would begin to hurt each other senselessly.

Crystal and I didn't go out the rest of that day except to take Jellyroll to the park. We listened to Benny Carter compositions. I'm very fond of his version of "Lover Man" from the 1985 recording *A Gentleman and His Music*. Maybe Mr. Carter will live forever. We didn't talk much; we ate Chinese food and listened. We did, however, make love, and, doing so, we felt the doubt and anxiety fade like storm clouds passing away over the horizon. Storms have a way of lurking out beyond the curvature of the earth and doubling back to clobber you when your guard goes down.

*   *   *

90

That night Crystal and Earle Grundy played high-stakes nine ball. Most of the regulars recognized Earle when he came in and sat down on a stool, ostensibly to watch Crystal and me play. Earle was hard to miss. He was a black man, very tall and slim. His graying hair was shoulder length and scraggly, and he always played with a pair of reading glasses perched on his crown. Crystal pretended not to see him. He went along with the pretense. I don't always understand these ritual preliminaries to gambling sessions, often as elaborate as aboriginal rain dances. Crystal beat me and immediately unscrewed her cue. I followed her lead.

"Oh, hello, Earle," she said.

"Hi, Crystal." His voice seemed heavy with some personal sadness. "Looks like you're in stroke."

"It comes and goes. Earle, this is my friend Artie Deemer."

We shook hands cordially, but he didn't smile. He and Crystal were doing business.

"Ready to go, Crystal?"

"You're too good for me, Earle."

"I'm way past my prime." He was no older than me.

I returned the tray of balls to Davey at the desk and paid the table time. When I returned, Crystal and Earle were sitting on adjacent stools, but they weren't speaking. The regulars were watching, waiting for serious action to enrich the routine of their lives. For once they were silent.

"One-pocket, Crystal?" Earle Grundy was one of the best one-pocket players in the country.

"I don't play that game, Earle."

Feedback tore through the room, and Davey said over the PA: "Phone call for Thumper. Thumper, you gotta call."

"Well," said Earle languidly, "I guess I'll go say hello to Davey. I haven't seen him in years. . . . Unless you want to play some other game. Like nine ball."

"You mean a friendly game?"

"Sure, just a friendly game."

"How friendly?"

"A hundred a set?"

Crystal didn't say yes, and she didn't say no. "I can't play you head up," she said finally.

The regulars were edging closer to hear.

"What do you need?" Earle wanted to know.

"The six."

"The six? Naw. I'll go say hello to Davey." But he didn't move.

"Well, we have to leave, anyway. We're late already, aren't we, Artie?"

I pretended to look at my watch. "Almost," I said.

"Maybe some other time," said Earle.

"Yeah."

"Better not wait too long. I won't have any eyes too much longer. Teeth, neither. So I'll give you the seven tonight."

"I'll take the seven and the break."

"Naw, your break's too good." Crystal was known to have a savage break. "I'll give you the seven, and winner breaks."

"Then I'll need the seven wild."

"Out of the question."

"That's okay, we have to go, anyway."

"The seven and the break. But I must be feeling generous. I don't usually."

"Hundred a set?"

"Want to make it an even two hundred, since you got the break?"

Crystal nodded. The preliminaries had ended. Let the games begin.

While Earle warmed up—by pounding in cross-side banks, never missing a one, then doing the same thing long-rail—the regulars descended on me to know the arrangements and the stakes. I told them. Spanish Jackie started making odds, waving bills folded between his fingers. The regulars placed their wagers, and Crystal pretended not to notice.

"Look at that guy bank," commented Outta-Town Brown.

"All black guys can bank," said Ted Bundy. "They're born with banking in their bones."

Feedback: "Phone call for Ernie's wife. Ernie's wife, you gotta call."

A hush fell around the table. Crystal crushed the balls. Two dropped. She stood staring at the rest. She had a clear shot at the one ball, and the nine had stopped near the corner pocket. The nine was makable off the one ball, but it was a dangerous shot, what good players call low percentage. Each nine-ball game presents a problem, and there is a crux, a one-shot turning point, to each. Sometimes the crux comes immediately, sometimes not until near the end. We were at the crux right now.

Play the one-nine combination or try for the run out? If she elected to run the balls, she'd have no trouble until she got to the six, which lay frozen against the eight on the foot rail. She'd have to figure out a way to break that cluster. She decided to run them. She leaned down to shoot the one, an easy cut in the side. She missed.

The crowd gasped. You could tell how the side betting had broken down. Those that had bet against her smiled. The others glowered. Expressionlessly, she sat down. She'd have to forget it, not let the early mistake defeat her. Earle ran the game out. They were playing what in the parlance is called a race to six games for the two hundred dollars.

Crystal broke, but nothing dropped. The table was open. Earle never got out of line. He left himself a straight, short shot on the nine. Crystal didn't even make him shoot it in. It was a foregone conclusion. She put her stick on the table between the cue ball and the nine, the sign of concession. The sweaters who had bet on Crystal fell silent and morose. Crystal broke, and again nothing fell. She never got another shot in game three.

She knew she was in big trouble, but nothing showed on her face. They seesawed back and forth in the next game. One safety was more devious than the next. Then Crystal made a mistake. Earle had a shot. That's all he needed. He was out. What was her problem? Was her head not on the match? Was the crowd making her nervous, or was Earle just too good for her?

I realized that Bruce was standing beside me.

"Hey, counselor," he said.

"Hey, Bruce."

"What's the action here?"

"Race to six for two hundred."

"What'd she get from him?"

"The seven ball and the break."

"Anything else?"

"No."

"Suicide." He went looking for Spanish Jackie. He didn't have to go far, not even out of earshot.

"No credit, no credit," said Spanish Jackie when he saw Bruce coming.

"Did I mention credit? Did you hear me say credit? Just tell me the line."

"Three to one on Earle, but you can't bet this set. Too late this set."

"Obviously, Jackie. Here's a hundred on Earle for the next set. No, make it a deuce."

Bruce counted two bills from a fat roll. Naturally, I figured he had all ones stuck beneath the thin skin of hundreds, a so-called Minnesota roll. But no. There were hundreds at the heart of the roll. He had several thousand dollars there. Bruce never had real money. Where'd Bruce get real money?

Spanish Jackie was asking himself the same question. He looked suspiciously at the bills, crinkled them, looked at them again, snapped them beside his ear. He even sniffed them before he accepted Bruce's bet.

"Could I have a word with you, Bruce?" I asked when he stood beside me again.

"You don't even need to say it, Arthur." He peeled off three more hundreds and stuck them in my shirt pocket. "Does that bring me current? Here, have another." He slid it into the pocket.

"Looks like you came into some money."

"Playing cards."

"I see."

Crystal was in dreadful shape. With only three balls left in game five, Earle had dumped her on the rail behind two balls. The one she needed to hit, the seven, was frozen on the opposite rail. She made a good try, going three rails, but she failed to hit the seven, a foul. Earle had cue ball in hand. Crystal didn't even make him shoot. She racked the balls. Earle's lead was insurmountable.

"Ever heard of Tiny Archibald, Bruce?"

Bruce blinked, but he didn't look at me. "The basketball player?"

"I don't think so."

"Why do you ask?"

"Just wondered."

"Tiny Archibald? Hmm. No, doesn't ring any bells. Seems like I'd remember a guy named Tiny Archibald. Why do you ask?"

"How about Chet Bream?"

"Chet Bream?"

"Yeah, a journalist. He's been doing a story on the CIA and the banking business. I figured you'd know him."

"Why?"

"He said he spoke to you about Trammell's death, you being the only witness."

Bruce shot a glance at me. You could see the wheels turning. "Would you like to step away from this gambling element?"

"Sure, Bruce." I saw Crystal pay Earle two hundred dollars. They were getting set to go again. Bruce and I walked over to the drinking fountain.

"This Bream, was he a twitchy fellow, did a lot of ChapStick?"

"Yeah, that sounds like the fellow." I told Bruce first about the cop's visit, then about Chet Bream's. I told him that both wanted to talk to him about Trammell's death, that both suspected Bruce had lied about the circumstances surrounding it. "Is there anything you'd like to tell me?"

"Trammell drowned, Artie. No shit. I didn't actually see him go down for the third time, but he wasn't on the boat and he wasn't swimming around it. He drowned."

"Okay. It doesn't matter to me one way or the other, but I thought you'd want to know."

"Okay, pal, thanks a lot."

"So where'd you get the money? You didn't get the money for bullshitting the cops about Trammell's death, did you?"

"I told you. I got the money playing gin with a fish at the Salmagundi Club. Nobody believes me. Why doesn't anybody believe me?"

"Because you're a liar."

"Listen, guy, you got to loosen up. Smoke some of this when the going gets tough."

"Okay, see you around." I had a drink of water, then went back to the game.

"What's the score?" I asked Thumper.

"Two to nothing in the second set. Crystal's down. Say, Artie, you wouldn't be interested in a Wagner Power Painter, would you?"

"When I came in here tonight, I hoped desperately someone would offer me a good deal on a Wagner Power Painter."

Bruce came out of the rest room. Head down, he strode to the front door, then out into the night. My heart sank. That was a very bad sign. If Bruce won the bet, Spanish Jackie would still pay off; it wasn't that. But betting on pool isn't like betting on a horse at OTB. You stay to watch. That's part of the point. Bruce wasn't staying. He was *walking out* on a two-hundred-dollar bet.

Earle sank the nine in a long combination off the five. Devastating. Three to zero . . . Maybe Bruce just went out for coffee. . . . They had excellent coffee right here. I kept looking over my shoulder at the door. He never returned.

The rest of the set lasted a mere forty minutes. Crystal never had a chance. On the rare occasions she got an opening, she failed to capitalize on it. She unscrewed her cue, paid Earle another two hundred dollars, and shook his hand. I let her sit by herself on a bench in the corner for a while, then I joined her.

"I was terrible," she muttered, staring out. "I was terrible in Philadelphia, and I was terrible here."

"Do you want to play him again?" I said after a while.

"I don't have any more money. I just dropped four hundred bucks."

"I do."

"Artie, I want you as a lover, not as a stake horse."

"I know. We don't need to make a habit of it. But if you think you can beat him . . ."

"You think I can?"

"He's tough. But the spot is fair. You never really recovered from missing that one ball in the first game. Maybe starting from scratch—but I get fifty percent if you win, plus I get to perform certain twisted sexual acts on your person."

"That's a hard offer to pass up."

I slid two of Bruce's hundreds out of my pocket and put them on her knee. She took a deep breath for courage and went after Earle Grundy.

It took all night, literally. The sun was well up when they finally quit. Crystal won that first set and paid me off right away. Then she won the next set. She was playing flawless, intelligent pool. She safetied Earle to death in those sets. She dumped him into one untenable position after another. It blew his patience. But no one ever said Earle Grundy lacked heart. He came back to win the next two. Side betting was very heavy. There must have been fifty people sweating the match. Even the bangers got in on the action. About four A.M. a quartet in evening clothes wandered in. Twenty minutes later they were calling for Spanish Jackie. It was an orgy of side wagering.

Most of the people in New York were shouldering their way to work when Earle called it quits by unscrewing his cue. His eyes were red and sunken. So were Crystal's, but the big difference in their eyes was that hers had won. Some players contend that in pool nothing else matters.

Earle paid off, congratulated her like a gentleman, and walked out the door, alone, into the raw daylight. By then the sweaters had diminished in number, but not by much. Some had taken a cold bath. The odds at one point went to four to one against Crystal. The losers sat silently, bleary-eyed, smoking cigarettes.

I could tell Crystal's adrenaline was still pumping even before she said, "I'll take you back to your place, where I'll let you perform—what was it?—twisted sexual acts on my person."

I was walking on my ankles by then. I didn't think I could come up with anything twisted, except my spine.

Driving up Amsterdam, she said, "I'll never be really good at this game, because I always feel sorry for the person I beat." We stopped at the light at Seventy-second Street. "And poor Earle didn't have anybody to go home with."

10.

THE TELEPHONE WOKE ME ABOUT NOON. A woman with a squeaky voice: "This is Lydia Segal. Remember me? With Bruce? From the pool hall?"

"Sure, Lydia." I always felt sorry for Lydia, an anorexic woman barely out of her teens who Bruce used to drag into the Upscale Poolroom after a weekend of debauchery. They'd stagger around the table, dribble coffee down their chins. On those rare occasions when she showed up straight, she was an intelligent person with psychological insight and a sense of humor. Now she didn't sound particularly straight.

"I was supposed to see him last night. I went over to his place. I saw light coming under the door, but he didn't answer. I went away. I came back today and there was still the light, but he still didn't answer."

If Bruce had been a normal citizen who pays taxes, I would have suggested that Lydia call the police. "I saw Bruce last night," I said. "He had a wad of money."

"Money? . . . Bruce?"

"He said he won it in a card game."

"I thought maybe since you live right around the corner, you'd be with me when I open the door. I got a key. I'm scared something happened. Cops have been around."

"Cops?"

"Well, one cop. And other weird people."

"Where are you now?"

"Up on Broadway."

"I'll meet you at his place in twenty minutes."

"What could I say?" I asked Crystal after I had related Lydia's call. "I couldn't just say no. . . . Could I?"

"I'm going with you," she said.

"No, there's no need for you—"

"Yeah, but there might be."

Bruce lived in a shitty brownstone on Ninety-eighth Street near Amsterdam Avenue. The usual members of the community were standing around. A wasted old man on a walker sang, "If you can make it here, you can make it anywhere." A group of kids played tackle football in the street. Crystal and I looked around for some kind of trap, but we knew that if there were one, we'd never see it. That caused the commonplace to assume an air of menace. I hate it when the commonplace assumes an air of menace.

Lydia was sitting on the stoop. Her knees looked like oranges in bags too narrow. She stood up when she saw us. Her eyes were black holes. Why was I involved with such people? Why didn't I move to Scarsdale or Greenwich, play golf and barbecue shrimp with those who hold traditional values and pay income tax?

"Lydia," I said, "this is Crystal."

"Hi, Crystal. We've met."

Crystal said she remembered. Crystal was tense and stiff.

Lydia unlocked the street door and led us down a dark hallway to a T at the end. We went left. Lydia knocked on the second door on our right. "Bruce! Hey, Bruce!"

"I hate you!" shrieked a woman to someone on an upper floor.

Bruce didn't answer. Lydia looked up at me. I motioned for her to try the key. She did, then pushed the door open. We hesitated there in the hallway, wondering what we'd find inside. Wait a minute, I suggested to myself, we didn't have any real evidence to assume there was something terrible waiting inside, just the fears of a largely unreliable burnout. I led the way inside.

I had never been to Bruce's place before, and it was worse than I imagined. The only furniture in the living room was a grimy beanbag chair. I'm not one to fault a person for the absence of furniture, but this was a different matter. Here there was no room for furniture because of all the stolen goods packed into the room. There were about fifteen television sets, most still in unopened boxes. There were stacks of car radios and boom boxes. A little path snaked through the hot stuff to the kitchen. I heard a sound, a sort of muffled mewing, coming from the bedroom.

"Bruce?"

"Mmmmfff!"

I picked my way cautiously around air conditioners, over cameras, moving bicycles from my way. I paused a moment at the bedroom doorway. I glanced back at Crystal and Lydia. Crystal, her mouth agape, peered at the hot stuff. Lydia's eyes were wide. I peeked around the threshold.

Bruce was totally naked. He lay on his stomach on the bare mattress with his arms and legs spread out and tied to the corners of the bed frame. Bruce had been whipped with something. Savage red welts, some oozing blood, latticed his back from the tops of his thighs over his buttocks to the tops of his shoulders. He whined and mewed. Then I saw that his mouth was sealed with flesh-colored tape. I felt Crystal and Lydia behind me. Both gasped at once. Lydia began to weep. The bedroom stank of urine.

I knelt beside the bed and pulled away the tape as painlessly as I could while Lydia whimpered behind me. Crystal had gone to the kitchen and returned with a butcher knife—in time to see Bruce retch twice and then disgorge a fat wad of bills from his throat with a full-bodied heaving motion, just the way Jellyroll disgorges seawater. The three of us froze momentarily in disbelief at what we had just seen, while Bruce gasped for breath like a beached bluefish. Then Crystal began sawing at the ropes tied around his ankles.

Before he was free, before he even caught his breath, he turned his head to Lydia, who had pressed herself against the wall, arms akimbo. "Where the hell have you been!"

"Don't talk to me like that!" she screeched.

Crystal cut his hands free.

He moaned when he turned over and tried to get a look at his back. "How bad is it?" he gasped. "Is it bad?" He curled into a tight ball as an answer to his own question.

Crystal knelt at the other side of the bed to examine his wounds.

Bruce picked up the wet wad of bills and shoved it under the mattress. "God, I thought I'd choke to death—" he muttered. "Choke to death on my own money. Bummer."

I try not to be too judgmental of my old friends, but I admit that I found this whole scene sordid and disgusting. I asked the obvious question.

"Is there bone showing?" Bruce wanted to know.

"No," said Crystal. "There aren't very many cuts."

I repeated the obvious question.

"Shysters," muttered Bruce.

"Shysters?"

"Loan sharks."

"Why?" I asked.

"Why? Because I owed them. I meant to pay up, but I didn't get around to it. I thought I'd have to lie here till I died. Thanks, Artie—"

103

Why didn't the shysters just take the wad of money, why tape it in his—?

"I'll get some antiseptic," Crystal said and headed for the bathroom.

"Bruce, why did they—?"

"Christ, I don't know. What do you think I am, a shyster shrink? They're nuts, that's why. Maybe they wanted to teach me a lesson."

"Did they?"

Crystal returned. "Bruce, there's nothing in the medicine cabinet but an evaporated bottle of Aqua Velva."

"They whipped me with a deep-sea fishing rod!" Bruce exclaimed.

"A fishing rod?" said Lydia. "Where'd they get a fishing rod?"

"They brought it with them!"

Something was wrong here. This didn't make good business sense from the loan shark's point of view, teach a welsher a lesson, but leave his money behind—in his mouth?

"Look," said Crystal, "I'm going to go to a drugstore."

"There's a Love Drugs on Amsterdam," Lydia offered. "I'll go with you."

I almost said no. I came a breath from saying, No, things aren't what they seem here, so we'll all go together or not at all. But I didn't. I was still trying to work out the sense of this scene when Crystal and Lydia left.

Bruce slowly, painfully unfolded himself. Wafts of urine stink followed him. Piss had darkened the mattress in a big circle. "Hell, I've been here since last night," said Bruce. He staggered and dropped to one knee. "They loved inflicting pain. Fucking sadist shysters."

"You want to call the cops?"

"Sure. When they get a load of all this stuff, I'll just tell them nobody beats the Wiz."

I helped him to his feet. He made a tortured trip toward the john, and I let him do that by himself. After he turned the corner, I lifted the mattress, propped it up against my shoulder, and sifted through the wad. Barely a third of the way through it, I had counted over two thousand bucks. Yes, this was wrong, all right. Where did he get that kind of bread to begin with, and, second, why did the shysters leave it here? But then, this was Bruce's life—

The door slammed open. Lydia shrieked twice. I stumbled over toasters getting back into the living room.

Lydia clutched her face with both hands. "They kidnapped her! They kidnapped her! They kidnapped her!"

I leapt at her, grasped her shoulders, gave her a shake I really didn't intend, and screamed, "Who!"

"I don't know! A Good Humor truck! Two guys jumped out of the Good Humor truck, they stuck something over her face and threw her in the back!"

Bruce, still naked, appeared from the direction of the john.

"No! No!" screeched Lydia. "It wasn't a Good Humor truck! It was a Mister Softee truck! They shoved me down into the garbage bags, and they drove off!"

Stupid with panic, I burst out the door, down the hall, and outside as if to stop ice-cream trucks of all stripes until I found one with my love aboard. I ran west, stopped, turned, ran east before I could think again. I ran back to Bruce's apartment.

"Phone!" I screamed at Bruce. Neither he nor Lydia had moved. Bruce's eyes were wide with panic—that was the only difference. "Phone!" I spotted it. On the floor in the corner. I shoved TVs out of my way. Glass shattered.

"Wait! Artie! What are you doing!"

"What the fuck do you think I'm doing! I'm calling the cops!"

"No, you can't do that!"

A terrible calm came over me. "Why?"

". . . How can I explain all this—?"

"Bruce, I don't care about your stolen goods. Crystal's been kidnapped. I'm calling the cops, and"—I turned on Lydia—"you're going to tell them what you saw!"

"Artie, please don't." Bruce began to sob. "If you call the police, they'll kill me."

I watched his shoulders heave for a moment. "Who will?"

He began to collect himself. I could see his wheels turning. He was searching for a line of bullshit.

I didn't wait. "Okay, Bruce, here it is. You tell me what's going on, tell me now, or I go straight to the police and tell them everything I've seen. Five seconds, Bruce."

He sat down on a TV box. He grimaced in pain. "You've got to promise you won't bring in the cops. They told me they'd kill me if I brought the cops in. They will, Artie. They don't give a fuck. They'll kill me and then go order out Chinese. Look what they did to me already."

"I told you, Bruce, I don't care about you. I only care about Crystal."

"They'll kill *her* if you call the cops," he said.

"You better tell me who, Bruce. *Now!*"

"Trammell's alive. We staged his death. He paid me to help him. That boat stuff—it was all bullshit." He folded his hands over his genitals, as if suddenly shy.

"Who's Trammell?" said Lydia.

"Those people who beat you—that's what they wanted to know?"

"How could I not tell them, flaying me with a fucking fishing pole! You'd have done the same thing."

"Who were they?"

"I don't know."

"What did they look like?"

"A black guy and a white guy, both big."

106

What was I going to do? I had to think, but suddenly I was exhausted. I sat down on a TV box. "What did they say while they were beating you?" My mouth was so dry I could barely speak.

"They kept asking me if Trammell was alive."

"What else?"

"That they'd kill me if I told anyone."

"Why didn't they just kill you after you told them?"

"They want me to find him for them."

"You know where he is?"

"Absolutely not."

"Why did they kidnap Crystal?"

"Maybe they think she knows where he is."

"You mean they're going to torture her like that?"

". . . I don't know."

"Bruce, as far as I'm concerned, this is your fault. If you don't tell me everything, I'll—"

"Come on, Artie, don't threaten me. . . . I've been through hell."

"And Crystal's just arrived there."

"I introduced you," he blubbered. "Give me a break. . . . Please don't call the cops. They probably won't kill her, they didn't kill me."

I stood up, trying to look like my knees were stable.

"What are you going to do?"

"I don't know." I walked out.

11

●

I SPED UP AMSTERDAM to 104th Street, then west, but I didn't feel the street beneath my feet. I didn't see street sights. Rage, fear, confusion overwhelmed them. I felt like screaming. I felt like smashing objects at random, like pushing people out of my way. Who could I vent this pain upon? Failing that, who could I hate? Hatred empowers the impotent. Hatred was made for the likes of me. Trammell, I could hate him, and I could hate . . . who else? Bruce? Why not, the twisted little fence? Sweat rolled under my glasses, stinging my eyes. This Tiny Archibald, he was hateable, and so was Chet Bream, wasn't he? I began to smell whiffs of myself, the stink of fear and indecision. I was nearly running now. I had to think! I couldn't just run around stinking up the neighborhood, dreaming of hatred and violence.

Jellyroll took one look at my face as I blasted, thinking, through the door, and his tail dropped. He cowered along the wall. "It's all right," I told him in a pinched voice he didn't even recognize. I didn't recognize it, either.

Where was DiPietro's card? That was the first thing to do, call the cops, no matter what I told Bruce I'd do.

Where was that goddamn card! In my shorts pocket. I went looking for my shorts in the bedroom, hurling clothes, throwing them behind me, digging like a panicky prairie dog, and that's when I saw the red light on the phone machine. Crystal! It must be Crystal telling me it was all a mistake—I leapt for it. Then, hand in mid-reach, I froze. I had been here before, a phone message from a woman I loved. She was dead before I heard it. . . .

I pushed the play button:

"Artie Deemer, you don't know me, but it looks like our life paths have crossed. I'm Norman Armbrister"—Norman Armbrister? Wait! Christ! He was one of the guys in the tape! Bream said he was the CIA guy—"I'm calling to tell you don't trust DiPietro. That cop dodge is one of the man's favorites. He's no cop, never was. I thought you should know. Listen, I'll get back in touch with you."

Rage faded. DiPietro was a phony cop? I fell into dispirited torpor. What was he really? Identity had lost its meaning. Everybody knew about me, but I didn't know about anybody. What chance did I have? What chance did Crystal have? Even now they were probably—I couldn't think about that.

I sagged onto the bed and sat staring at the patterns in the patch of peeling paint under the window. Jellyroll slunk in to see what I was doing. He sat down in front of me and stared fearfully into my eyes. He remembered this look on my face; he remembered when my last lover died. . . . Jellyroll is so sensitive to human mood that sometimes I hide my feelings so as not to upset him, but that of course has more to do with me than the presence of an extraordinarily attuned dog. "It's okay." I grinned weakly. He of course didn't buy it. He cocked his head from side to side. This is what Uncle Billy meant when he said a dog like that could break your heart.

I thought about verifications. Why should I believe a

voice on a phone machine? Norman Armbrister? Who was Norman Armbrister? How did I know that *was* Norman Armbrister, just because a voice says so. Why should I believe him about DiPietro? How did I even know Norman Armbrister actually existed, except that Chet Bream told me so? Why should I believe Chet Bream? DiPietro seemed like a cop to me. How could I verify?

I keep taped to my telephone in the kitchen a list of emergency numbers, among them that of the Twenty-fourth Precinct. I held the number on DiPietro's card up beside the precinct-house number. They weren't even close. I called DiPietro's number.

"Hello, this is Detective DiPietro," said a recorded message, "I'm not in now, but if you leave a message—"

I didn't. What did that prove? He wouldn't give me a phone number that, when called, would reveal him to be a phony. However, if I could put an address with that number, I'd know where DiPietro lived. Or worked. Why would I want to know that? Maybe, if they hurt Crystal, I'd want to murder him. My hands were trembling. Now what?

Calabash! Now was the time for heavy firepower, no matter what happened next. If you can't beat 'em, kill 'em. Calabash was no killer, but he had a keen sense of justice. Injustice pissed him off, turned him deadly. I'd seen it before. Calabash lives in the Bahamas. I called him there. Our connection was tinny.

"They kidnapped my girlfriend, Calabash!"

"Only one way to reason wid dat kind," he said after pausing to give the matter some thought. "I'm leavin' now."

I nearly wept with gratitude. "I'll have a ticket waiting at the airport. . . . Thank you, Calabash."

"Don't do nothin' crazy till I get dere."

I called American Airlines and paid for a first-class ticket by credit card.

What could I do now that wasn't crazy? I called Islip, Long Island, information and asked for DiPietro. They had no such person listed. Hell, that proved nothing. I didn't believe that family-outing-from-Islip bullshit when I thought DiPietro *was* a cop. . . . The obvious finally occurred to me. I called the Twenty-fourth Precinct house. A Sergeant Brannigan answered.

"Detective DiPietro, please."

"Who?"

I repeated it.

"Nobody by that name here. Can I help you?"

"Well, this isn't business, it's personal. I'm the alumni director from his old high school, and I'm trying to get in touch with him about the class reunion. Maybe I have the wrong precinct. Do you have a general department directory?"

"Yeah, I went to my twenty-fifth reunion. Hated it. Hang on. . . . DiPietro. Yeah, here we go, DiPietro, Seventy-fourth— Nope, wait. Monica DiPietro. That don't sound like the party you want."

"No others?"

"Nope, that's it."

"Thank you."

The phone rang.

"Artie?"

"Crystal!"

"I've been trying—busy."

"Are you all right! Where are you!"

"I'm . . . I'm down by my car. Where we parked it." Her words were slurred. Why were her words slurred? "Please come and get me!"

"I'll be right there. What did they do to you, Crystal?"

"They . . . drugged me."

"But you're all right?"

"Yes, I—"

"I'm on my way—" Oh, relief! They only drugged her, the fuckers! My step was breezy, I felt giddy, like chuckling to myself. I was dancing for the door when I stopped, stood silently, thinking. I turned on my heel and went into the kitchen, pawed around in the knife drawer, but chose instead an ice pick. I'd need some kind of point guard. Is that an ice pick sticking in your thigh, or are you glad to see me? I opened an indifferent bottle of red wine for its cork. If I was giddy with relief, why was I so frightened? Why was I arming myself?

I sprinted to Riverside Drive. Crystal had parked on the east side of the drive near the western terminus of 104th Street, but I didn't go there directly. I ran up to 105th and approached from the north on the opposite side of the avenue. . . . I didn't see anything funny, funnier than usual, that is. A man slept in a refrigerator crate on a bench, only his bare feet sticking out. His worldly goods were packed into two shopping carts tied together with string. The other end of the string was tied around his big toe. Another guy was singing, "Seventy-six trombones led the big parade," as he pissed over the wall into the park below. Car alarms blared and whooped and whined. "No Radio," said signs on the windshields. "Already Stolen." Yesterday a sanitation truck had swerved off Riverside Drive and smashed into an elm tree. I saw the elm tree up ahead, torn to shreds. The driver had failed the drug test. Then I saw Crystal's car.

She was in it! She was sitting on the passenger side, her head leaning against the window. I jogged across the street, dodging a crazed cabbie who swerved to get me, and I climbed in behind the wheel.

"Darl—!"

She turned her face to me—

I gasped. It wasn't Crystal at all! It was a man in a wig.
He was a thick-browed simian fucker with no neck. He
grinned at me. Brown teeth. That face under the Crystal
wig was the most obscene sight I'd ever glimpsed. Re-
pulsed, I sat there staring at him, frozen. He began to
chortle.

From the rear seat, somebody—he must have been lying
on the floor—clapped a rag over my face and jerked my
head back against the rest. Ether. I'd smelled that smell
before. Trammell and Bruce used to do ether in law school.
I never did. I didn't like the smell. It reminded me of a
hospital in my youth. My mother was there at my bedside
with some crew-cut pilot. She told me I'd be fine, everybody has their tonsils out, as a nurse put the wire-mesh
mask over my lower face. . . . My peripheral vision went
first, in shimmering waves of light too bright to look at
directly, but I found the handle in my jacket pocket. Could
I get it out; having gotten it out, could I get the cork off
the point?

The asshole in the Crystal wig was trying to pin my arms
to my side, but he was clutching me around the biceps.
My lower arms were free, if I could just get the goddamn
cork off—

I did! Corkless, it was in my hand, and my hand was
free. Now all I had to do was muster the strength before I
crashed to stick—

I brought the handle up to the level of my chin and
plunged it into his thigh. That was all I could hit just then.
He let out a long, falsetto wail. The Crystal wig fell off his
head into his lap. The anesthesiologist in the backseat lost
his grip on my face. I shot forward in the seat and came
up hard against the steering wheel. Crystal's car began to
spin. I jerked the ice pick across my body all the way to
the door, and then I swung with everything I had left. The
man went "huuufff," like a punctured pair of water wings.

I didn't actually see it hit him, but it went in deep—I felt his clothes against the bottom of my fist. He howled, grabbed the Crystal wig, clapped it over his wound, and howled again. I felt so satisfied at the sound of that second howl that I decided to get a little sleep before I considered my next move.

12.

BLARING WHITE LIGHT and primordial darkness swirled in a contradictory combination, so I decided to ignore the inexplicable and get a little more sleep. When I woke up again, the light/dark sequence hadn't changed. All light fades eventually of its own accord. I'd wait it out right here.... Then I began to ruminate on just where "right here" might be. Normally, one determines that by empirically perceiving one's surroundings and then checking whether they looked, smelled, felt—taste didn't seem applicable—familiar.

Trees! Aha! Those black shapes, tops swaying gently, were trees, and that meant I was outside. I was outside, and I was sitting down—in a chair, a lawn chair. The trees were not green but black. That meant night. Progress. But what about this light? This light could only be artificial light, electric light, Thomas Edison.... But something was wrong with my arms.

When I realized there was nothing wrong with my arms except that they were chained behind my back, the world around me came into sharper focus. That was bad. I was chained. I was sitting in an aluminum lawn chair on a concrete deck that circled a large swimming pool. The water was lighted from below the dead-flat surface. There was lawn all around, woods in the distance. We weren't in Manhattan anymore. Now all I needed to do was get a move on, beat it out of this country club to the nearest train station. Could I get my money out of my pocket with my hands cuffed behind my back?

"He's all yours, Henry."

The voice came from behind me. Apparently, this Henry fellow was back there as well. I spun as quickly as I could. I saw a black man, but he wasn't Henry, apparently, because he was addressing Henry.

Henry was a white guy who wore a minute black-and-red bathing suit. I squinted at him as he passed through a dark patch and into a bright one. It looked like he had a tugboat hawser stuck down the front of his suit. His upper torso looked like an alpine rock face.

"He the gink I'm supposed to drown?"

"Yeah," said the black guy, "that's him."

Drown? Did he say drown?

Henry was on me. He clamped the back of my neck and jerked me to my feet. With a powerful sweeping motion, he hurled me into the swimming pool. I believe I skipped once or twice like a flat stone across the surface. I stood up in nipple-deep water. Henry jumped in on top of me.

We came up face to face. His was crazy with activity. The chewing muscles at the hinges of his jaw were twitching a mile a minute; his mouth, brows, and forehead were ticcing rampantly, but his eyes were flat, like dead fish eyes. No compassion in those eyes. He was almost entirely bald. Even the skin on his crown jerked and wrinkled, flattened and wrinkled again.

He whipped me around, clutched the chain between my cuffs, and hoisted my hands high up my back, causing my face to slap the water. An immense force shoved me under. This was it, the termination of my life, right here, for something I didn't even understand, in heavily chlorinated water. But I struggled, jerked and twisted around to get at him, to kick him in the hawser. The effort was hopeless, a waste of oxygen, but I wanted to hurt him in some lasting way before I died. He held me under with ease. I relaxed, gave in.

But he hoisted me back up into the air. I gasped a single, mostly liquid breath, and before I could take a drier one, he ducked me again. He was going to drown me by bits! I thought for an instant I'd just inhale a lungful of water, get it quickly done. He yanked me out again.

"Stop!"

Somebody was shouting and waving his arms, coming toward us from what in my limited vision appeared to be an enormous mansion.

"What the Sam Hill are you doing, Henry!"

"Why, I'm drownin' this gink. Rufus said he was the gink—"

"Rufus said, Rufus said! Rufus is a dick-up! This is *not* that gink! This is a different gink entirely! This is Artie Deemer."

I flopped against the side of the pool. I watched two black ants weave their way along a gorgelike seam in the concrete. I didn't know ants came out at night.

"Oh, shit," said Henry in a thick, stupid voice.

"Oh, shit is right. Get Mr. Deemer out of that pool this instant. Rufus! You come help!"

I tried to get a look at the man who had saved my life. Or pretended to. I squinted. He was large. His body was shaped like a pear.

A black man came through a gate in a white picket fence I hadn't seen before.

"Rufus," said the fat man, "this is not the drowning gink."

"You sure?"

117

"Of course I'm sure!"

"Oh, shit."

"Will you two fuck-ups get Mr. Deemer out of that pool right now!"

Rufus had a big grin on his face as he leaned over me and pulled me up, while Henry hefted from below. I didn't think my legs would support my weight, so I sat on the concrete deck and tried not to throw up.

"Hey, boss," said Rufus, "while we're on the subject of the pool, we had frogs again this morning."

"Damn, how many?"

"Ten."

"Ten?"

"Yeah, I called Posh Pools. Guy said 'bout all we could do is build a small-animal fence around it." Rufus giggled. "A frog fence."

"We've got a real frog problem this summer," the fat man said to me. "Like a biblical plague on the suburbs. Frogs hop in the pool thinking it's a country pond, I guess. Well, they can't get back out. Next morning we got dead frogs on the bottom. Rufus, you and Henry get on out of here while I talk with Mr. Deemer."

"Handcuffs," I said in a chlorine-burned voice.

"Why, hell, I almost forgot. Rufus—"

Rufus unlocked me and took the handcuffs away. Deep red rings circled my wrists, but I didn't rub them.

"Rufus, we'll have two iced teas made the way I like it, with a sprig."

The fat man pulled up two director's chairs. His ass strained the wooden arms apart as he sat in his. He had a brush mustache. Dripping, I sat in the other chair. We sat facing each other in a puddle of weird white light shining down on us from the tree trunks. "I'm glad we can have this talk, Mr. Deemer. I'm sure we can straighten things out, but time is of the essence. People, you see, are closing in on me. I have this closed-in feeling—"

"You probably need a bigger chair."

"Ha! Good one. Some robust fellows like myself take exception to fat jokes and grow nonplussed. Not me. I take them in the spirit they were meant. You see, the fact is, I'm in trouble, I'm in deep shit, as someone as crass as Henry might put it. I need to take extraordinary measures. Normally, I don't snatch people I want to talk to off the street. Normally, I invite them to lunch, talk sense with them, not drown them. The world is out of joint, as the bard used to say."

"So you snatched Crystal, too?"

"I'm afraid so."

"What have you done with her?"

Rufus arrived with the iced tea. I drank it to ease the burning at the back of my throat.

The fat man looked up at the sky as if it displeased him. "Rufus, the lights are too bright. Take them back to the late-dusk effect."

"You got it, boss."

"I want my glasses," I said.

"Where are his glasses, Rufus?"

"I don't know. Lost in the scuffle, I guess," said Rufus, and then he left. Soon afterward the lights dimmed.

"I heard about the scuffle," the fat man said to me. "I heard you stabbed Barry with an ice pick. Got him good, I hear. You're a violent man."

"I carry that ice pick to gouge dog shit out of the treads in my shoes."

"So we're talking raging septic infections in Barry? No matter, Barry's an asshole. You know the type—attends martial arts classes, collects Nazi paraphernalia. But then sometimes that's just the kind of man one needs."

"You're Tiny Archibald, aren't you?"

119

"The sarcasm of that application troubles me some, but I know it's widespread. Reggie is my real name. Reggie Archibald. You recognize me. I still find it gratifying to be recognized."

"What have you done with Crystal?"

"Nothing. Restrained her, that's all."

"What do you mean you restrained her? Like you restrained Bruce?"

"Personnel management is the hardest thing in business. How can a man control the way his employees go at things? Their methodologies? They're just following orders. My orders were to find out if Bruce Munger—vulgar surname, huh?—was stupid enough to help Trammell stage his death. Sure enough. So you recognize me? I used to be in show business. You're in show biz, too. Trammell was in the biz as well. Remember? Here, I'll do it for you: 'Come on, son, we'll get that old motor going yet.' That ring any bells from your cultural past? One can't have grown up in the U. S. of A. without recognizing that. Part of our cultural currency. 'The Mayhews.' Everybody's heard of 'The Mayhews.' Bingo and Milt Mayhew. Their adorable son, Timmy. Trammell was like a son to me, not just a TV son, a real son. Now look how he's betrayed me. It hurts an old man to lose his son. Don't think it doesn't."

"How?"

"How what?"

"How did he betray you?"

"He made a videotape—TV is the tumor that will kill this country; I've seen your dog on TV—a videotape which, let's just leave it, would incriminate me. I'm not an honest man, Artie."

"No shit."

"But with me, there's a philosophical component. I love to corrupt. Or assist people to corrupt themselves. I expose the darkness at the core, the intrinsic darkness of humanity. It's deeply satisfying work."

"Let Crystal go, and I'll give you whatever I've got, I'll do whatever you want me to do."

"Gee, that's very cooperative. Trammell was cooperative like that, but then, look what he went and did. . . . Trammell is alive. That makes for a big problem. I don't have any problem with Trammell skimming a few hundred grand off the top, but this tape business, that's a different matter entirely. That could lead to publicity, if not prosecution. Some of the folks I deal with tend to shun publicity. The dark of night is their milieu. A few of them want their money back—I can take care of that—but they all want silence. The tape is the problem. For all I know, Trammell's taken the tape and entered the witness protection program; however, the half-assed manner of his going, with some poolroom lout as the only witness, suggests haste. In any case, my customers feel they're in danger."

"The CIA?"

"Oh, sure, they need the services I offer to cover their extracurricular activities, which in most cases are stupid as shit, but then I'm not my customers' keeper."

"So you run a bank for criminals?"

"I know you disapprove of me. All honest people—both of them—disapprove of me. Sometimes I disapprove of me. But that brings us into philosophical waters, and you've already had a swim. Let's remain on concrete ground, hmm?" Tiny Archibald must have weighed 350 pounds buck naked, which would have been an unappetizing sight. He was wearing a natty blue suit with a red tie and a matching pocket handkerchief. His loafers were fashioned from the skins of endangered species.

"Why did you kidnap Crystal? I don't see what that gains you."

"Crystal is bait in the search for Trammell Weems. And,

of course, there's you. I understand you and Crystal are in love. I understand further that you used to hang out with Trammell. In law school." He giggled at that notion. "I also know that your records weren't stellar among students of jurisprudence. I have nearly unlimited access to information. I know every move you make. I know about your dog. You're well placed, for my purposes. Trammell's going to get wind of the fact that Crystal's been kidnapped. He cares about Crystal, don't mistake that. He's going to come looking for her. If I were him, you'd be one of the first people I talked to. When he does that, call me, and then I'll return Crystal to you."

I pretended that we were talking about a real estate deal in which I had only financial interest. "You're going to hold her prisoner until Trammell turns up?"

"Right. Like I said, I'm usually a congenial fellow, but I don't have time for social niceties now, so there we are. What do you think?"

"Presumably you're going to let me go?"

"Absolutely." He began patting himself for a pen. He found one, then laboriously extracted his wallet. He thumbed through a sheaf of business and credit cards, but he didn't seem to find the one he wanted, so he picked another. He turned that one facedown on his knee and wrote on it a telephone number with a Manhattan area code. "I can always be reached here."

"Where are you keeping Crystal?"

"Now, come on, Artie, do you take me for an imbecile?"

"I had to ask." I smiled falsely. "You know how it is, Tiny, you'd do the same thing in my position. Good tea. I have one request, no, one stipulation. Crystal and I have been followed. I'm still being followed. I want you to get everybody off my tail. I won't have any room to operate, and I'll get that same closed-in feeling you have. Besides,

Trammell's not going to approach if he sees twenty assholes trailing me. See what I'm saying, Tiny?"

He cocked his big head suspiciously to consider me out of the corner of his eye. "Well, okay."

"Is Crystal comfortable?"

"She's not uncomfortable. She won't be harmed or molested in any way, but she won't have complete freedom of movement. If this works out, all she will have been is frightened, maybe a little bored. Anything else?"

"No, I guess that'll do it."

"Now I'm going to call Rufus out here to handcuff you again."

"Why?"

"Then he's going to blindfold you. It's either that or another dose of ether."

I stood submissively while Rufus gathered my arms behind my back and clicked the handcuffs snugly around my wrist bones. He pulled a black hood over my head and down around my shoulders. Utter blackness. I began to pant in fear.

"Just like for your execution, right, Artie?"

"Tiny—?" Did the hood smother my voice?

"Yeah, Artie?"

"I just want you to know that I pissed in your pool."

From far away, on the other side of the dark, I heard Tiny laugh heartily. "That's okay, everybody pisses in my pool."

13.

THEY REMOVED MY HANDCUFFS and shoved me, still hooded, out the door.

"Ta-ta, now," said Rufus. By the time I yanked off the hood, threw it down, the van had already pulled back into the traffic heading south. I might have gotten the license number, but without my glasses I could barely see the cars. I stood soggily, trying to figure out where the goons had dropped me.

Two emaciated winos stopped mid-swig to watch me. "Neighborhood keeps gettin' weirder and weirder."

"Where's it gonna end?"

There was a major intersection forming a square. There are dozens of squares formed by major intersections in Manhattan, but I couldn't really be sure I was in Manhattan.

Though blurry, this square looked vaguely familiar. I walked to the nearest street sign and squinted up. West End Avenue and Broadway. Okay. This was the northern terminus of West End Avenue where it merged into Broadway. The cross street would be 106th. I was only two blocks from home. How convenient.

My shoes squished all the way. I took the elevator to the eighth floor and walked up the rest of the way, slowly and quietly. There was no one lurking on my floor. I quickly opened the door, slipped into my apartment, and flipped about $300 worth of dead bolts to the locked position.

Forlornly, Jellyroll lay in the dark in the foyer with his chin between his paws. I made a big fuss over him so he wouldn't worry, but you can't fool this dog. He followed me into the bedroom, stopping to sniff each wet piece of clothing as I shed it en route. Naked and uncertain, I returned to the living room, sat in my morris chair, and pondered the question at hand. I was pissed. I rolled up a thin gasper for objective perspective, but I remained fuzzy-headed and pissed.

A bloated felon named Tiny Archibald had kidnapped Crystal. The question for me was, what was I going to do about it? Try to forget anger, fear, outrage, and think strategically. I could call the cops. That was the usual response when your lover (not to mention yourself) gets kidnapped. But how could I know how the cops would handle it? If they acted crudely, Archibald might make Crystal disappear forever. He said himself the heat was on, that he felt closed in upon, the miserable runny-ass, arrogant, obese son of a bitch—wait, that was anger. Anger was a luxury Crystal and I couldn't afford, anger would lead to missteps, and missteps could get Crystal killed. But why did I think I could handle it better than trained professionals on the police force? . . . Pros like Detective DiPietro.

I retrieved my wet shorts from the living-room floor and found Tiny Archibald's card in the pocket. His number was running blue ink, so I wrote it on the wall near the phone. 555-4100. Wait, that rang a bell. I knew that number. Why? I fumbled DiPietro's card out of the kitchen drawer where I'd stowed it earlier. His number was 555-4200. I called Archibald's number—

"Hello," said another recorded melodious woman's voice,

"you've reached Mr. Archibald's line. Please leave a message after the tone."

I put on some thinking music. I wanted to hear a lot of notes, and I wanted them *fast*, I wanted hard-driving, brain-blasting bebop, goddamnit. I cranked up the volume. For vocalists I picked Babs Gonzalez and King Pleasure. Thinking: what did I know about Tiny's location? I knew that he went to some extremes to keep it a secret—the blindfold and so forth—unless that was more for intimidation than secrecy. What else did I know? That it was about an hour's drive from New York City. Chet Bream might know—the tape he'd described on the beach sounded as if it might have been shot at Tiny's place. But I didn't want to get mixed up with Chet Bream, because journalists tend to publish things, and an article in a major metropolitan newspaper didn't seem in Crystal's best interests. So what else did I know? There were a lot of trees. And the big swimming pool . . .

I found a New York area road map in a drawer in the kitchen. An hour's drive: let's say roughly fifty miles. I cut some twine from a roll and tied one end to a pencil. I measured a fifty-mile length of string on the map scale. I held the end on the Upper West Side of Manhattan and drew a circle with that diameter. To the east the circle enclosed the expensive suburbs and towns in Connecticut. North, it encircled Westchester County and the river towns on both sides of the Hudson, and to the south and west, the radius went well into New Jersey. A lot of ground. Crystal could be anywhere in that radius. Or beyond it. I had picked an hour's drive almost randomly. I really didn't know how long I had ridden chained and blindfolded in that van. What else didn't I know?

There was a lot of frogs. Frogs! What did that asshole Rufus say about the frogs? He said he'd called about the frog problem. He mentioned a name, something pools.

LUSH LIFE

What was it? It was alliterative, I remembered that. What *was* it?

Posh! Posh Pools.

I told Jellyroll we weren't going to the park, that this was "a hurry-up," and though disappointed, he pissed in the gutter. I was touched nearly to tears by his desire to please. We walked around to Riverside Drive. Crystal's car was still there. The effects of the fiscal cutbacks were beginning to bite. They seldom swept the streets these days, so her car wouldn't have been towed, but I was surprised it hadn't been stolen, especially since the keys were still in the ignition. This time I peeked in the window before I hopped behind the wheel. Jellyroll wagged with excitement. We were going somewhere— I gasped when I saw the bloody wig on the passenger seat. Maybe that was the reason nobody had stolen the car—"Forget that Toyota, man, somebody got scalped in that Toyota." As we drove away, I picked it up by a single strand of hair and dropped it out the window.

One reason I hang around the Upscale Poolroom is for the comforting sense of solidity it affords, the feel of timelessness. Nothing changes in the Upscale Poolroom. Change scours the outside world like a glacier, but in here you can't tell whether it's day or night unless you open the door and look.

The regulars were lined up on the bench in the back. I didn't see Thumper, one of the people I'd come to see, but I was fairly certain he'd show up. Jellyroll went off to work the room. I sat on the bench. Chinese Gordon was playing a serious-looking game of one-pocket with a big fleshy fellow I didn't know, so I asked Outta-Town Brown who he was.

"You don't know who *that* is?"

"Would I have asked?"

"That's Ed the Greek."

"He's good. Where's he from?"

"Greece."

Thumper hobbled over from somewhere and sat down. "Hey, Artie."

"Hey, Thumper."

"Artie, would you be interested in a nice outdoor gas grill complete with accessories and built-in rotisserie? I can get you eighty-five percent off wholesale."

"Thumper, you have a mistaken impression of my lifestyle."

"Everybody can use a good gas grill. Who's that guy?"

"That's Ed the Greek."

"Where's he from?"

"Greece."

"Yeah? Where in Greece?"

"I don't know, Thumper."

"That's where my father was from, Greece, the rotten son of a bitch. You could put your gas grill right beside your aboveground swimming pool with trouble-free filtration system."

"I might be interested in some other things."

"You might?" That seemed to delight Thumper. "Like what? I got everything, and what I don't have, I can get. It'd be my pleasure to fulfill your needs with no questions asked."

"I'm not sure what I'll need."

"Feel free to browse. I'm conveniently located in the Red Hook section of Brooklyn."

Burns was the other person I'd come to see. Burns was one of the straight-pool intellectuals, real students of the game who played nothing else, looked down on nine ball because luck figured into the outcome of nine-ball games. Luck was not a factor in straight pool. I don't really know how to play straight pool. I don't know which ball to shoot when, and I don't have enough cue-ball control. Now Burns was playing an intensely serious game (the straight-pool intellectuals never gambled) with Lenny, a Federal Express deliveryman. I hung around watching them do a safety seesaw that seemed to go on for two days. They nodded cordially at me, but, concentrating, they didn't want to talk. I waited for a break in the inaction.

Burns worked as a computer operator for a securities firm on Wall Street. I don't know how he managed his workday, because he played straight pool all night. On many days, I'll bet, he got by on looks alone. He looked like a sixteen-year-old choirboy with a peaches-and-cream complexion and blue, seemingly guileless eyes. But Burns lived on the fringes of the law.

The SEC had been asking questions about Burns around the Upscale Poolroom in the mid-eighties. Something about insider trading. Everybody was very close-mouthed about it, but rumor held that Outta-Town Brown, Chinese Gordon, and a couple of the straight-pool intellectuals were buying stock for Burns and taking a percentage of the profits. For a while, well-thumbed copies of the *Wall Street Journal* could be found on the benches, guys were talking about stock splits, leveraged buyouts, and mergers and acquisitions. Play would almost cease entirely when the Nightly Business Report came on NPR stations. I don't know what happened to the SEC's investigation. Since I didn't want any of the action, I wasn't privy to the upshot.

Burns screwed up a safety, leaving Lenny a break shot. Lenny made it, spread the balls. While Lenny, one of the slowest players in the room, stood staring at the table, Burns came over and stood beside me.

"What say, Artie? How's show-biz life?"

"Grueling, Burns, grueling. How are you hitting them?"

"There's nothing I can't miss."

"I know that feeling. Say, Burns, if I had two phone numbers, could you get me addresses to go with them?"

He flashed a suspicious glance at me, but I pretended not to notice. "Local?"

"Yes."

"We're all connected," he sang. "I'll have to charge you a fee."

"Goes without saying."

"Something cooking?"

"No, just curious."

"Curious, right. I can call into the system from here—if fucking Lenny *ever shoots.*"

"I'll be around for a while." I gave him Tiny Archibald's and DiPietro's numbers with my own number written below them in case I left before Lenny shot. "Thanks, Burns."

I went to the john.

"The R-r-ruff Dog. My, my, my. Must be something owning the R-r-ruff Dog." He was a short, heavily bearded man I'd never seen before. He had appeared at the adjacent urinal, but he didn't look at me, stared instead at the chrome flush handle.

"Yeah," I said dryly.

"I bet. Yes, I do, uh-huh, I'd take that bet." He was short, not taller than five foot six, but he was built solidly, like a tallish fire hydrant, with great bulging forearms, as if he'd had somebody else's forearms grafted on, somebody like Popeye. The coarse hair of his beard ascended almost to his eye sockets. The beard didn't look real to me, and that made me nervous.

I flushed and went to the sink, where I could see the man's back in the mirror. He wore sockless boat shoes and khaki shorts that dropped baggily below his knees. A neat, round bald spot, about the diameter of an orange, rose at the back of his skull. The bald spot was encircled by a jagged purple scar. It looked as though sometime in the past someone had tried to scalp him with a rusty spoon. His shoulder muscles bulged beneath his white T-shirt. His face looked sixty, but his body looked much younger. Aw, I was being paranoid. There was no reason to assume anything scary about this guy. A stranger in a phony beard making chitchat in a pool-hall rest room.

"They kidnapped your girlfriend," he said without turning around. "Maybe you aren't aware of that, but I think you are."

I froze. I didn't reply, just watched him in the mirror. He didn't turn around. I didn't like the confined quarters. "Shit happens," I said. I turned and walked out the swinging door. I figured he wouldn't leave it at that, so I sought out a seat near but not on the regulars' bench.

I watched him approach. He walked in a jerky, stiff-legged fashion, as if on a ship's deck in a seaway. He sat down beside me. "We can't talk here."

"This is the only place we can talk."

"Security."

"Yes."

He giggled. He had strange powder-blue eyes that seemed genuinely amused. "If I was out to do you, you'd never have seen me. I'm Norm Armbrister." I couldn't see his mouth move under his beard. He stood up to pull a folded news clipping from his hip pocket. He unfolded and presented it to me.

It was the obituary page from the New York Times, dated six months earlier:

Spengler—Captain Adam R., who will be fondly remembered by his shipmates, was declared missing and presumed drowned after he was washed from the deck of his trimaran Raven in high seas 400 miles southeast of New

131

York en route to Bermuda. Captain Spengler served with distinction aboard the light cruiser USS *Thurgood* in the Tonkin Gulf and aboard the destroyer USS *Ranger* in the Arabian Sea. "Oh, hear us when we call to Thee/For those in peril on the sea."

"You're dead, huh?"

He grinned and nodded with boyish delight.

"Didn't you just say your name was Norman Armbrister?"

"Most people call me Norm. What do you think of the style?"

"What style?"

"The obituary style. I wrote it myself. You don't think it's too stark, do you? I hate flowery obits, but I didn't want to go too far in the other extreme."

"You drowned, huh?"

"Just like Trammell Weems. Nice thing about drowning is there's not necessarily a body. Did you get my message about that cop?"

"Yes."

"I was right, wasn't I?"

"I guess so."

"I'm right about your girlfriend, too."

"You know a lot."

"I used to be in intelligence." I couldn't see any teeth, but his eyes still seemed amused.

"Naval intelligence?"

"Army. Also the National Security Organization, Department of Defense, and Central Intelligence Agency—I've been in them all. I served my country with distinction, like in my obit." He grinned at me. "I'm retired." His eyes seemed full of jollity and goodwill, but he probably learned that in spook school. "So what are you going to do about it?"

"Do about what?"

"Crystal. Aren't you going to get her out? Are you a man or a mouse?"

"That's not the question here. You're the question. Even if I was going to do something, why would I tell you, a man who fell off his own boat under an assumed name?"

"Because I'm offering my services. Men, weapons, vehicles. What do you need? You need an Apache gunship? Depends on how you want to go in. Do you want to go in hard, or do you want to go in soft?"

"Why would you want to help?"

"Let's say personal reasons, for now. Our relationship is still young. Candidness may follow. Depends."

"On what?"

"Mutual trust."

"How do you know so much about Crystal and me?"

"I told you, I used—"

"More specifically."

He paused, giving that some thought, leaning forward to place his elbows on his knees. He motioned with his head for me to join him. I leaned down. "How many of these guys do you know, the guys around us?" he whispered.

"All of them."

"How long?"

"Years."

He nodded. "Okay, I'll tell you something further as a basis for a mutual trust-type relationship. Remember that no-neck cretin you stuck with the ice pick?"

"Well, gee, I've stabbed quite a few cretins lately. They tend to blur."

"I'd have done the same, the only difference is Barry'd be dead. That's his name, Barry. Barry was working for me. Kind of a double agent I planted in Tiny's camp, but Barry's got no brains. Additionally, he's an unstable acid freak with psychopathic proclivities. It's tough for dead guys like Captain Spengler to hire reliable, top-rank help. Barry won't be of any further use to me as an inside man. You see, all he wants to do now is go after you."

"What!"

"Because you stabbed him."

"He was trying to kidnap me!" I hissed.

"Of course. I know that. You know that. On some certain level even Barry knows that. But Barry's not a rational adult. You can't reason with Barry. No, he'll be coming after you, if I know my Barry."

I felt like moaning out loud, but I suppressed it.

"I respect you for it. It takes a certain kind of individual to use an ice pick. Get right up close and *stick* it in, close enough to smell a man's after-shave, but you'll probably have to do it again. If you don't mind a word of advice about technique, go for an upper thrust to the thoracic region. Then twist it up and down and all around. Takes a special sort. I respect that. That's why I figured you'd have the nerve to go after your girlfriend. Maybe I was wrong."

"You were." There was a revenge-crazed acid freak on my ass. . . .

"Okay, I hear you. Why trust me, right? Let's see what I can give you as another sign of goodwill. William Spivey. You know him? Crystal's uncle."

"What about him?"

"He knows about the money."

". . . What money?"

"Trammell robbed a bank before he left. Not your average bank, but, like most, it kept money. Now it's gone. Being dead, I know how hard it is to even get a checking account. Trammell would have that same problem. Even your crookedest banker would shy away from the dead guy who ripped off Tiny Archibald. Trammell'd have to make some arrangements for a cover. He'd need another person who was alive."

"He used Billy?"

"I'm not certain yet, but if I had to say yes or no right now, I'd say yes."

"Is Billy in danger?"

"Sure. But he's got one thing going for him. He's retarded. His actions won't be predictable. Another thing. What are you going to do after you break her out? I mean, you can't come back here and play pool with these bums like nothing happened."

I had recognized that. "You got a lot of guts calling these guys bums."

"I take your point. My apologies."

"What do you suggest?"

"I have a boat, the one I drowned off of, but don't let that bother you. She's intrinsically sound. She's docked out in the Bronx, place called Cuban Ledge Marina. Eastchester Bay. My wife and I live aboard. We're about to get in the wind for tropical climes."

"I still don't see why I should trust you. How do I know this isn't a setup? How do I know you aren't working with the people who kidnapped Crystal?"

"You don't need to trust me for us to work together. Who can trust anybody? Our interests intersect. That's more important than any abstraction like trust. Spheres of intersecting interests make the world go round."

"How do our interests intersect?"

"Tiny Archibald and I used to be professionally associated. At one time, our interests intersected, but he doublecrossed me, and I had to die. I realize that damages my point about intersecting interests, but everything has exceptions and everything changes. I've been looking for an appropriate mode by which to reenter Tiny's life, and this is it."

Despite its irrationality, I gave that some thought. I leaned back against the wall. "I'll tell you what. If you keep Barry away from me, I'll think about it. That's not to say I'm going after Crystal. I don't have any experience in such things. I'd be crazy to do something like that."

"I have a lot of experience." He grinned.

"Is that beard real?"

He gave it a sharp tug. "Real is as real does," he said.

"How do I get in touch with you?"

"I'll be around."

"In the shadows with the rest of the spooks?"

His eyes twinkled. He stood up. "Remember when we were trying to kill Castro with the exploding cigar?"

"Yes."

"Well, it wasn't my idea."

"I'm much relieved."

He walked out. On the way, four regulars hit on him. "Want to play a little? For fun?"

Burns sat down with me, holding his cue between his knees. "Say, Artie, I could be of use to you if you got something going. I'm well placed."

"What do you mean?"

"What do you mean? That's what they all say, innocently. Those two phone numbers were both from the same place."

"Yeah?"

"Yeah. Concom International Securities."

I could tell he was watching my eyes for a reaction. For that reason I felt I should have one, but I didn't. I'd never heard of Concom International Securities. "Do you have an address?"

"Yeah, Nine nineteen Third Avenue. I tell you what, Artie. The phone search is on the house, but if you need someone with information at his fingertips, you know who to talk to, right?"

"Sure, Burns. What is this Concom Securities?"

He just winked at me, stood up, and returned to his game, where Lenny was staring at the balls motionlessly.

Jellyroll was enjoying himself in the center of a clot of petters. I felt too tired to move.

14
●

I BARELY SLEPT. Two hours before dawn I looked up "Pools" in the yellow pages. It said, "See: Swimming Pools." I did. Posh Pools (or variants) was not listed. I hadn't expected it to be listed in the New York book, but I found a number for the American Association of Swimming Pool Designers and Contractors. I drank coffee and brooded until business hours.

"Hello, I'm trying to locate Posh Pools—"

"One moment, please," said the receptionist before I could say more.

She came back and said they had five, three in southern California, one in Tempe, Arizona, and one in New Canaan, Connecticut.

New Canaan lay easily within range. "Could I have the New Canaan address, please?"

She told me it was 134 Church Street.

Then I called Jennifer, an ex-girlfriend, the one who told me about the prohibition against visible toe cleavage on fast-track female feet in the business community. A fast tracker herself, Jennifer had objected to my lack of ambition. "You don't *do* anything," she had said to me one morning, as if she'd suddenly recognized the fact, while

I watched her dress for work at Sedgwick, Marwick and Hardwick—she liked to wear very naughty lingerie beneath her pin-striped suit. I was vulnerable on that score, all right.

Jennifer viewed most men as frat-boy assholes who learned their masculinity from Bud Lite commercials. That was a hard proposition to argue with, there being so much evidence to support it. Jennifer intended to beat men at their own game by getting promoted over them for her greater intelligence and diligence. That I lived off my dog made her edgy because it implied contempt for her striving. I didn't mean it that way. She left me, saying we had "a fundamental conflict of desires for the future." It hurt me, her leaving, but her reason was difficult to argue with. Frankly, I think she found it harder to part with Jellyroll than with me.

I called Bushwick, Harwick and Warwick.

The receptionist said it was Harwick, Marwick and Sedgwick. I asked to speak to Jennifer Pratt.

"I'm sorry, sir, she's no longer with us."

"She isn't?"

"Can someone else help you?"

I tried Jennifer at home. I felt fondly nostalgic at the sound of her voice. "They laid me off, the frat-boy assholes."

"Gee, Jennifer, I'm sorry to hear that." Like other fast trackers who thought it would never end, Jennifer had bought things in the eighties, an expensive condo on Central Park West, a BMW, a place in Fire Island. If I knew Jennifer, she was panicking. But she didn't want to talk about it.

"What's up?" she snapped.

"Well, I don't want to impose, but I wondered if you knew anything about Concom International Securities."

Long silence . . . "Why, Artie?"

"Well, a neighbor of mine got in a little trouble, and he asked me to ask around. I thought you might know."

"What kind of trouble?"

"SEC trouble."

"Figures."

"Why?"

"I've heard rumors."

"Rumors?"

"I'll make a couple calls for you, but that's all I can do."

"Thanks a lot. Do you need cash, Jennifer?"

". . . No, I'm fine. Goddamnit, Artie, I was a top producer. They kept guys who sat on their thumbs and rotated all day. They laid me off. I'll get back to you."

I wished her luck.

I was on the road before the rush hour was over, heading north against the traffic on the Henry Hudson in Crystal's Toyota. Incoming commuter traffic, one person to a car as if it were still 1962, had congealed and halted entirely, festering in its own pollutants. Jellyroll hung his head out the window, ears and tongue flapping in the wind. He loves car trips; he doesn't need to give a shit about the folly of the American road. I felt stiff and sore and pissed. I put WBGO on the radio and listened to the seminal musical genius of the century, Thelonius Sphere Monk: "Crepuscule with Nellie," "Epistrophy," "Lulu's Back in Town," and afterward I felt a little better, clearheaded at least. I took the Henry Hudson to the Cross County, thence to the Merritt Parkway. Forty-five minutes later I had my choice of three New Canaan exits. I took the middle one.

Car commuting as a way of life was born in these suburbs along the Merritt—Weston, Westport, Wilton, Greenwich, New Canaan—after World War II. They spared trees in those days, and from most of the winding roads mature oaks and maples hide even the existence of homes. There are New England rock walls, quiet lanes, and produce stands, but rustic charm is the style, not the reality, of these places. They exist in their present form because New York, from where all blessings flow, lies forty Mercedes miles down the road.

I asked two adolescent suburban urchins throwing rocks into a little roadside brook how to get to Church Street. They didn't know, so I drove randomly until I came to a Sunoco Station, where I repeated the question. The young attendant, decked out like a surfer, neon-green baggies, ponytail, and peace-sign earring, told me I was on Church Street, what was I looking for?

"Posh Pools," I said.

"Two lights up, be on your right in a little shopping plaza." Long Island Sound surfing must be really exciting. Hey, dude, surf's up, medical waste down. I was feeling surly again, so I searched the dial for some jazz, vainly. Fuck it, I was here.

Nobody seemed to be following me as I pulled into the parking lot, but I sat in the car and waited for a while. I should have worn a disguise, I decided. Perhaps a Long Island surfer—Ray Bans, toxic-waste suit. Posh Pools, Ace Hardware, and Gilbert's Lawn & Garden Supply shared the little strip, all the needs of suburban life except the gin. I knew that wasn't a fair view, but I didn't care.

Posh Pools was painfully air-conditioned. The smiling young woman who called me sir when she asked if she could help me wore a down vest, as if this were Maine in midwinter. The place was loaded with gear: strainers, skimmers, ladders, diving boards, umbrellas, rafts, water wings, bathing suits, goggles, tanning lotion and other unguents for the outdoor life. The walls above the display racks were lined with two-foot-square color photos of pools, which Posh apparently dug themselves. They had titles like "Ionion Motif," "Tahiti Revisted," "Traditional," and "Kidney."

"You folks do pool maintenance, don't you?" I asked the chilly young woman. "Chlorine levels, frogs, and so forth?"

"Oh, we're a full-service pool company."

"Yes, I see. You come highly recommended. I think Mr. Archibald is a client of yours. He says you do terrific work."

"Oh, that's nice." But there was no recognition on her face, so I tried again.

"I'm new to the neighborhood, just transferred in from Seattle, and my wife wants a pool in the backyard. Archie says you're the folks to dig it."

"Maybe you'd like to speak to my father. He'll here any minute now. He's the expert on digging."

"I'm particularly interested in your 'Olympic Racer' model." I pointed to the photo over our heads. "Well, I'll stop back with the wife. Actually—it's kind of embarrassing—I'm on my way over to see Archie's pool, but I've lost the address. Maybe you have it in your records. He's an old customer of yours."

"What did you say his name is?"

"Archibald. A largish fellow."

She went behind the cash register, hefted a big looseleaf notebook onto the glass counter, and thumbed pages until she found my old friend Archie. "Yes, he has a fullservice contract with us. Number Seventeen Sylvan Brook Road."

"Where is that, please?"

She gave me a truncated set of directions. "Welcome to New Canaan," she said.

The directions fled from my head when I spotted a Posh Pools van parked near Crystal's car. I circled it. It was a tan van. The logo—crossed palm trees and "The Full-Service Pool People"—was painted on both sides.

I drove down endless unnamed, tree-lined streets while Jellyroll sat beside me, his head pivoting this way and that as if he, too, were looking for Sylvan Brook Road. I came upon the two urchins still throwing rocks into the water. Could their target be Sylvan Brook? I asked them.

"Yeah, this is it. Who you looking for?"

"Archibald."

The boys looked at each other blankly. "The fat guy?" one muttered. "Oh, yeah, the fat guy," said the other one. "That's his driveway back there. You can see his mailbox." I could hear them giggling ("Fat, fat, the water rat—") as I turned around.

I pulled to a stop on the berm beside Sylvan Brook. I couldn't see the house from the road because of the mature forest in the way, but the country-style mailbox said Archibald on the side. The flag was up. What more could I ask for? I resisted the temptation to drive up the gravel road to have a look.

I retraced my route back to the city, but I continued down the West Side, took the Brooklyn-Battery Tunnel, and emerged back aboveground near Red Hook. From New Canaan, Connecticut, to Red Hook, Brooklyn, was a journey to the polar extremes of American society. From posh pools to chop shops, from Sylvan Brook to the Gowanus Canal. Red Hook rotted in the shadow of the elevated Brooklyn-Queens Expressway, its gigantic concrete support columns poking out the heart of the neighborhood, leaving it gutted, demoralized, vicious. Here I didn't feel so inclined to ask directions of strangers, and I didn't see any towheaded youths chucking stones into minor tributaries. After some experimental turning, I found Thumper's place.

It was a fenced lot that ran along the Gowanus Canal, waterfront property. A twelve-foot-high chain-link fence topped by spirals of razor wire surrounded the lot. It took me a while to find the front gate. There was no sign. I drove right in. Two black guys in coveralls with nothing visible underneath sat on the hood of a wheelless pickup truck.

I didn't know Thumper's real name, and I hesitated to call him Thumper, the appellation Outta-Town Brown had laid on him. "Hello," I said. "Is the owner around?"

"Hey, Thumper," called the smaller guy.

At that moment, Thumper was hobbling out of a rickety wooden building, no more than a shack, which I hadn't noticed until then. Dodging puddles of oily water, he carried a silver tray of demitasse cups.

"Artie, welcome," called Thumper. Jellyroll ran at him. Thumper placed the tray on a bank of welding gas tanks, did a little jig, and clapped his hands together. Jellyroll jumped to kiss him. Thumper knelt to accept. Greetings winding down, Thumper said graciously, "Artie, these are my associates, Boo and Randolph." The two black guys slid off the hood in unison. "This is my friend Artie Deemer. And do you know who this is? This is the R-r-ruff Dog."

"No shit?" said Boo or Randolph.

"None," I said.

"Lookit that. That dog's smiling!"

And he was, too.

"Coffee, gentlemen?"

Tractor-trailer traffic roared sixty feet overhead.

"I got a batch of new espresso machines. Nice ones. Scenes of It'ly painted on 'em."

I turned down coffee, because Thumper had only three cups on the tray. "However, I could use a van."

"We have vans. What kind of van could you use?"

"A tan van."

"A tan van. Yes. Have we got a tan van, Boo?"

"Got a brown van."

"What shade, Boo?"

"Shit."

"Hey, boss," said Randolph, sipping, "this ain't outstanding mud."

"Maybe you got to have a knack with the valves and spouts."

"Maybe we got burned on the beans."

"Maybe," said Thumper. Then to me, "I bought four hundred pounds of coffee off an associate of mine. He said it was one hundred percent Kona."

"He lied," said Randolph.

"Well, let's us go see the van," Thumper suggested. They threw their coffee into the dirt.

We walked down a dirt path between rows of vehicles. Some were reasonably new, with paint still intact, and some were rusted hulks, wheelless and forlorn. Not only did he have cars and trucks, but speedboats, snowmobiles, forklifts, backhoes, pile drivers, golf carts, motorized wheelchairs, even an ancient Zamboni machine, and around the machinery, under it, among it, there was a substrate of decaying metal objects, most gone beyond recognition. Five hundred years after his death, Thumper's place would be a career-making find for some Brooklyn College archaeologist. There were three vans similar to Posh Pool's full-service vehicles, but none the exact shade of brown. Shit-brown was the closest.

I showed the Posh Pools card to Thumper, Boo, and Randolph. "Could you paint this on both sides of the van?" I asked.

They studied the card. "How big you want it?" Boo wondered.

"The whole side."

"Hunnert bucks," he said.

"By tomorrow morning?"

"Hunnert and a half."

I gave him cash on the spot. He liked that very much. "I'll get my gear." He headed for the shack. Jellyroll sauntered off at Boo's heels.

"How much to rent the van, Thumper?"

"Well, I'll tell you, Artie, that depends on the degree of damage."

"Damage?" I hadn't considered damage.

"I don't ask to what use you intend to put this vehicle. That's one of the services I offer—lack of inquisitiveness. Therefore, I can't assess the degree of damage potential till you bring it back. Also the degree of heat. I can't assess that. If it comes back so hot I got to retire it into the Gowanus Canal, then that's a total loss, and your total loss is a different matter altogether, feewise."

"How about if there's no damage?"

"Just that pool hooey painted on the side?"

"Right."

Thumper produced a notepad from his pocket and did some figuring. "For you, a hundred a day prorated hourly for any period thereafter."

"Okay. I'd like to park my car back here for however long I need the van."

"Sure, we'll put it near the back outta sight."

Boo returned, Jellyroll on his heels, with a big carpenter's box full of paints and brushes. We watched while he taped the card to the side of the van at eye level and then began to grid out his work. Boo seemed full of the confidence of an artist.

"Say, Artie, how about some pool supplies?"

"There's a thought. What have you got?"

"Skimmers, plungers, pumpers, maybe a sucker somewhere."

146

"How much?"

"Well, that again depends on degree of damage and extent of loss." I didn't want to keep hearing about damage. "Undamaged, I give 'em to you for free, if you take an espresso machine off my hands for twenty-five bucks. It's got brass nozzles and spouts, nice I-talian mountain scene in color."

"Fine."

He made a note on his pad.

"Oh. Uniforms," I said. "I almost forgot uniforms."

"Uniforms. Check. White coveralls?"

"Okay. Put some phony names on the tits?"

"Goes without saying. How many?"

"Uh, three." I gave Thumper a hundred and fifty dollars down—against damage.

"Pleasure doing business with you, Artie. You too, Jellyroll."

A car had blown up in the northbound lane of the West Side Highway, so during the miserable bumper-to-bumper lurch back uptown I had time to run my plans over and over in my head. Jellyroll didn't like the trip, because there was no wind to ruffle his ears. Every now and then, I'd check the mirror for suspicious motorists, but that was ludicrous. How would I recognize a tail in stalled traffic?

The Ninety-sixth Street exit from the Henry Hudson in sight, it took another half hour to get off. People did this every day of their lives. That made my plans seem sensible and conservative by comparison. I left Crystal's car in the hands of the downtrodden attendant at a nearby parking garage. He clearly hated me, and after I tipped him five, he still hated me.

I had been recklessly roaming the metropolitan area in a daze all day, in a dream that could turn to nightmare. A nightmare was just a dream with a higher degree of damage. What was Crystal doing right now? Suffering? The fat fuck said she was "restrained." What did that mean precisely? Tied naked, spread-eagled to a grotty cot, at Henry's service? Chained in a painful ball? Caged? Hang on, Crystal. I fingered the handle of my ice pick as I took Jellyroll for a quick shit in Riverside Park. Took a special kind of guy . . .

On the promenade, two testosterone-twisted adolescents swung on a cherry-tree branch until it snapped. They jumped up and down and whooped like crazed cannibals after the kill. I walked down by the river near the tennis courts, because the tennis courts were always crowded. I watched the flotsam and jetsam bob upstream on the tide. Two gulls rested on a floating railroad tie. Corralled in a tidal eddy, errant tennis balls went round and round, turning gray. Three used condoms drifted by, mouths up, like a school of short, dead lampreys. The day was beginning to seem long. Jellyroll picked up an ancient pizza crust and began to chomp contentedly until I told him, "Drop."

I sat down on a bench, envied the couples playing tennis, and felt sorry for myself. It seemed hopeless. We'd had fun for a time, we were growing to love one another, and then reality interceded, if this could be called reality. Our interests intersected with those of crazies. I thought about our first night together almost mournfully.

Jellyroll spotted him coming before I did. He stiffened, pricked his ears. I stood, spun, and backpedaled, putting the bench between me and whatever my watchdog had seen.

A man on crutches was moving at me with alarming speed, swinging his heavy body along almost lopingly. It was Barry! I'd never forget that fleshy, pocked face grinning at me in Crystal's car, with the Crystal wig on its head.

"Jellyroll, come!" I turned and bolted north—Jellyroll and I could outrun this guy—

"You can run, but you cain't never hide," Barry called after us, coming hard, crutches flicking in the setting sun. "I know where you live—"

That was a nightmare of mine—to be hunted down in my own neighborhood, to feel the commonplace take on the air of menace because nowhere was safe, not even my own home. I still had the ice pick in my pocket. I could try to stick him again. He was obviously pissed about the last time, but maybe this time I could stick him somewhere vital to life itself. However, there were an awful lot of witnesses on the promenade. I looked back over my shoulder—was he gaining?

No. Barry slowed, then slowed further. Something was wrong with Barry. I stopped to watch. His head lolled forward, back, but since he had no neck, it couldn't loll far. I thought I saw his eyes roll as well. He seemed now to be walking in quicksand on crutches. Each step came with comedic deliberateness, just putting one foot in front of . . . the other foot, move the crutches. Then Barry stopped altogether. He flopped onto the nearest bench. He propped the crutches against the seat, but they clattered to the concrete. Barry couldn't seem to pick them up again. Eyes open, he sagged sideways on the bench. His head thunked against the wood. He didn't move again. Nobody looked twice. Tennis players, Lycra-clad joggers, blade skaters, mothers pushing baby carriages—they saw people sleeping on benches every day.

Jellyroll sat at my heels. That's what he does when he gets frightened. Me, I melt into a puddle, flooding my sneakers. My hand started trembling first, like a bongo player's at the crescendo. Something had happened to this Barry. He hadn't merely gotten tired chasing me up the river on crutches and decided to catch forty winks before he got on with it.

My head darted around, but my eyes didn't see anything

in the watery blur. I stopped it darting, clenched my eyes into focus—

Calabash! He stood on the walkway near the front gate to the tennis courts. I could have blubbered with relief. Calabash was built like a subcompact automobile and weighed only slightly less. He was my friend and body-guard. Apparently, he had seen what had just happened to Barry. Calabash looked at me and nodded minutely. Then he looked at Barry there on the bench. Calabash's face was tense.

I sat down about six benches from Barry, mainly because my knees had melted. Calabash sat on Barry's bench and nonchalantly crossed his legs, a giant Bahamian taking in the sunset over New Jersey. Several passersby glanced at him, but that was only because he was too big to go any-where without people glancing to him. No one glanced at Barry.

After a time, Calabash reached out—about five feet out—grasped Barry by the back of his neck, and drew him effort-lessly up into something like a sitting position. He held Barry like that for a couple of seconds, then he abruptly stood up and walked toward me. He didn't look at me as he passed. I didn't look at him either as I stood up and fell into step behind him. We both had similar ideas: get the fuck away from Barry and whatever had happened to him before it happened to us. Jellyroll sniffed the air in Calabash's wake.

"Good to see you," he said without moving his mouth.

"That's putting it mildly," I said.

"Dot guy was dead."

"Dead?"

"Dead."

"How?"

"I don't know. I only know he's dead."

I stopped, placed my elbows on the rail, and watched

New Jersey. Calabash stopped a short way on. Here was a dead guy with at least one ice-pick hole in his person, and here was me—a special kind of guy—with an ice pick in my pocket. . . .

Now Jellyroll recognized Calabash, gave out a little snort of joy, and jumped on him. Never seen each other before. Slick. I reached in and covertly extracted the ice pick, flipped it in the river, and watched anxiously to see if it would sink. It did.

A Hispanic guy appeared beside me, but he was too short to lean his arms on the rail. He was built like a fire hydrant. Naw, couldn't be—the Hispanic guy had beautiful long black hair brilliantined straight back from his high forehead. He had a little black pencil mustache. The Hispanic guy had powder-blue eyes, which twinkled at me.

Calabash was circling around behind him, but the Hispanic guy saw him doing it. He offered Calabash his hand. "Norm Armbrister—" he said.

"Calabash."

"Calabash?"

"Dot's a fruit."

"Don't I know it. Where you from, Calabash?"

"De Bahamas."

"I thought so. Like whereabouts specifically?"

"De Exhumas."

"Oh yeah, I've been all around down in there, the wife and I. Poor Joe Cay—"

"You been to Poor Joe?"

"Oh, sure."

"Did you kill dot guy on de bench?"

"No other way to reason with men like him. I'm trying to convince your friend Artie to take me along when he goes after his girlfriend. That's probably why you're in town."

Calabash looked at me.

Norm Armbrister was a silent killer, a spook who killed, how, by sheer force of will? That was just the sort of man I needed.

"How can I get in touch with you?"

Norm handed me a card with a phone number penned on it.

"I'll call you at nine o'clock tomorrow morning, and I'll tell you where we'll pick you up."

"Security?" He giggled.

He went south, we went north, leaving Barry on the bench. I wondered if Barry had friends or loved ones who'd miss him. Probably not.

15.

SHORTLY AFTER FIRST LIGHT, I took Jellyroll for a walk in the park. The homeless still slept on the hillside in cardboard boxes and refrigerator crates. Some stirred, peeked out of their crates for a glimpse at the new day that held nothing new for them. Others would probably never wake up. Due to the cutbacks, the city didn't collect the dead with regularity. I picked up Jellyroll's shit—healthy—with a Chinese-restaurant menu, and as I dropped it in the basket, I felt intense melancholy for those in the crates, for the city, for myself, and for Jellyroll. This might be the last shit I'd be around to shovel. Who could predict what would happen out there in the wilds of New Canaan? Back at the apartment, I kissed him goodbye, and I could tell he was wondering, What's the big deal about today? Dogs love routine, but today was decidedly different.

I phoned Norman Armbrister at precisely nine. I told him to meet us—on foot—at the Riverdale side of the toll bridge across the Harlem River. He giggled at my security measures and said, "Okay, Captain, I'll be there."

I was acting by rote, paying the man behind the bulletproof glass for the overnight garaging, starting Crystal's car in the gloomy garage recesses, and driving it toward the light. Like my dog, I've always been fond of normalcy. There could be no more normalcy. Here I was, an eccentric hermit who habitually thought through even the simplest of day-to-day actions from all possible perspectives before deciding to do nothing; any other decision seemed too complicated. Now I was leading a covert incursion against a racketeer's suburban mansion to rescue my lover who may or may not be there. I didn't hold out much hope of success. Hopelessness—yes, that was the feeling I was trying to repress by living in the moment—step on the gas, step on the brake, as needed, don't wreck the car driving around to Broadway to pick up Calabash. At least stave off the ludicrous.

It had taken most of last night, a bottle of rum, and more than one gasper to explain the events of the past several days to Calabash. I told him about Trammell's disappearance, Bruce's beating, Crystal's kidnapping, my own kidnapping, about Chet Bream and the tape. Then we began to talk about the plan.

"Hmm," said Calabash after I'd finished. I didn't take that "hmm" as a sign of enthusiasm. He began to unpack lethal objects from his black gym bag, to clean and load them. Hmm . . .

Calabash was clutching that gym bag when I picked him up on Broadway. He scrunched into the Toyota, his head bent against its roof. We drove south on the Henry Hudson in light traffic. I almost missed the Brooklyn-Battery Tunnel entrance. Tunnel entrances require a degree of driving precision.

"You okay?" Calabash reasonably wanted to know.

"Oh, sure, fine, great."

"We don' want to get killed on de way."

*　　*　　*

"Still a little tacky," said Boo, his head cocked, touching his work with his index finger.

"It's beautiful," I said.

"Yeah, it come out pretty good." He nodded approvingly. "But that one palm tree there, it could be some better. Palm trees is tough. It's the fronds, you know. Fronds is hard. You don't have time I can do it over, do you?"

I tipped him fifty bucks.

The van rode like a stagecoach. It shimmied and shook and pulled to the left. Before we left Thumper's place, we'd checked the brake lights and such, so we wouldn't get stopped for minor infractions, but there was no time for a test drive. "I been in ten-foot seas calmer den dis," commented Calabash. An ominous grinding sound from the stern made my teeth itch.

The shit-brown van got us to the Harlem River. I paid the toll with the exact change, and we crossed the bridge into the Bronx, looking for the murderous spook. Calabash had tactically removed himself to the backseat.

Norman Armbrister stood beside the road just beyond the bridge abutment. He wore his original getup—baggy shorts and the enormous beard that obliterated his features. He also wore an unseasonably heavy—in every sense—jacket. I pulled over and pushed open the passenger door for him. Norm clanked as he got in and buckled his seat belt. I heard an ominous metallic click from the backseat. A tight-knit commando unit on the move. I felt like opening my door and throwing up the lemon yogurt I'd forced down for breakfast.

"Seat belt," Norm said to me. "It's a law in this state. Always want to observe civil law when you're operational. Posh Pools, huh? Great. I like it. We used to do Con Ed. We'd disappear down that manhole, leaving nothing but a puff of steam."

Belted, I drove on north toward the Cross County Parkway, which would take us to the Merritt Parkway.

Norm was hanging on to the window post in the turns. "I hope we don't get killed on the way. How would it look with all these arms? Calabash, I presume you're armed."

"Yes."

"Yes, so I hear. . . . Hell, what can one expect in the way of vehicles? It's not like the old days, once you're dead." There was a lilt in his voice. This guy was having a ball. His eyes beamed. "In the old days, there was no end to the matériel. I just loved the Russians. They loved us, too. If it weren't for us, they wouldn't have gotten all their good shit. And vice versa. You needed a deuce and a half for your gear, an APC for your guys, you wanted some air support, Cobra gunships, you wanted some arty, just call it in. Never mind the expense to the taxpayers. The taxpayers loved it, too. We *got* to have all this gear or the Evil Empire will poison your daughters and fuck your bird dogs. But those times are gone forever, at least in this lifetime. Want an apple juice? I brought apple juice. Yes, times change after you die. That's one of life's inevitables. Juice?"

Calabash, I could see in the mirror, was looking at the back of Norm's head as if it belonged to a spook from another planet.

"So what's the plan?" Norm wanted to know, all grins.

I told him.

"Well, simple is good."

Was there an edge of sarcasm in that? This psycho probably hated my plan. My plan probably failed to consider things every freshman spook knew by heart. My plan was probably suicidal. Anxiety scraped my nerves raw. I felt like I was bleeding internally. I began to obsess on Jellyroll. I had made no arrangements for him. What if I got . . . killed? What would happen to him, waiting endlessly for my return? . . . Would it be better for my associates' morale for me to vomit all over my Posh Pools coveralls or to fall down sobbing like a colicky infant?

"We'll be there in what, twenty minutes," he said, "barring the freaky-fluky?"

"Yeah, barring that."

"Okay. We have a chance to talk turkey. You're probably still asking yourself, 'Why's this fellow Norm want to help us free Crystal, anyhow? What's in it for Norm?' Am I right?"

"Well, to tell you the truth, Norm, we don't really give a shit as long as you don't betray us. We just want Crystal back. If we can get her out and if they'll leave us alone after we get her, then you and the rest of them can do whatever you want to each other."

"I hear you. Apathy. Apathy is not an unreasonable response to the events of the late twentieth century. But as for your first if, we *can* get Crystal out. If he's got her at his place, we'll break her out. If he's got her somewhere else, we'll take Tiny and make a trade, even steven. Frankly, I don't think he's harmed her. Murder is not Tiny's métier, but then you never know. The second if, however, is a bit more dicey. Tiny's not going to be happy if we snatch Crystal back. He's going to feel stupid. How do we keep him off your ass? That's where Norm Armbrister comes in. I can help you there. Tiny likes to live. He loves the seven deadliest, particularly gluttony and avarice. It'll frighten Tiny to learn I'm alive and angry with him. But that leads back to the original question—namely, *why* does Norm Armbrister want to help? The answer is twofold. One: Trammell Weems. Two: the tape."

As he said "the tape," he looked at me for a reaction. I watched the road without any. "What tape?"

"A videotape. One or another of these treacherous banking bastards made a tape of a meeting held at Tiny Archibald's place in late July 1990. In the wrong hands, that tape would be embarrassing at best, incriminating at worst. That tape is the reason I died. As it says in my obit, I had a proud career. I don't want it sullied."

"Do you think Trammell made the tape?"

"Maybe. Maybe Tiny. Maybe Trammell. You see, I suspect that Trammell didn't drown. I suspect that it was a put-up death."

"Sort of like yours?"

"Right. Does Calabash know about my death?"

"Yes, I told him."

Norm Armbrister pulled his obituary from his shirt pocket and handed it to Calabash, who was watching Norm with one eyebrow arched. Calabash read while Norm went on: "Here we have Crystal, who used to be married to Trammell; we have Crystal's uncle's boat; and we have you, his old friend. You seem to be in a position to answer the question, 'Is Trammell dead or is Trammell alive?' That's why I'm helping you—to get that question answered."

"Trammell's alive."

Norm nodded. "What makes you think so? Have you seen him?"

"No."

"Bruce Munger?"

"Yes."

"So Trammell paid this Bruce Munger person to witness his drowning?"

"Apparently."

"Tell me this," Norm said with a note of skepticism. "How did Munger think he'd get away with it?"

"You'd have to know Bruce."

"An asshole?"

"Yes."

"Well, asshole-ishness explains a lot of things these days."

I told him about Bruce's whipping and about the wad of bills taped in his mouth. "I had assumed that was Tiny's work."

"But you don't now?"

"No."

"Why?"

"Because you had Barry spying for you. If Tiny did it, wouldn't Barry know about it and tell you?"

Calabash passed Norm's obituary back to him. "You was in de navy?"

"No, that's bullshit. Barry was setting up your kidnapping. Your sticking him with the pick rendered him useless to me. So Tiny could have gotten to Munger without me knowing about it."

"Who else might have done it?" I risked losing control of the vehicle by taking my eyes off the road to look into Norm's eyes. "Concom?"

He snapped his head around to look into mine. "What do you know about Concom?"

"Nothing, except that Tiny Archibald and the phony detective both gave me phone numbers belonging to Concom."

"I was hoping we could keep it out of Concom's hands. I'm sure that's what Tiny was hoping, too."

"Why?"

"Trust me when I say it would be best for you and Crystal and Calabash to pretend Concom doesn't exist."

"Gladly." I swerved off the highway at the New Canaan exit. Everybody held on.

"Artie, one last item. Do you know where Trammell is?"

"No."

"Does Crystal?"

"No."

"Okay, I believe you. But let's say we're successful here.

Let's say we get Crystal out safe and sound. Will you tell me if you find out?"

"I won't be looking, Norm."

"I hear you, but suppose it just comes to pass that you learn his whereabouts. Will you tell me?"

"Yes."

"Hey, Norm—?" said Calabash.

Norm pivoted, looked over the headrest.

"I gonna be watchin' you close."

"I hear you, big guy." Norm was actually grinning.

I had recently read a book about Horatio Nelson, who, during a short peace in those wars with France, watched the Danish fleet assemble in Copenhagen Harbor and assumed that when the peace inevitably failed, the Danish navy would go in on the French side. So Nelson attacked— and destroyed the Danish fleet at its moorings. For a time in the early nineteenth century, "Copenhagen" became a verb in the English language. It meant to strike first, to destroy your potential enemy before he has a chance to become your actual enemy. That's what I should do to this crazy spook—Copenhagen his ass after he helped us rescue Crystal. Could I do that? Copenhagen him in cold blood?

16.

THE FRUGAL YANKEE INN was one of those darkly oaken restaurants decorated with Colonial furnishings, agrarian gewgaws, creaky floors, and help who say, "Hello, my name is Darrell, and I'll be your waiter today." I had picked the Frugal Yankee because it was located on a corner lot at the intersection of Cherry Grove Lane and Sylvan Brook Road, within sight of Tiny Archibald's driveway.

Thumper's uniforms must have been tailored for wear in the pituitary-case ward. Calabash's fit him fine. I could have gotten a couple of close friends in there with me and still had room to squat. Norman had nearly disappeared in his. "Hell, this isn't a disguise," he said, "this is a *hide*out."

Since our hosts at Tiny's place had seen me before, my disguise was a tad more elaborate than I would have liked. I wore silver-mirrored sunglasses and a hot-pink baseball cap backwards, with a phony blond ponytail stapled under the brim. My disguise was modeled on the Long Island Sound–surfer motif. I felt more ridiculous than anonymous stumbling over my uniform cuffs into the lobby of the Frugal Yankee.

I felt somewhat less ridiculous when I saw how the poor sod inside was got up—Puritan suit: flat-brimmed hat with buckle, big brass buttons, wooden clogs, knee britches, and starched bib. "Posh Pools?" he said. "Great. Where you been? I been calling you all morning." He had a surly Long Island accent.

"Do you have a pay phone?"

"We got frogs again. You know, *dead* frogs. Totally grossed out the guests."

"I just need to make a call first."

He pointed to an anachronistic phone on the wall near the hayrick—

Henry answered.

"Artie Deemer. Let me speak to Tiny."

" 'Bout what?"

" 'Bout how you're still sniffing girls' bicycle seats up at the middle school." Maybe I *could* Copenhagen that bastard Henry.

Tiny came on the line after a short wait.

"I'm looking at him right now," I said.

"Trammell?"

"Isn't that who you wanted me to find?"

"And where might you be?"

"Kennedy. He just checked about ten pieces luggage aboard a Varig Airlines flight to São Paulo. It doesn't look like he's going for the weekend. There, I've done my part, now let Crystal go."

"Please don't insult my intelligence. All I have right now is you on the telephone. When I have Trammell, then you get Crystal. I'll be disappointed if I don't see you at the airport, too."

"Look, I'm just trying to do what you said. All I want is Crystal." I thought I should protest a little to make it look good.

"And you'll get her. If you play square with me, I'll reciprocate in kind. You can trust me on that."

"I'll be here, right beside the duty-free shop. But you better hurry or he'll be gone."

The Puritan blocked my exit. "Pool's out back," he said.

"I got to make a quick stop before I get to you."

"What, is the surf up?"

"No, this is an emergency. You think frogs are bad. These people have *piranha*. Stripped the flesh off this guy's wife and kids in about thirty seconds."

When I climbed back into the Posh Pools van, Norm was watching Tiny's driveway with a miniature pair of rubberized black spook binoculars and Calabash was sorting through his gym bag. A panicky grackle flapped its wings in my stomach. "Do you think they hurt Crystal?" I asked Norm.

"I don't know," he said without taking down the binoculars. "Depends on the disposition of the tape. Trouble with telling Tiny Trammell's at the airport is that Trammell could be sitting on the couch right across from him. It's that kind of conspiracy."

I hadn't thought of that. The bird flapped hysterically. "Why the fuck didn't you say so!"

"Get a hold of yourself," he snapped.

I turned to Calabash. "Do you want to forget the whole thing?"

"Looks like Calabash can take care of himself," grinned Norm.

"I didn't ask you!"

"You're panicking. No room for panic when you're operational."

"We do it," said Calabash evenly. "But I want dis CIA spy fellow to know one t'ing clear. If it go wrong, den de first t'ing I do is shoot big smoky holes in his hideout."

"Oh, sure, Calabash, I never doubted that for a minute. And if you ever want a job—here they come."

We didn't need binoculars to see the black Buick pause at the bottom of Tiny's driveway, then roar up Sylvan Brook Road toward the Frugal Yankee Inn.

"They're going fast. That's a good sign. That means they bought it."

The car passed us, accelerating.

"Tiny's not in the car," said Norm.

Rufus was driving, a white guy was riding shotgun.

"So who's that leave?" asked Norm.

"Henry," I said.

"Henry's twisted. Henry's not sane."

I pulled the Posh Pools van into gear and drove slowly toward the driveway.

"I know it's a little late to tell you guys, now we're operational, but I'm gonna sneak off at some point and bug Tiny's house. He won't be able to spray one without I hear the tinkle."

"I don't care what you do. I just want Crystal safe."

"I hear you."

We fell silent and watchful as we ascended the driveway, winding our way up through an oak forest with great lichened boulders left over from the last glacier. My mouth was so dry I couldn't part my lips. The trees suddenly gave way to a sunlit clearing, an impeccably groomed lawn, a gentle hill. The house stood at the top.

I had seen ads for such places in the back of the *New York Times Magazine*. Twenty rooms, plus guest cottage, gardener's quarters, stables, six acres of land, $4,000,000. Even the hotshots in the animal-movie business didn't live in places like this. Georgian-style with Corinthian columns. Tiny's house was too elaborate to understand from only the front view. Two-story wings flapped off in all directions. This was the aristocracy of the American criminal class. We couldn't see the pool from the driveway, but we could see the white picket fence. I remembered the white picket fence.

I flinched as if at incoming artillery when something big moved at the edge of my vision.

"Get a grip on yourself," said Norm.

"Shut up," said Calabash.

It was a woman posting by on the back of a beautiful black horse. She too was beautiful, though I only caught her profile. She didn't even glance our way, service employees here to do something with the amphibian corpses in the swimming pool.

We circled the bottom of the hill before we climbed it toward the front door, an enormous red thing that would barely have covered the entrance to St. Patrick's Cathedral, but we stopped short of that, in front of the white picket fence. Birds flitted and chirped in the Norfolk pines.

We climbed out of the van. Calabash opened the rear door, pulled out the pool gear, and placed it on my shoulder—he wanted to leave his gun hand free, I realized. Adrenaline was blasting though the passages of my body like the Columbia River. My knees were rubbery. Unbalanced, the pool tools kept sticking in the grass ahead, bringing me to comedic halts. Operational, I felt like an idiot. But Calabash and Norm looked strong, eyes darting alertly from side to side. They opened the gate. Into the valley of the shadow of death. We sank to our ankles in the luxurious lawn. Every blade of grass was uniform. Tiny's gardener probably plucked out the aberrants on his hands and knees.

The water was roiled, as if someone had just gotten out of the pool. Calabash and Norm spotted her. I'd missed her entirely—a woman in her twenties wearing a tiny bikini, her body lithe and athletic. She had been lying on a bath towel along the edge of the pool, but at our approach, she sat up. Her perfectly shaped breasts made all effort to escape their tiny triangles. "Hi," she said.

"Hi," I said. "We're with Posh Pools. Is Henry here?"

"Somewhere. Is it the frogs?"

"Yes. It is. The frogs."

"Good. Henry's got a frog up his butt."

"Hey, look at this," said Norm, pointing. "There *are* frogs."

I looked into the pool. So did Calabash and the woman in the bathing suit. Four large ones, legs outstretched behind, lay on the blue concrete bottom in a ring around the drain grate as if it were a poisonous trough from which, having supped, they'd dropped simultaneously dead. I thought it one of the saddest sights I had ever seen.

"About fuckin' time." It was Henry, coming up behind us in his thong suit. The woman wrinkled her nose as if Henry stank and went back to her beach towel. "I been on the horn all morning to Posh. I got better things to do. There's a pant load of pool firms out there. You can't deal with the frogs, we'll find one that can!" The muscles in his face twitched and jerked as if little animals were running in panic beneath his skin.

"I hear ya, dude," I said. "Those frogs, they're history."

"Yeah, well, you keep an eye on that big nigger there. It's well known niggers is scared of frogs." Henry turned to walk away—

But before he completed one whole step, there came a terrible flash of movement, a dull thunk, a sweeping follow-through; it had a grandness about it, like the calving glaciers you see on the Discovery Channel. Henry took another step and a half before his knees packed up. His body remained upright for a moment, wavering left, then right, head lolling, before he keeled forward. The impact must have done some nasty work on his nose.

"Well sapped," admired Norm.

"Only way to reason with fooking racists."

The woman in the bikini leapt to her feet. Reflexively, she covered her breasts with her arms. "Please don't hurt me—"

"We're not going to hurt you," I said.

"You're not?"

"What do you do here, sweetie?" asked Norm in a gentle voice.

"Nothing. I don't do anything, and I don't know anything. I'm decoration. I mean, I'm really an actress, but times are tight. Tiny pays good money for me to sit around his pool in a bathing suit. No sex. He's just trying to impress his guests that he has friends."

"Where are the guests?" Norm seemed to have taken over the questioning.

"They're not here yet."

"Who's in the house?"

"Tiny. He's there. The housekeeper's there, but she's like a hundred and six."

"Anybody else?"

"Two of his stooges just left. Look, I'll vanish, I promise. I'll move to Helsinki, Norway, anywhere, you'll never see me again—"

Calabash edged over to the house, peeked in the first window, then the next, his right hand thrust into his jacket.

"What's your name?"

"Cecily."

"Mine's Norm. We'd appreciate it, Cecily, if you'd just sit down like nothing happened. As far as you're concerned, nothing did."

She squatted tensely on her towel, terrified that we were there to kill Tiny and, having done so, couldn't leave her alive to testify. But what could I do to reassure her just then?

"We'd also appreciate it if you'd call Tiny outside."

"Oh, Jesus—"

"Don't worry, we're not going to hurt him."

"I don't care what you do to him. He probably deserves it. Just don't do it to me. Please!"

"Call him out, Cecily."

"He doesn't come when I call."

"You're an actress. Pretend Henry just had a heart attack," I suggested, "and you've got to call for help."

"I probably wouldn't."

"Then pretend it's your father who had a heart attack."

Her eyes looked off into the sky. She was preparing. She screamed. All three of us hunched our shoulders against the piercing blast. She let fly another that set us back on our heels. Norm was grinning broadly. Calabash was sneaking along the side of the house to the sprawling screened porch, which was elevated about six feet above the lawn. A heavy door slammed somewhere in the house, then a screen door, closer—

Tiny, wearing a dark blue three-piece suit with a cravat, appeared on the porch, waddling full speed.

Calabash would be behind him when he emerged into the pool area. The woman had closed her eyes. She didn't want to see what the impact did to Tiny. But she let out another throat-scarring scream. I hoped that would be the last. Tiny hotfooted it down the stairs, onto the lawn, and through a gate in the picket fence. "What—!"

Tiny froze when he saw Henry facedown on the concrete. He glanced from me to Norm, back to me, then behind, but too late. Retreat was now blocked by Calabash towering over the fence, staring at him.

"Hi, Tiny," said Norm.

"Who's that? That's not—?"

"Sure is."

"Norm? Norman Armbrister? . . . But you're—"

"Go ahead and say it. I love when they say it."

"—dead?"

"This is Artie Deemer. He wants his girlfriend back. And the gentleman behind you, he wants to eat your young."

Tiny nodded. He got the picture. "What do you want, Norman?"

"The tape."

"The tape?"

"Where," I insisted, "is Crystal?" I didn't want this to degenerate into a quarrel among spooks and bankers and conspiratorial assholes over a tape. We were here for Crystal—

"You've got balls, Norm," said Tiny, "coming to me about the tape, when you're the one who made the thing in the first—"

"I did not—"

Calabash kicked the gate open. "Fook da tape, I'm gonna crush dis guy—"

Slack-jawed, Tiny looked up at personified doom approaching and screamed, "Noooo—!"

Calabash grabbed Tiny, spun him around, and enfolded his neck from behind in great rippling ebony arms. "I'm gonna snap dis guy's neck for kidnapping Crystal, den I gonna t'row him in wid de frogs—"

"Haaa! No, Deemer, tell him no!"

"He doesn't answer to me. He does what he feels like. He feels like snapping your fat neck."

"I didn't hurt her! I didn't hurt her! A few tranquilizers is all! Please—!"

Norm, I suddenly noticed, had vanished.

"I'll show you! She's fine!"

"Is she here?" I screeched. I was about four inches off the ground, I was flying downstream on Class-6 adrenaline rapids. There was no turning back now. There was a crazy sharp-edged clarity to all I saw—the house, the trees, the pool, the woman in the bathing suit, prone Henry, Tiny's terrified face—

This might actually come off! She was here! I felt on the verge of a semihysterical giggling fit. "If you take us to her, we'll drive away with her and we won't hurt you!" I was shouting. I had to get a grip on myself.

"What about Norman?"

"What?"

"Will he kill me? He's a psychopath, you know. You ought to watch who you hang around with. Do you want a job with me—?"

"Look, I told you—I want Crystal. I better start seeing her or he's gonna twist your head off!"

"The garage apartment! She's in the garage apartment!" He pointed to a building out beyond the picket fence on the edge of the great lawn.

I bolted in that direction—

"Artie, wait." It was Calabash. He was right. I was getting giddy. He escorted Tiny toward the fence, whispering something in Tiny's ear. Whatever he said made Tiny's eyes bulge.

"No, no, no tricks, I swear!"

"Somebody's out dere, Artie. I saw somebody move."

We edged toward the fence, looked out . . .

Norm. He was loading two bulging garbage bags into the van.

I could barely keep myself from sprinting down the hill. Finally we were there. The garage door was raised. There were no cars inside, just a sit-down lawn mower. Tools for gardening, auto repair, and home maintenance hung on pegboards along the wall, all neat and clean. There wasn't a drop of oil on the concrete floor. A flight of carpeted stairs led up to the apartment. Calabash called me away from them.

Norm jogged up, big grin. "I'll take Tiny off your hands."

Calabash released him to Norm and stood at the bottom of the stairs with a gun in his hand. His other hand made the *shhh* sign at us.

"Here," Norm whispered to Tiny, "come sit on this tractor."

"What?"

"Come sit on the tractor, take a load off. Handsome machine. What is that? Is that a Toro Lawn Doctor?"

Tiny waddled over and after two false starts managed to hoist himself astride the tractor. He gripped the handlebars and peered up from under his bushy brows with frightened deer eyes. His jowls trembled.

Calabash cringed with each creak as he cautiously climbed the stairs. All eyes were on him. He was reaching for the doorknob—

Norm, meanwhile, was screwing the cap off a gallon can of gasoline, but that didn't really register then. I was concerned with the door. What would we find behind the door? Calabash slowly, silently turned the knob, then shoved. The door banged against its stop. I bolted up the stairs without touching a one of them and followed Calabash inside.

She was asleep. She looked like a little girl, curled on the bed in a loose fetal position. She wore the same clothes I'd last seen her in, seemingly months ago. I dropped to my knees beside the bed and put my cheek against hers.

Gun leveled and cocked, Calabash went to search the bathroom.

"Crystal," I whispered, "it's Artie. We're here to take you home." I felt like a fairy-tale prince.

She moaned.

I brushed a shock of hair from her eyes. They opened and immediately closed again.

Calabash returned from the john with a warm, wet towel,

which he handed to me. He leaned over to see her face. "Can she walk? We better be gone."

"I'll carry her," I said. "Crystal—" I swabbed her brow. Her eyes opened and stayed open.

Her head rose. "Artie! . . . It's you?"

"Absolutely."

Smiling, she sagged back onto the pillow. "What happened to your hair?"

"It's a disguise." I picked her up. She hugged me around the neck and hummed in my ear as I carried her to the head of the stairs. I hoped I could make it down. They were steep. That would be a hell of a note, rescue Crystal only to fall down the stairs and break both our collarbones.

The stench of gasoline hit us in the face like a wet mop, but I tried not to question the reason for that until I navigated the stairs, tried not to look at Tiny sitting absurdly on the Toro Lawn Doctor. My legs were shot at the bottom of the stairs. I needed to sit for a minute.

The Toro, I realized, was soaked in gasoline, and so was Tiny's lower body. His chinos were dark with it. Norm stood nearby, same grin, puffing deeply on a fat black stogie. The end glowed in the gloom of the garage.

I carried Crystal away from the scene.

"I'm gonna barf," said Tiny from the fumes.

I had brought a sleeping-bag pad, a pillow, and a blanket and had already made them into a bed in the back of the van. There was a sweet smile on Crystal's face as I laid her down. She held me around the neck, so I lay down beside her.

Calabash climbed behind the wheel. "I told dat freaky spy I leavin' in thirty seconds, no matter what." I cringed as he turned the key. It started on the first crank. Relief. I'd pictured us putt-putting out of there on the Toro Lawn Doctor.

I looked out the back door to see Norm sauntering across

the lawn toward the van. Over his shoulder I saw Tiny roll off the tractor like a bag of water and crawl away from it on his belly. Then I pulled the door shut. Calabash had us going before Norm shut his door.

"Stop," said Norm at the foot of the driveway.

"Why?" asked Calabash as he stopped.

Norm reached into a bag on the floor between his little feet and extracted from it a nasty star-shaped object, like a Christmas-tree decoration. He placed it on his palm. The thing had five brutally sharp points. I understood its design: no matter how it landed, one of those points would stick straight up. Norm got out of the van and spread the stars all over the driveway behind our van.

17.

"AW, SHE'S PRETTY," said Norm, leaning over his seat to look back at Crystal. "Sleeping like that, you know, she reminds me of my daughter. My daughter married an ophthalmologist, lives out in Scottsdale, Arizona, a fine upstanding family, Rotarians. Personally, I'd commit suicide first. But who am I to criticize? You won't need to hide out after all."

"What? We won't? Why?"

"I made a deal with Tiny. Back there astride his steed. I told him you have no knowledge of the tape. I mean, so you told me, and so I told him. He agreed to leave you alone. You two can get on with your love affair. Tiny's not such a bad sort, as these wealthy patrician criminals go. He swears he didn't make the tape. He assumed I had. So who did? Trammell? Danny Barcelona?"

Or the Fifth Man? But I didn't say anything because I remembered I didn't care one way or the other. "What have they done to Crystal, Norm? Let's talk about that."

"Sure. Her pupils dilated?"

"Yes."

"She slightly warm to the touch?"

She was.

"Yeah, it's the usual. They probably gave her a tab or two of laboratory acid to loosen her up, but that's worn off by now. Probably followed it up with a pocketful of tranks to keep her quiet." His tone was light and breezy, like he was talking about the view. "No sweat there."

I studied Crystal. Her breathing and color seemed normal. I wanted to believe Norm, but I didn't. Was it irresponsible not to take her to the hospital, regardless?

Norm seemed to be reading my mind. "There'd be repercussions to a hospital visit."

"I told you what I cared about when we started out. If she doesn't snap out of this we're going straight to the hospital, fuck repercussions."

"I hear you. But why don't you trust me on this? Who made the deal with Tiny to leave you out of it? I had your interests in mind, even if not *foremost* in mind."

Calabash took his eyes from the road and stared at Norm.

"You don't even need to say it, big guy."

We rode in silence for a while, then Norm said, "You're not speeding, are you?"

"No, I ain't," Calabash snapped.

"Christ, everybody's so hostile. We just launched and successfully completed a covert operation. Where's that sense of camaraderie, the old all-for-one-and-one-for-all spirit? Hmm? You're beginning to hurt my feelings." Pause, then: "Of course, Tiny could be lying about the tape. However, I don't think he's got the steely nerves to sit there, the Human Fireball, and lie to me while I'm stoking my stogie. My stogie made me kind of dizzy, I was stoking so hot. No, I don't think he's got that degree of nerve. I guess the time of our parting draws near. I only hope you'll fill me in on any future activity with respect to the tape. I'm sure you will, after all we've been through together. Nothing like covert camaraderie to build trust. There's just one thing before we part. I don't have a TV on the boat."

He had put the garbage bags in the back. I reached over and squeezed one. It contained things shaped exactly like videotape cassettes. I told him it wouldn't be so convenient to watch television at my place, what with Crystal and all, plus we had to return the van to Brooklyn and get Crystal's car.

"I tell you what. I'll return the van. I'll drop you at your place and go on to Red Hook. When I come back, we'll peruse those tapes."

"Red Hook? Who said anything about Red Hook?"

"Isn't that where you got the van and the phony paint job?"

"Yeah, but how—?"

"Little munchkin with a savage limp?" Norm grinned playfully.

"I'll go with you," said Calabash, and as an act of friendship that touched me deeply.

"Happy for your company. We can ruminate on Bahamian sunsets, one of my favorite things in this hemisphere."

I was beginning to feel sad, now the adrenaline river had gone dry, weak and weary, now the covert operation was over. I was only too glad not to drive to Brooklyn and back, even if Norm did have something up his coveralls.

I knew it was hopeless. I knew we'd never make it in unseen. The elevator door opened on Mrs. Fishbein. She, of course, wore her Siberian-winter gear. She could barely move in it. Her ratty fur earflaps were pulled down around her face and tied under her chin. Temperature in the high eighties, humidity hovering around eighty-five percent.

"Ach! Ar-tie. Wif a *woman!*"

At that point I was almost carrying Crystal. "She's just arrived from Finland. Serious jet lag." I edged Mrs. Fishbein out of the elevator.

"Is it cold in here?" Crystal muttered.

"Wif a *woman!*"

On the way up, Crystal talked unintelligibly about a childhood swimming competition, which apparently she lost. By the time we were inside, she could walk with the support of a wall. But her eyes still weren't focusing.

Jellyroll came sprinting down the hall to greet us, but he took one look at our condition and skidded to a stop on the polyurethane. I was delighted to see him. I knelt and hugged him tight. He lapped at my face.

"Oh, Artie, I love Jellyroll," Crystal cooed. "And I love you." She bobbed and weaved toward the bathroom. "Let's take a shower."

"Sure." That seemed just then the single most erotic proposal I'd ever heard.

"Are those men coming back?"

"Yes, but not for a while."

"Then let's go."

I had no idea that covert incursions were so sexually arousing.

"Do you have candles?" she asked.

"Candles?"

"Let's put candles all around the bathroom."

"Great. Candles. Terrific." Giddy with expectation, I peeled off to the kitchen to rummage for candles. Crystal continued toward the bathroom. I had candles. Somewhere. Jellyroll, head cocked, watched me rummage. "Have you seen the candles, boy?" I found several in various conditions, culled the citronella, collected matches, and made for the bathroom, shedding shoes and shirt, dropping candles en route.

Crystal was already in the shower, moaning with pleasure at the hot water running over her shoulders. Her clothes were wadded up and stuffed into the wastebasket. "Artie, who were those guys in the truck?"

"The big guy is Calabash, my friend from the Bahamas. The other guy is a spook from the CIA."

"You'll tell me all about it?"

"Sure," I said, stepping out of my shorts.

"But not now."

"Definitely not now."

She opened her arms to me. Water coursed over her body, spilled off the ends of her nipples in deflected drops, flowed down her belly and away between her legs. Oh, Crystal. I hugged her close, sipped droplets off her breasts. She cupped me gently in the palm of her hand, and the sensation blasted through my—

Crystal's eyes rolled back—for an instant, absurdly, I thought, Gee, I've never had such an effect on a woman before. Then her eyes refocused, but not for long—"Artie, I can't. I thought I could, but I—I think I'm gonna—please get me out of this shower."

I picked her up. Another chance to break our collarbones. I wavered, sat us down prudently on the side of the tub, flipped my feet over onto the floor, and stood up again. Our dripping limbs extinguished candles. I carried her into the bedroom and dried her off as thoroughly as possible before I tucked her under the covers. Crystal and I nestled together like spoons. . . .

A heartbeat later, it seemed, Jellyroll's high-pitched visitors-are-here bark woke me. Crystal stirred but didn't wake up.

I peeked out the viewhole.

Calabash and Norm stood in the hall like a comedy team, Norm in front, the crown of his head ascending to Calabash's sternum. Norm clutched his garbage bags by the neck, while Calabash held a steering wheel hooked in his index finger. A steering wheel? I opened the door.

"Hi, how is she?" asked Norm, breezing in. "Nice place. . . . I like the sparse look."

Calabash rolled his eyes as he handed me the steering wheel.

"One must always remove one's steering wheel," instructed Norm, "or assholes steal your vehicle." Norm was heading for the western window to check the view.

"Thank you," I said quietly to Calabash.

"You welcome. Dot mon's nuts."

"I know. Maybe we can be rid of him soon."

"The Hudson River," said Norm at the window. "Hell of a river, the Hudson."

"Hey, Norm, if she's not up and around in an hour, I'm taking her to the doctor."

"Don't worry. She will be. So where's the TV?"

"It's in the bedroom, but that's where Crystal is. I'll bring it out here."

"I'm here," said Crystal, leaning against the doorjamb. She was wearing a pair of my sweatpants and a T-shirt.

"Are you okay?" I went to her.

"I'm okay, a little dizzy."

"Crystal, this is Calabash."

"How do you do, Crystal?"

They shook hands.

And then I introduced her to Norm Armbrister, who bowed graciously.

"Are you in the CIA?" Crystal asked.

"No, I'm retired. I'm beyond retired—" He pulled out his obituary and, grinning impishly, unfolded it for Crystal to read.

She glanced at him suspiciously as she read it, and returned it without comment. "Well, dead or alive, thanks."

"We couldn't have done it," smirked Norm, "without Artie's brilliant plan."

I let that slide. "Would you excuse Crystal and me for a few minutes? There are things I'd like to explain to her."

"Sure, sure," said Norm.

"I'll take de occasion to mix us up a pot of rum swizzles."

I put Jimmy Heath on the box, because I hadn't heard his soaring big-band compositions in a while and because I wanted him to cover our conversation.

We sat close together on the edge of the bed. I told her about Barry on the park bench.

"He . . . just died?"

"Without a sound. Crystal, I wouldn't be surprised if Norm were bugging the apartment right now. Otherwise, it doesn't make much sense for him to come over here to watch the tapes."

"What tapes? You mean the tapes Chet Burns told you about?"

"Bream. I think his name is Chet Bream." In a whisper, I told her that DiPietro was a phony cop. Then I took her hand and told her that Norm suspected that Uncle Billy knew something about Trammell's stolen money.

"Oh, Jesus," was all she said.

"Do you believe it?"

"I don't know. Trammell wouldn't hesitate to take advantage of anyone, even somebody who loved him. Artie, I'm going to call Uncle Billy right now."

I suggested she do it quietly.

No one answered at Billy's home. Then she called Aunt Louise, who told her that Billy had left, but she didn't know where he'd gone. She tried the Golden Hours. Someone Crystal knew named Mark answered. Mark told her that Billy had gone out to Montauk bluefishing with one of his cronies, someone named Arnie Lovejoy.

". . . I've been neglecting Billy," she said.

"Let's take the TV and the VCR into the living room, get this over with. I want to close off the bedroom to Norm. I can't lock the door, but we can watch him when he goes to the john."

She nodded. Her hands were folded in her lap. Her knuckles were white.

"Christ Almighty," said Norm as we ran the first of over a hundred tapes. "It's 'The Mayhews.' Remember that piece of shit?"

I could still hum the sickening-sweet theme music. I could still see, even before it had come up on the screen, the tugboat *Jolly Roger*. The Mayhews lived aboard the *Jolly Roger*. It was a rust bucket, meant to be endearingly folksy. Milt and Bingo Mayhew were the salt of the earth circa 1962. They stood for all that was straight and true, all the solid-upstanding-Christian-traditional values in American society that people killed for. "The Mayhews" was conceived to affirm the status quo and to keep everybody in their place. Bingo and Milt Mayhew had an adopted son, Timmy, played of course by Trammell Weems, who attended junior high school in the "Valley." People from the Valley put on airs, subscribed to fads, valued status over character, appearance over reality, form over substance. The Valleyites bowed down to graven images, worshiped money, and never said grace before dinner. The Valley was bad; the Mayhews were good.

Every half-hour episode was the same. Timmy would go off to the Valley, there to become temporarily polluted by brazen displays of superficial wealth and conspicuous consumption. He'd come back aboard the *Jolly Roger* imitating, comically, the denizens of the Valley. Just before the commercial at the fifteen-minute mark, Timmy would inevitably say, "Gee, why can't you be like other guys' moms and pops?"

Milt would wipe his hands on his oily rag—he was always working on the engine, which never ran—exchange knowing glances with Bingo while she cooked a wholesome meal from all four food groups, and then we at home knew Timmy was about to learn a lesson in humility, perseverance, thrift, honesty, modesty, truth, justice.

Having learned it, baby-faced Trammell would, before the final commercial, say, "Gee, you guys are all right after all."

Milt and Bingo would exchange another look. Then Milt would say, "Come on, son, we'll get this engine going yet."

"Jesus," said Norm, "you don't think *all* these are 'The Mayhews'? . . . Hell, we've got to watch them all, I guess. I'd rather get mugged. We can fast-forward, but Tiny could have edited the tape in there anywhere, the sneaky bastard."

Down on the street a car alarm blared.

"Listen, Norm," I said, "if the tape's here, it's not in our interests to see it. I don't want to be inhospitable, but why don't you take them somewhere else to watch? If you don't have a VCR, take mine with my thanks."

Norm grinned at me. "Well, there's still a few items that warrant discussion. There could be trouble, and I don't want us to go off half-cocked."

"But you said—"

"I said Tiny's not going to come after you, and I stand by that. But I can't speak for the others."

"Mr. Armbrister, do you know my uncle Billy?"

"Norm. Call me Norm. No, I never had the pleasure."

"Did you tell Artie that Uncle Billy knows about Trammell's stolen money?"

"I've been meaning to talk to you about your uncle Billy, but I wanted to wait till you were sprier. Let's say Trammell decided that he was better off dead, all things considered. Hell, I can relate to that. Let's say he didn't have a lot of time to plan out the details of his death." Norm paused to put in another tape. He fast-forwarded through the theme music and the *Jolly Roger* bullshit. "Trammell stole maybe ten, maybe fifteen million bucks from VisionClear before he disappeared. You can't be moving money around offshore banks after you're dead without attracting some attention. You need a living person to do that."

"Not Uncle Billy—?"

"I don't know for sure. But I happen to know there's an amount in the National Bank of the Bahamas in the name William Barraclough. Billy Barraclough was a secret shareholder in Tropical Trust while he was head of the accounting firm auditing Tropical Trust. Tricky relationship, patently illegal. They fished Billy Barraclough out of a south Florida drainage canal four years ago. They finally identified him by his dental records."

"But what's Barraclough got to do with Uncle Billy?"

"That's what I hoped you could tell me about."

"Nothing. I never heard of anybody named Barraclough."

In this episode, Trammell went to the Valley and came home a surfer. He was talking about hanging ten down at the pier, shooting the curl with the hodaddies, while Milt and Bingo rolled their eyes. There was no way to get rid of Norm. Norm was part of our lives now. That realization washed over my back like a sticky liquid substance.

"See," he said, "Trammell used Barraclough to move his money overseas. Even after Barraclough vanished, he was moving money. But then, just before Trammell vanished, the Barraclough account—thirty-four million bucks' worth— got closed out. That money's been moving around offshore since Trammell vanished."

"Are you saying Uncle Billy has that kind of money?"

"Maybe, maybe not. Let me explain something to you, Crystal. I don't care about the money itself. My beloved wife and I were about to sail off around the world when I heard about the tape. I can't go while that thing's out there unaccounted for. The tape's a loose end, and so am I since I'm on it. Loose ends wind up dead. Maybe it wouldn't happen tomorrow or even next year, but eventually some-body would come after me. It might be somebody I know. He might show up in Tahiti, say, with a glad hand and a smile on his face. My body would never be found. Boy, would my wife be pissed. However, as in most of these criminal episodes, you can't go far wrong if you follow the money. So that's why I'm asking you about it. When did you last see your uncle Billy?"

"The day after Trammell disappeared. Look, I'll make a deal with you. I don't care about the money either. You leave my uncle alone, and in return, I'll find him and ask him about the money and anything else you want asked. Then I'll tell you. But you have to leave him alone. What say?"

Norm fast-forwarded, thinking. "Okay, Crystal, you've got yourself a deal. We still have to watch all these Mayhews. The thing could be right here."

By dark, I'd had it. "The Mayhews," episode after epi-sode flashing by on fast forward, were making me crazy. I began to feel like a child again; nameless boyhood anxie-ties turned the room dark and dreary. It was time to stop with the rum fizzles.

Crystal had gone to bed hours ago. I went in to make sure she was breathing normally. I kissed her. "I hope Trammell's alive so I can kill him," she muttered before she turned over and went back to sleep.

Trammell as a rock-and-roll drummer. Trammell as a child fashion model. Trammell as an actor. Trammell as a rocket scientist. Trammell as a country and western singer. Calabash was asleep at the dining-room table. Every now and then he twitched. "Come on, son, we'll get that engine going yet."

There were four episodes on each tape. When one finished, Norm would stick in another, but the unseen pile seemed never to diminish.

I took Jellyroll to the park.

Norm ordered Chinese food, but the Mayhews had killed my appetite.

At some point in the evening, Norm, watching Trammell, a young businessman selling lemonade in the Valley, try to wipe out his competition, said, "You wouldn't have any idea where Trammell would go if he had to disappear, would you?"

"No."

"No special place he had?"

"We didn't have that kind of relationship."

"When did you see him last?"

"The day before he—you know. I saw him at the poolroom. He came to rent Uncle Billy's boat. We spoke two sentences apiece. Before that, I hadn't seen him for twenty years."

"Want any more moo shu?"

"No."

"Mind if I—?"

"Go right ahead."

Long after Norm had eaten the moo shu pork, the phone rang. I took the phone into the bathroom so as not to wake Crystal. A couple of candles still burned.

"Hey, babe, Chet Bream here. Innocent bystanders, you told me. Nothing to do with it, you told me. Now here you are hanging out with Norman Armbrister?"

"This isn't a good time, Chet. You promised you'd leave—"

"Yeah, but that was before I knew you were pals with Norman Armbrister. He's after the tape, isn't he? Lemme come up and talk to him—"

"No! Don't you dare! Look, I'll talk to him, see if he wants to meet you. If you barge in, he just might kill you."

"You got a point there."

"I'll talk to him and meet you at the poolroom tomorrow. How's that?"

"Okay, when?"

"About noon."

"Promise?"

"Yes."

"Just tell me this. Is he after the tape?"

"Yes."

"I knew it! I knew that tape would shake the shit out of the trees!" He was giggling as he hung up. He was probably slathering on ChapStick.

18.

JELLYROLL WOKE ME next morning with a wet nose in the eye.

"Hi, pal."

I scratched Jellyroll's neck while I propped myself up against the headboard and watched Crystal sleep. I was filled with love-song sentiments. Birds seemed to sing. She slept on her back, her left arm up over her head, her right folded across her stomach. I had read somewhere that people who sleep on their backs tend to be open and emotionally available. I sighed with pleasure at the sight of her sleeping. She caught me watching. Her eyes were clear.

"Hi," she said.

"Hi. Do you feel better?"

She stretched as if to find out. "Yes, I do. I guess Crazy was right. It wore off. But I feel like I just walked away from an airplane crash. What were you doing?" she asked coyly, pulling the covers up over her nose.

"When?"

"Just now."

"Watching you sleep."

"Why? ... Because you love me?"

"Yes."

187

"I'm glad."

I slid under the covers with her. But we hadn't walked away from the crash yet. We were still strapped into our seats, yet I moaned with abandon when she touched me.

The doorbell rang.

"Think we can make ourselves some kind of reservation?" Crystal asked.

"That'll be Calabash. At least I hope it's Calabsah." He had spent the night in Jerry's apartment. . . . What if it wasn't Calabash? After Norm had left at dawn with his library of Mayhew tapes, before Calabash went to sleep upstairs he left me a gun, a black and nasty automatic. He had shown me how to cock the thing by pulling back the slide mechanism—I had seen idiots on-screen do it numerous times—and he said, "Start low, aim at de guy's knees and jus' keep shootin'. De recoil'll bring de bullets right on up de body." I pulled on a pair of khaki shorts and a white T-shirt, picked up my gun, and went to the door with it. Calabash. He asked how Crystal was doing while he petted Jellyroll hello.

"De police came wid a warrant for dat Jerry fellow. I didn't answer de door. Is it jus' me or is dere an unusual amount of crooks in dis town?"

I made him scrambled eggs and coffee.

"I been dreamin' about dem fooking Mayhews all night."

I felt warmly indebted to this enormous man and told him so.

"You don' need to keep thankin' me. I kinda enjoyed it. Besides, you did some nice t'ings for de kids on Poor Joe."

"That wasn't me, that was Jellyroll." Last summer, he built them a preschool with playgrounds and an aquarium. I made double-strong coffee, the way Calabash likes it. Jellyroll kicked his empty bowl. I decided to try him on the New & Improved formula.

"Artie, dot spook said a t'ing troublin' to me. He said

188

dot de crooks put all de stolen money in Bahamian banks. My uncle Fergus, remember him?"

"Sure." Poor Joe Cay lay a hundred and fifty watery miles from the government in Nassau. Places as remote as Poor Joe, Calabash had told me, cannot expect much hands-on help from Nassau. Those places tend to form unofficial governments run by the wisest, the best, and the brightest on the island. Uncle Fergus ran Poor Joe Cay.

"Uncle Fergus don't like our banks taking de white man's crooked money. He t'inks it corrupts us all, even while de common people don't get shit outta de deals."

I remembered Uncle Fergus. He was about five feet tall, but he had wild eyes that made him seem bigger even than his nephew. "What do you want to do, Calabash?"

"I gonna look into dat money."

"Will you stay around for a few days?"

"Sure. Dis ain't over."

"No."

The phone rang.

"Artie? Is it *really* you?" It was Shelly, Jellyroll's agent. "What, you don't return messages anymore? Does he have a new agent behind my back? Am I Shelly non grata?"

"No, Shelly, I—"

"The R-r-ruff idiots are semifrantic. They've been trying to get you for days!"

"I've been busy, Shelly, I—"

"Wait! I've heard that before, that 'busy.' Is it a woman? I had to tell them JR was under the weather, you took him to the vet. He probably had a little stomach thing, that's why he didn't eat the food, I told them."

I glanced at Jellyroll's bowl. It was empty! "He ate it, Shelly."

"What? The new R-r-ruff? Really? Terrific. I'll tell that fool Fleckton. You got a shoot today, remember?"

"Tell him I can't make it today."

189

"Did you just say you can't make it today?"

"Tell them Jellyroll still has a little stomach thing. To-morrow, he'll be fine tomorrow."

"Artie—"

"Tell Fleckton he's eating it, and we'll be there tomorrow."

"How about this evening? Could he do it this evening?"

"Okay."

"Artie, I say this for your own good: you're getting to be an eccentric hermit."

"Thanks, Shelly."

"For your own good, Artie. Okay, gotta scoot. Love to JR."

Crystal came out of the bedroom. She was wearing my clothes. Calabash stood up. "Good morning, Calabash."

As I poured her coffee, I placed a note on the table be-tween them that said, "Bugs!?"

They both nodded. This was no way to live.

"Is Calabash your real name or a nickname?" Crystal asked.

"A nickname."

"What's your real name?"

"Oswald."

"Oswald?" I said. "You never told me that."

"I don' go tellin' dat to everybody."

"So I'll start callin' you Ozzie."

"You can, but den I snap your leg bones off." He wasn't smiling.

The phone rang:

"He's eating it? Is he really eating it!" Hysteria nibbled at the edges of Mr. Fleckton's voice.

"Yes, he just ate it."

"Oh, merciful Father! Thank you! And you, too, Artie, thank you, thank you! You don't know what this means to me. The assassins were on my tail! See you this evening at six?"

"Okay."

"Thank you, thank you—" He hung up.

Then the phone rang again.

"Hello, Artie."

"Hello, Jennifer. Did you learn something?"

"Yeah, but I need you to tell me the truth before I go into it."

"Okay."

"Do you have financial or other interest in Concom or any of its affiliates?"

"Absolutely not.'"

"Good."

"Why?"

"I spoke to a guy I know who used to work in the DA's office back when the RICO law was first being used to go after organized crime. Remember?"

"Sort of."

"My friend was involved in the Sammy 'The Neck' Randolucci prosecution. The cement case."

I remembered. Apparently the hoods had a piece of every pound of cement that got poured in this town, and during the eighties a lot of it got poured. You had to hand it to the hoods—they always picked the fundamental urban stuff to corrupt: cement, garbage, and, most recently, windows.

"Well, my ADA friend said that Concom kept coming up in the investigation. He wasn't free to go into much detail, but he implied things. He implied that Concom— there's about a dozen permutations of the company—he implied that Concom had illegally acquired a string of banks and savings and loans here and abroad. One of the banks was laundering money in Miami for the wiseguys. Once the trail had led to this bank, every time they turned around there was another Concom subsidiary. He said it took his office four years before they even got to the name

Concom, it was so deeply buried. While he was working on the RICO case, somebody else was working on a bunch of illegal arms purchases by Middle East countries, and this guy would ask my friend if he'd heard of such-and-such companies. They were all connected to Concom. Then the same thing'd happen with somebody else who was following the paper trail to big-time drug laundries. There'd be another Concom company."

"Did they ever bust Concom? It sounds like they had a strong case."

"Yeah, you'd think so. My friend thought so. But then his informant in the Randolucci case disappeared right out of the Federal Witness Protection Program. And then they found Randolucci's bullet-riddled body in the Meadowlands. And here's the punch line. My friend goes to his boss and says, 'Look, at the bottom of all these unrelated cases, there's Concom International Securities.' Three days later both my friend and his boss were transferred off the case and out of the state."

"By whom?"

"Good question. Somebody with bigger clout than the district attorney. Much bigger. My friend was pretty disillusioned. He was also a little scared. He thought people were following him for a while after he was transferred. You can't repeat any of this. Okay?"

"Sure. I promise.

"So, who's your friend?"

"Pardon?"

"Your friend. You said your friend had gotten into SEC trouble, and Concom had come up."

"Oh, yes."

"Is your friend a woman?"

"Yes."

"You tell her to be careful."

"Thank you, Jennifer."

"Ah, Artie, you mentioned money when we talked—"

"Sure. How can I help?"

"Think Jellyroll could loan me a thousand dollars until things loosen up some? I hate to ask."

"He'd be happy to."

"You know I'm good for it."

"Of course you are."

"Just until I get a job."

"Sure, I'll send a check right away. Jennifer, did any names come up for Concom? I mean, like owners."

"I asked, but my friend didn't want to talk about that. I miss you, you know?"

"Me too."

"So who's Jennifer?" Crystal wanted to know after I hung up.

I wrote another note: "Let's go in the bedroom and talk."

While we fumbled with Crystal's steering wheel, a Hispanic transvestite with hairy hands was ranting about Iranians. At least it sounded like Iranians. I was wondering if Norm had bugged Crystal's car.

"It's loose," Crystal pronounced when we were done affixing the wheel.

We went back at it, got it right this time.

Off to Sheepshead Bay—Crystal driving, Calabash riding shotgun with his knees under his chin, Jellyroll and me in the back—I wondered who was following us now. Billy didn't answer his phone; maybe he was still off fishing, maybe not. The purpose of this trip was more emotional than practical. Crystal felt she had to do something concrete—like make sure he wasn't dead in his apartment. Also, she needed clothes. I began to fantasize, heading down the West Side Highway, that we'd find Uncle Billy hacked to pieces. Or maybe Trammell. My imagination flew from one gory corpse to the next. Almost everybody

I ever met was dead in that apartment, stacked up like Lincoln Logs. A lovely day in the neighborhood.

Crossing the Brooklyn Bridge, I noticed that Calabash and Crystal were also tense and silent. Crystal's eyes kept darting from the road to her rearview mirror. These fuckers were pros. We could have a line of spooks back there the size of the Godfather's funeral procession and never know it.

"Why don' you let me out near de place while you go around de block, like we don' know each other. Den I can watch your back when you go in."

"Uh, actually, Calabash, you'd be pretty conspicuous in my neighborhood. It's not like Manhattan."

"No?"

"We'd better go in together."

Unlike at the Upscale Poolroom, where gamblers would still be going strong from last night, the Golden Hours was nearly empty. Players at the three active tables stopped and waved to Crystal. She greeted them by name, trying to seem friendly, normal. No corpses yet.

A young woman with a long ponytail was sitting behind the desk. "Hi, Crystal, I haven't seen you for ages."

"Hello, Sally, how are you?"

"Pregnant."

"Congratulations."

"*Again.*"

"You're pretty fertile, Sally."

Crystal introduced Calabash and me to Sally.

"Say, have you seen Uncle Billy?" Sally asked. "The Coke guy was in yesterday. He says he won't deliver no more till he gets paid. Also, there's other bills." She took a stack of business envelopes from behind the desk and handed them to Crystal.

Her brow furrowed as she thumbed through them. "Look

194

at the postmarks on these," she said to Calabash and me. "Some of them are two weeks old."

"Pardon me," said Sally, "but isn't that the R-r-ruff Dog?"

Jellyroll was sitting staring up into Sally's face.

"Yeah, that's him," said Crystal.

Sally clutched her face and squealed. "I *love* the R-r-ruff Dog! I heard he was here—can I pet him!"

"Go see," I said to Jellyroll. He and Sally smooched as we looked at postmarks. He followed us up the stairs while Sally tried to call him back.

There were two doors at the top of the landing. Crystal went right and knocked on that one. "Uncle Billy—" No answer.

"Is that your place?" I asked about the other door.

"Yeah. You've never been there, have you? Uncle Billy—?" She put her ear to the door. Silence. She led us to the other door and unlocked it. The three of us gasped at the sight, and our gasps brought Jellyroll, sauntering in, to an abrupt halt.

Crystal's apartment was a cramped studio with a tiny alcove kitchen. I had wondered on occasion how Crystal lived when she was alone, but even as I looked, I still couldn't tell, because her place was completely wrecked. Devastated. Wasted. Crystal began to whimper in the doorway.

Calabash gently moved her aside by the shoulder as he pulled a gun and went in. Adrenaline surged as I watched Calabash look left, right, then go into the bathroom gun first. He came back out. We were alone with the wreckage. We stood silently staring at it.

Drawers had been yanked from the dresser, their contents hurled around. The splintered remains of one drawer lay at the foot of the opposite wall, against which it had been smashed. Likewise, kitchen cabinets had been emptied, the contents broken. Shards of glass and utensils covered the black-and-white linoleum floor. The cushions from the convertible couch had been sliced open and disemboweled, tufts of stuffing strewn about. The bed had been pulled out, its mattress gutted. Crystal's clothes covered the wreckage as if blown there by a horrific wind. She began to cry softly. I put my arm around her shoulders.

Calabash, thinking, pulled the door closed and bolted it.

I tried to think, too. What kind of way was this to search for something? If I were searching someone's apartment for a thing—a thing like Barraclough's bankbook, say—I wouldn't sling stuff around like this. I'd conduct an orderly search, area by area, take things out, put them back. The object I was searching for might otherwise get covered in the rubble of my own destruction. . . . That was thinking. . . . But maybe this wasn't a search.

"Crystal—"

"Huh?"

"Is there a back way out?"

"Through Billy's place. There's stairs down to the little patio in back. . . . We had a pool out there when I was a kid—" She pointed at the window. "You can see it down there."

"Why don't you pack some things and let's get out of here?"

"This is where I live! They came where I—and did this! Bastards! I've had it with these fuckheads, Artie!"

Calabash peeped out the window. So did I. Nothing below but an empty, leaf-littered patio, where once Crystal had splashed in the pool.

"While you pack, could we check Billy's place?"

She handed me a key ring, Billy's key isolated between her thumb and forefinger. The rest rattled in her trembling hand.

I kissed her. "Keep Jellyroll with you. Lock this door behind us, okay, darling?"

Calabash's gun reappeared in his hand as Crystal did so. We approached Billy's door, the landing creaking loudly beneath our feet. Calabash took the keys from me. He pointed to the hinged side of the door—that was where I was to stand. I stood precisely there.

Calabash stood to the other side of the door, put the key in the lock, turned it—then he shoved the door all the way open against its stop. At the same time he held up an enormous hand to tell me to remain where I was. I didn't need to be told twice. He remained where he was, the gun muzzle pointing up at the ceiling. I heard pool balls click below. Compared to banks, poolrooms seemed places of innocence and goodwill. He slid down the wall and crouched with his knees under his chin. From that level, he looked in over his gun hand. No shots got fired.

We walked in. The same search-and-destroy tactics had been applied in here. We closed the door behind us but didn't relock it. This was a much larger place. The living room and dining room were visible. Beyond, I could see the doorway to the kitchen. A hallway led back to the bedrooms and bath, I assumed. I could see the traces of French doors that had been walled up to separate Crystal's little adulthood apartment from her childhood home, both now wrecked. Calabash disappeared down the hall.

The furnishings were all 1940s era. Brocaded chairs with doilies on the arms, heavy fabric curtains, floor lamps with yellowed shades, knickknacks and porcelain objects decades out of fashion. Most of these things were broken, sliced, or overturned. I crunched across broken glass into the dining room.

Crystal knocked on the door and called my name. I opened up. She had an overnight bag in one hand and a pillowcase in the other. Jellyroll slipped in, but Crystal surveyed the destruction from the doorway. "He's not dead in here, is he?"

"No." Of course, he could be dead somewhere else. "Are you okay?"

"I guess so. Artie, look at this—" She knelt and spilled the contents of the pillowcase onto the rug. . . . It was her lingerie. Jellyroll sniffed until I eased him aside. I picked up a pair of black panties. The crotch had been sliced out. There was a matching bra. The nipples had been sliced off. I sifted through the pile. They were all mutilated. I looked up at Crystal. She was clutching her mouth. "Who are these people, Artie?"

"Come look at this," called Calabash.

Crystal and I shoved the ravaged underwear back into the pillowcase and then went to see.

Calabash was in the first bedroom off the hall. He leaned out and gestured to us. The room was ransacked, but we were used to that. That wasn't what he wanted us to see. He was pointing at the wall above the bed:

POOL IS SATAN GAME

It was scrawled across floral wallpaper in red spray paint, letters two feet high. But the letters were ill-formed, as if written by a non-English speaker.

"What . . . ?" asked Crystal.

All around that statement other letters were painted. But these weren't English letters. I copied them on the back of my laundry slip, checked to be sure I'd gotten them right, and returned the laundry slip to my wallet.

"What is it?"

"Arabic."

"Arabic? What do the Arabs want with Uncle Billy? . . . And my underwear?"

"Let's get out of here," I suggested.

198

19.

WE SPED HEADLONG up Ocean Parkway.
"They're making me very angry, the fucks!" snapped
Crystal. "They kidnap me, shove drugs down my throat.
They kidnap you! They ruin my place. They might al-
ready've killed my uncle!"

"Dey don't deserve to live," agreed Calabash.

"What do you want to do?" I asked. "Do you want to go
to the police? Maybe we could get a real one this time."

That met with silence.

Crystal swerved into the right lane and stopped behind
a car full of Hasidim vacating their parking place. The
Hasidim hit the car in front, setting off its alarm, then hit
the car behind, doing the same thing. Then, having gotten
a feeling for distance, they pulled out. I had thought that
was the Manhattan method of close-quarter maneuvering—
hit the car in front, hit the car behind—but it seemed to
obtain in Brooklyn as well. Crystal took the spot. We sat
between the wailing alarms with the engine running. This
was a pleasant, tree-lined neighborhood of large red-brick
apartment buildings where the races seemed to mix in reasonable harmony.

"Where are we going, anyway?" Crystal snapped. "Do we have any kind of *purpose*?"

"I told Chet Bream I'd meet him at the poolroom. We could blow him off, but if we do, he'll be knocking at my door by dark."

"How are we ever going to get out of this? Huh, how? This'll never end. They'll just keep doing things to us! Do you believe these goddamn alarms! They're trying to make us crazy on top of everything else!" Shouting over the noise, Crystal slammed both hands down on the steering wheel. I ineffectually put my hand on her shoulder. I hoped she wasn't cracking.

"We could blow dem up," suggested Calabash.

"We *could*?" That idea clearly appealed to Crystal.

"I got de goods."

"You *do*?"

"Sure."

"I think there's more here than we could blow up," I said, the voice of restraint.

"Yeah, we'd have to get more o' de goods."

"If they've hurt poor Uncle Billy, then let's blow them up," said Crystal, jaw set. I looked at her in the rearview mirror. I saw there the face of a woman capable of pushing the plunger, or whatever you do these days to set off the goods.

"Can we think of anything else?" I asked.

"We could go to Poor Joe Cay. There ain't no dangerous strangers dere. We keep track of 'em on de Cay."

A black car had pulled up behind us. Two men sat in the front seat and watched us. They were wearing uniforms, but not from the military or the police. We watched them. Even Jellyroll watched them.

The driver got out and stood beside his car. Calabash reached inside his jacket. But the driver didn't approach, merely stood beside his open door. His uniform was from one of the private security agencies. "Hey, lady, you leavin' or what?"

"No," Crystal snarled. "Get outta heah!" Trouble brought out the Brooklyn in Crystal. I liked it. But the alarms were turning me morbid. I suggested we leave this place.

"I've got another uncle," Crystal said after a few blocks. "His name is Ray. He's in the rackets. Small time, a bookie, like that. Uncle Ray can be a loudmouth asshole sometimes—he drives around the neighborhood in a pink Lincoln with a Continental kit on the back. But he knows people, and he loves me. He could put out some feelers for Billy, it's just I'm not sure he can keep his mouth shut."

"What's a Continental kit?" Calabash wanted to know.

"A spare tire in a stupid case. . . . Maybe I should bullshit Ray. Maybe I should tell him Billy got into money trouble or something."

"What about Danny Barcelona?" I asked. "Do we mention Danny Barcelona? He's in the rackets, too."

"Yeah. . . . You don't like the idea. I can tell."

"It's not that exactly. It's just you said he had a big mouth."

"What do you think, Calabash?"

"It just depends how much you trust dis Uncle Ray. 'Course you could tell him if he fucks us over den we blow up his Continental kit with him inside."

"Where would we find Uncle Ray?"

"He minds a pizza parlor in the East Village, on Avenue A. I think the place is a money laundry."

"Lotta dat goin' around," said Calabash.

Through the rearview mirror, Crystal looked me in the eye. "I told you that first night my family was tacky."

We turned south off of Twelfth Street, and there it was, two doors down from the corner on Avenue A. Ray's Absolutely REAL Original Pizza Parlor (Believe It, said a sign

below the name). And there was the pink Lincoln, with
Continental kit, double-parked in front, along with five
other gaudy gas-guzzlers. Hard-looking guys hung around
the cars talking and smoking cigarettes. A couple of guys
were eating pizza slices, leaning over to keep the grease
from running down their silk shirts. We cruised past to
check it out before we committed ourselves. . . . We
seemed to be free of tails.

There was a crack store across the avenue masquerading
as a bodega. You can always spot the crack stores by their
bereft shelves and by the clots of jittery youths bobbing
around on the sidewalk out front waiting to use the pay
phones—just like you can spot the crooked pizza parlors
by the wiseguys and the pink Lincolns loitering in front.
There was a dreary Ukrainian restaurant on one side of
Ray's, Madam Casbah's, Fortunes Told, on the other.

The wiseguys watched us park. Crystal's Toyota was
dwarfed by the Cadillacs and Buicks. Crystal left the engine running and got out alone. She said hello, by name,
to a couple of the wiseguys as she went in. I think they
made rude remarks about her ass as she did so. Calabash
and I stared straight ahead.

Five minutes later, Crystal came back out with Uncle
Ray, a fat man of several chins and arms that didn't touch
his sides. He wore a blue three-piece suit, expensive but
still ill-fitting in the shoulders. He was bald on top, but
he'd made a futile attempt to cover it by combing sparse
strands of black hair over the hole. When Uncle Ray saw
Jellyroll, he stopped dead in his tracks in the gutter and
clapped his hands together.

"Christ, it *is*!" he exclaimed, chins twittering. "Crystal
tells me, I think she's kidding her old uncle!"

I rolled down the rear window. Uncle Ray stuck his big
face in, and Jellyroll licked it. Uncle Ray squealed.

We got out of the car.

"Hey, you guys, here, look here!"

A half a dozen wiseguys gathered. They all wore pegged pants and silk shirts buttoned up around the neck. I wondered where they hid their guns.

"This is my niece, Crystal, and *this* is the R-r-ruff Dog!"

"Naw—"

"No shit?"

"Jumpin' Jesus, it *is*!"

"Lookit that smile! That's him, all right!"

"Can I pet him?"

"Holy shit, I petted the R-r-ruff Dog. I'll never wash my hand again!"

"Okay, boys," said Uncle Ray, "beat it."

They dispersed, chattering, and Ray was clearly pleased with his power to assemble and disperse lackeys.

Crystal introduced Calabash and me.

"You *all* get in that little car together!" He bellowed laughter. "Welcome Calabash, welcome to Ray's *Real* Original Pizza Parlor, where I'm Ray. Say, Artie, how much you want for that dog? We can come to terms on this. Cash, services, you name it, pizza for life, whatever. Gimme a starting figure on which we can bicker—" He laughed and clapped me on the back with a fat, soft hand. "Come on in." He put his other arm around as much of Calabash's shoulders as he could reach and led us into the pizza parlor-cum-money laundry. He stopped in the threshold, turned, and said, "Hey, you guys, keep an eye on that Toyota."

Wiseguys sat at round Formica tables and dropped cigarette butts into cups of Coke. Two Mexicans cooked pizza behind the counter. They humbly averted their eyes as the boss and his entourage entered. Ray led us around behind the counter, between the ovens.

"Hey, Jesus. Hey, Pancho. Look here, this is the R-r-ruff Dog!"

The cooks looked sheepish, grinning uncomfortably.

"El pero de R-r-ruff? . . ."

They returned blank stares.

"Never mind—"

He led us through a beaded curtain, into a closet-sized back room. It was already crowded to capacity by a little Formica bistro table, four mismatching chairs, and ceiling-high stacks of Coke cases that seemed to loom over us like Stonehenge. We squeezed in and took seats at the table.

"How 'bout some wine? I mean good wine. Want some top-of-the line wine? Jesus!"

A Mexican man appeared at the beads.

"Wine, Jesus. The good stuff. You know. El vino primero."

Jesus went to fetch it.

"Gee, it's good to see you, Crystal. I ain't seen you in, what, must be two years, since at Billy's birthday party."

Jesus returned with a bottle of Chianti and four glasses. He poured a taste for Uncle Ray, who swilled it around like mouthwash. "Mmm, good." There wasn't room for Jesus to enter, so he reached an arm in through the beads and poured from without.

Uncle Ray was right about the wine. He arched his eyebrows and nodded, wanting us to like it.

"Excellent," I pronounced.

"It's Billy I'm worried about, Uncle Ray."

"Billy?" Uncle Ray looked at Calabash and then at me. He was wondering, no doubt, what we had to do with Crystal. I looked in his eyes. This guy was no fool, even if he acted like one. Acting like one might have been his strategy for survival.

Crystal, too, was thinking, debating silently. "Remember Trammell Weems?"

"Sure. He drowned, right?"

Crystal paused. "I think he's alive."

"I'm glad you're not trying to kid me, Crystal. That would hurt my feelings."

"I thought about it, Uncle Ray, but, no, I'm not going to kid you. It's possible Uncle Billy was—or is—involved with Trammell."

"Uh, would this have anything to do with a bank?"

"I'm afraid it does."

Ray nodded gravely.

"Why, Ray?"

"There's talk on the street. Professionally, it ain't in my best interests to get near the banking business. . . . Where's Billy now?"

"I don't know. That's why we came to you. I thought maybe you could ask some questions around town."

"Where was he last seen?"

"An employee at the Golden Hours told me he went bluefishing up to Montauk with Arnie Lovejoy."

"Arnie Lovejoy, the lush?"

"I hear he quit. Talk to me, Uncle Ray. What are they saying on the street?"

He paused, considering. . . . "Crystal, who are your friends?"

"Artie is . . . my boyfriend." She glanced at me to see if I minded her putting it like that. I certainly did not. "We haven't known each other that long, but we like each other. Now my ex-husband's crooked business affairs are ruining it. Calabash is Artie's friend. He's here to help us."

"I'm de bodyguard of dem both."

Ray nodded again. "So you got no other interest, like financial interest? You ain't kiddin' me?"

"We're interested in being left alone," said Crystal. "But I want to find Uncle Billy. I want him to be safe, too."

"I'm a pizza man. I ain't in the banking business. I'm in the pizza business."

"Okay, Uncle Ray, I wouldn't want you to get in trouble."

"Of course family is family, blood is thicker than what-have-you. Marinara sauce."

"There's something else I should tell you, because maybe you've heard of him. The name Danny Barcelona has come up."

This didn't seem to surprise Uncle Ray. "Who raised it?"

"A guy who used to be in the CIA. He's one of the people we want to leave us alone."

"CIA, huh? I told them not to get mixed up with those guys, they're crazy. But they wouldn't listen to me, a pizza man. Uh, what about the name Archibald? Tiny Archibald? Did that name come up?"

"Yes, it came up."

"I heard things. On the street."

"That's why we came to you about Uncle Billy. Maybe you heard something."

"Not about Billy." He looked down into the surface of his wine, and his head hung, at least as far as his chins allowed, in silence for a while. "We got to do this carefully. Little cat steps . . . But hell, he's my relative. No reason why I can't look around for him, right? Hey, Jesus—"

Jesus appeared behind the beads.

"Jesus, call Ronnie Jax in here."

Ronnie Jax was a hood in his late twenties with an unsuccessful mustache and long, slicked-back black hair. "Yeah, boss?"

"I want you to go over Sheepshead Bay and find an old guy, late sixties, gotta big booze gut, name of Arnie Love-joy. Tell him I wanna talk with him. Bring him back here if you can. But be polite. If he can't make it, tell him get in touch with me, tell him today."

"You got it, boss." Ronnie Jax left.

"Uncle Ray, somebody ransacked my apartment and did the same to Uncle Billy's place. We just came from there."

"Who did?"

"I don't know."

"You mean like they were looking for something?"

"Yes."

"But you don't know what?"

"No."

"Where should I get in touch with you?"

I gave him my phone number.

He leaned down to pet Jellyroll, then he straightened and said, "Crystal, it's good to see you. I been missing you."

20.

WE RODE IN ANXIOUS SILENCE across town to the Upscale Poolroom. I stared out at the hot city as it passed, so many paths crossing, and I longed to accept Calabash's invitation to Poor Joe Cay. When Jellyroll and I visited him there last year, we stayed in a rustic, one-room hut thirty feet from the transparent ocean, our only neighbor. The hut was a place of exquisite isolation. We had been at peace there. Jellyroll placed his chin on my knee. He'd loved the hut as much as I did. Of course, there wasn't much going on around Poor Joe Cay, no major cultural events of the first water. I'd probably get bored in about thirty or forty years. The only thing I'd missed of the modern world was music. You don't hear much jazz on Poor Joe.

The poolroom was a radically different place from the island hut, but I felt a vaguely similar kind of peace in its unchanging rhythms. Balls clicked together, some fell, some didn't. Jellyroll went off to work the room. The regulars were there. They greeted us.

"Okay, Artie, come on. I'll play you one set for Jellyroll," said Outta-Town Brown.

"What are you putting up?"

"My business."

"Just what is your business, Brown?"

"Successful."

Piercing feedback bounced around the room. "Phone call for Thumper. Thumper, you gotta call."

Never-Miss Monroe sat smoking his rubber cigar, all fifteen balls racked and ready on his table, whitey on the head spot.

"No loitering," said Ted Bundy, just to get a rise out of poor Monroe.

"Loitering?" replied Never-Miss. "You got some fat nerve, Bundy. Loitering. If we was to play, they'd sweep you up with the cigarette butts at the end of the session. You wouldn't get a breath of air. I'd crush you like a Dixie cup on the innerstate."

"Okay, one game for a t'ousand, right now."

Nobody moved.

A couple of the intellectuals—Burns, the computer crazy, and Morris, a man of unknown occupation—played gravely serious straight pool. All was as I knew it. There were few strangers.

Calabash entered, pretending not to know us, and took a stool in the center of the room. Chet Bream was not there. Crystal asked me to play some straight pool until he showed up. I got us a table and a tray of balls—

Bruce Munger, Attorney at Law, came out of the john, sidled over with his hands in his pockets, and said, "If it isn't the couple of the year."

"You're looking better than the last time we saw you," I said.

"Yeah, I've been meaning to discuss that with you. Crystal, I'm glad to see you safe and sound." He said it brightly, casually, as if he were talking about her cold. "You had me worried. Nasty business . . . getting kidnapped."

"You're insane, Bruce."

"It's not just me. They're all crazy. That's what I wanted to discuss with you. Remember I told you Trammell was alive?"

"Gee, no, Bruce," said Crystal. "Refresh our memory."

"Well, between us, just because we're old friends, I'll tell you the truth. He drowned off Billy's boat. Just like I said originally. I kept telling those guys he was dead, but they kept beating me with the fishing rod. It became clear that that wasn't the popular position on Trammell Weems. Everybody seemed to want him alive, so I told them he was alive. But he isn't. Alive. Unless he grew some quickie gills."

Crystal walked away.

"What's she so exercised about? I didn't kidnap her."

"If he drowned, where did you get all the money they stuffed down your throat?"

"Playing cards."

There was no purpose in talking to Bruce, so I went to get my cue.

Bruce hovered around as Crystal and I began to play. I could tell he had a million questions to ask, but he couldn't stick to that card-game story and still expect answers from us. Anyway, in this, Bruce and his knowledge were obsolete. I couldn't concentrate on our game, and neither could Crystal, but by the time Chet arrived, I was losing 68–12.

I barely recognized him. He looked terrible, porcelain pale, his features pinched in his already too-narrow face. I might not have recognized him at all were it not for the ChapStick he was smearing on his desiccated lips. His legs barely sustained balance. He took a stool near the head of our table, and it seemed a big relief to sit.

"I'm sorry I'm late. I'm sick."

I'd expected Chet to leap upon us with questions. His hands lay limp, palms up, in his lap.

"Do you have the flu?" I asked.

"I hope so."

Hope so? Why? As opposed to what? I didn't really have the energy for this talk with Chet, and neither, apparently, did Crystal. She was listening but not participating, shooting the balls around without caring if they dropped or not.

Nor did Chet seem to have the energy. I was about to suggest that under the circumstances we forget the whole thing when Chet said, "So Armbrister was after the tape?"

"Right. He's retired and ready to leave the country with his wife, but he can't while the tape's out there making him look foolish. That's what he said. How's that sound to you?"

"Like a load of horseshit . . ." He was still trying to do the worldly-wise reporter number, but there was nothing behind it now, no enthusiasm. The Chet on the beach was enthusiastic, if jumpy. This Chet was spent, but I liked this one better.

"So he's not retired?"

"No."

"What's he do?"

"He's a gunrunner. Have you come across Concom yet?"

"No," I lied for no clear reason.

"Yeah, well, you will. Concom's at the bottom of this, you watch. I've been saying that for years. Would anybody listen? Concom owns everything. For instance, remember back when we were supposed to give a shit about Nicaragua?" He fumbled with the ChapStick applicator, having trouble removing the cap. "Well, Norman Armbrister and the rest of the spooks were down there selling SAMs to the Contras, and at the same time selling choppers to the Sandinistas. See the pattern here? Shoot down the choppers with the SAMs, then you sell replacements for both. You duplicate that pattern all over the world—and Armbrister did—you stand to make some real money."

"But what did Concom do?"

"Concom bankrolled the deals! Then used VisionClear, which it owned, to launder the profits. And how do you keep the law off your ass while you're illegally selling American arms to anybody with the money to buy them? You buy it. The law, I mean. You buy the law, or you become it."

I didn't know whether to believe him or not. But one thing was clear—he believed it. I glanced back at Crystal. She looked like she was about to throw up.

The ChapStick dribbled from his hands and bounced on the cigarette-burned carpet. I picked it up for him. As I straightened, I realized that Chet was sobbing silently. His body jerked. His eyes were clenched, but tears still poured from the slits. His lips were drawn away from his teeth in a rictus grin.

"I wish I'd never heard of the bastards! I had a family, a kid, but I fucked it up. I could have been a family man, love and all that, Little League games, but now I'm going to die alone, goddamnit!"

"Aww," I said like a fool, "it's just the flu. It really gets you down—"

"No, I think they've killed me!"

"What?"

"I never thought they'd kill me!"

"Who?"

"Concom!"

"Killed you?"

"Hell, I can hardly lift my arms."

"How? I mean, how—?"

"Look, I'm going now." He slid off the stool and stood unsoundly. "I'll call you or something." He snaked a path to the door.

"Chet," I called, but he waved me off.

One of the regulars hit on him for a game before he left.

Calabash joined us. "What was dot?"

I told him. He said, "Hmm."

Bruce was heading our way, so I whistled for Jellyroll and we left. We were back in Crystal's car and on the move uptown before I realized I still had Chet's ChapStick clutched in my sweaty fist.

We found a parking place near my building, but then decided to put the car in a garage, where you pay exorbitant overnight rates in the hope that your car will be there when you want to drive it again.

Calabash watched our backs as we walked up to Akmed's newsstand on Broadway. Akmed and Jellyroll made their daily fuss over each other.

When the greeting subsided, I handed Akmed my laundry slip and asked him to translate. His brow furrowed as he read.

"One pants . . . Two shirt—"

"I'm sorry, Akmed, the other side."

He turned it over, looked at the writing I had copied from Uncle Billy's living-room wall, then looked back at me.

"I don' understand," he said.

"Isn't that Arabic?"

"No."

"What is it?"

"Nothing. Squibbles. How do you call it?" He drew "squibbles" in the air.

"Thank you, Akmed."

As we headed for Riverside Drive, Crystal said, "That sounds like something Trammell would do. Write 'Pool Is Satan Game' and a bunch of phony Arabic bullshit on the wall. This is making me very depressed, Artie."

"I've got to do that R-r-ruff shoot now," I said. I'd thought about calling in sick, and with the slightest en-

couragement from Crystal, I would have. "Do you want to
go?" I asked when she offered none. She seemed numb.
"Can I stay at your place in case Uncle Ray calls?"
"You can stay at my place forever."
"Thank you." She put her arm around me. A fine
romance.

Mr. Fleckton pounced on us before we'd finished signing
in at the security desk in the lobby.
"Is he *eating* it?"
"Yes, he—"
Mr. Fleckton seemed to levitate with joy and relief. His
two lackeys, James and Willard—I can never get straight
which is which—clapped each other on the back and made
those pumping-piston moves with their fists you see so
much these days as signs of masculine delight on beer
commercials. After the day I'd had, I was glad to spread a
little happiness. Jellyroll wagged his tail with a "what's
up?" look on his face. He cocked his head from side to
side.
"Look at that wonderful animal! Will you just look at
him!" Mr. Fleckton giggled like a seventh grader. "And
he's eating it!"
"Congratulations, Mr. Fleckton," said James or Willard.
Mr. Fleckton turned to them. "James, Willard, Willard,
James—it's been a grand campaign. I couldn't have done
it without you."
It was almost touching. Jellyroll looked up at me for a
cue as to what was going on. I didn't know what to tell
him.
We went into the studio.
"Clippity-clop, clippity-clop," went the soundtrack as
lights came up on a painted backdrop: the fruited plain.
The pioneer prairie. Yellow hills faded away in forced per-
spective all the way to the shining Rockies. A yellow

wagon-rut road, also in forced perspective, curved across the studio floor. There was a bowl of New & Improved R-r-ruff at the end of the road.

Then horses, *real* horses, four of them, came on from stage left. I'm no student of horseflesh, but these horses looked like the kind you'd put King Arthur on if you were doing a King Arthur thing, magnificent creatures with rippling flanks and huge tossing heads. . . . They were pulling a stupid Conestoga wagon made out of plywood with a muslin cover. "R-r-ruff or Bust" was painted on the muslin.

The Pioneer (ex-Space Traveler) sat on the wagon seat going "Giddy-up, giddy-up" to these glorious animals. The Pioneer's full-leg cast was covered by a big set of leather chaps. (Somebody had suggested to the director that you don't wear chaps while riding on a wagon. "Who gives a rat's ass?" he'd replied.) A happy grin on his face, Jellyroll sat beside the Pioneer. No matter how absurd the humans' concept, Jellyroll always seemed to enjoy himself, smiling, glancing around the studio until he caught my eye. That attitude takes a lot of guilt off my shoulders.

"Won't be long now, R-r-ruff, boy," said the Pioneer in a bullshit general-western accent. "We're in New-and-Improved territory now, boy." Clippity-clop, clippity-clop. "Whoa! Whoa!" The Conestoga wagon came to a stop. The horses fidgeted and flared their nostrils.

I glanced over at Mr. Fleckton. He stood in the light spill behind the cameras with both hands pressed over his mouth. It wouldn't be long now.

"There it *is!*" said the Pioneer from his perch, pointing at the bowl of New & Improved R-r-ruff as if at the Promised Land.

At this point, Jellyroll was to jump from the wagon, which he did, and run to the R-r-ruff. Originally, the Pioneer was to have jumped down as well, but that was out of the question with a fresh compound fracture. Everyone held their breath as Jellyroll approached the bowl. . . .

He slowed, sniffed, approached, leaned down—and he began to eat heartily. Everyone in the room cheered—silently, but you could feel the vibrations—as he ate. The cameras rolled. But then he stopped abruptly.

His stomach heaved. Uh-oh. I'd seen that move at the beach. That's how it always began. Now his whole body heaved, and he began to retch. As the room watched, Jellyroll threw up this horrible, wet, brown mass of congealed New & Improved R-r-ruff. Silence. Interminable silence. He sniffed his expulsion and walked away.

The room trembled with the pressure of suppressed laughter. Then it started at one of the camera positions. A titter. Somebody else giggled, and that was enough. All at once it burst out, bellows of it, paroxysms of giggles and cackles. Jellyroll loved it. He delights in human mirth. He pranced.

Once started, there was no stopping it. The place was paralyzed with hilarity. But the laughter, or something, seemed to be spooking the horses. The horses were growing restive, agitated. One's agitation spread to its adjacent teammate, and in that way it built. They sputtered, stomped, shook, and neighed. Fear fed on itself. One of the lead horses, a huge white one, reared up on its hind legs. Handlers sprinted from the back to calm their horses, but they were driven back by flying hooves.

"Get me off this fucking wagon!" screamed the Pioneer/Space Traveler, hanging on for dear life. "Get me off—! Jesus, please! Get me off—!"

The wagon lurched violently. I saw the white of his cast as it was hurled over his head and he disappeared into the back of the wagon. Another wave of handlers rushed onstage. They had black horse hoods in their hands. I called

Jellyroll away from the wild horses so he wouldn't get his snout kicked off.

Finally the handlers got their horses quieted and under control. Techies hefted the Pioneer, rigid as a railroad tie, out of the back of the wagon. He was babbling and whimpering. The giggles took hold again. They quickly spread. The people in the control room had their heads down on their consoles, lurching with silent laughter.

Mr. Fleckton leaned against the back wall, staring off into space like a shell-shocked doughboy. James and Willard wrung their hands and paced around him:

"We could cut right before he threw up."

"Sure we could!"

"It was great up until then—"

"Excellent until then."

"He was eating it—"

"Until then."

But Mr. Fleckton didn't even blink. He was looking into the *nihil*. What could I do? I had troubles of my own.

There was a pink Cadillac double-parked in front of my building when I returned. Two wiseguys were hovering around it. The day would never end.

21.

THE MOOD WAS tense, but then that was nothing new. Tension was our life now. Crystal and Calabash were there. So were Uncle Ray, his man Ronnie Jax, and another wiseguy who went unintroduced and who looked just like Ronnie.

The clear focus of attention was sitting in my morris chair. He was a man near seventy with a beer gut, bald head, a reddish-purple nose with bad veins, and black eyes that darted here and there. The others were gathered loosely around him. The man's head was down. He had the demeanor of a man who'd been badgered. When I opened the door, he looked hopefully up at me as if I were there to extricate him.

Crystal met me in the foyer as Jellyroll went directly to the man in the middle. Jellyroll can recognize focus. "I hope this is okay with you," she whispered. "They just showed up at the door. What could I do?"

"It's okay, don't worry. This is what we're doing now. Arnie Lovejoy?"

"Yeah. Wait'll you hear."

Jellyroll was sniffing Arnie's shoes for a clue to his identity. "This is himself, isn't it?" Arnie said to me as I approached.

"Yes, that's him. He likes you."

Crystal introduced us. Arnie Lovejoy stood up and gripped my hand with both of his. Frightened puppy eyes peered up at me from under his brow.

"Okay, Arnie," said Uncle Ray gently, "tell him what you told us."

"Well . . ." Arnie sat back down. "Uncle Billy drowned."

What? I looked to Crystal. She rolled her eyes at me.

"We was fishing way out on Baltimore Canyon, but we ain't catchin' nothin', and . . . and he fell overboard. I go down to get us our sandwiches, and I hear a shout and a splash. I come runnin' up on deck and, sure enough, there's Billy in the water. I throw him a life ring, I get my hands on him and try to get him back aboard"—he leaned forward in his chair as if over the rail of a boat and hefted at the man in the water—"but the current carried him off . . . and he went down."

"Did you report the drowning to the cops?" Ray asked.

". . . No."

"Did you report it to anybody?"

"No."

"Why not, Arnie? Thing like that ought to be reported to the proper authorities. It's the law of the sea."

"Because it never happened."

"Billy didn't drown?"

"No."

"He didn't even fall off the boat, did he?"

Arnie shook his head. "Hell, we didn't even go fishing. But that's what Billy wanted me to say. He sorta wanted to disappear. Billy was scared to be seen anywhere."

"Why?"

"He didn't want to say." He turned to Crystal. "I known

you all your life, Crystal. From the neighborhood. I ain't one to betray his friends."

"Sure, Arnie."

"I just couldn't go tell the cops about how he drowned. I mean, it just didn't sound like a good idea to me."

"You did the right thing, Arnie," said Uncle Ray.

"You really think so?"

"Yes, I do. They wouldn't of believed you."

"Where is he now, Arnie?" Crystal asked.

It was happening too fast, and I was too tired. What if Norm had bugged my living room?

"City Island. He's livin' on my boat up to City Island."

"You mean up in the Bronx?" said Ray.

"Yeah, you know, like near Co-op City and Pelham and like in there—"

City Island is an incongruous piece of New York City, a thin peninsula hanging off of the Bronx into the waters of Long Island Sound at its western end, near where it passes under the Throgs Neck Bridge and becomes the East River. City Island looks more like a shabby New England fishing village—seafood restaurants, marine-supply and antiques stores, boatyards, and several yacht clubs—than a Bronx community.

"Zuzu's her name." He turned again to Crystal. "That's what I used to call my wife. You remember her, don't you? My wife?"

"Sure, Arnie, I remember her."

"Zuzu. That was like a—whattaya call it?—a pet name. She's been dead fifteen years now," he said to me. Then back to Crystal he said, "Billy didn't want me to tell nobody except you. I was supposed to tell you he didn't drown."

"Would you like something, Arnie?" I asked. "A drink or something?"

"God, I'd love a drink. But I don't do it no more. It didn't help."

"Some orange juice?"

"I don't want to put you to no bother."

I got him orange juice and put some water to boil for coffee. It was too late now. If he was listening, Norm knew by now. "Hey, Norm, you fucking spook," I said, but not too loud, "you want some OJ?"

"Arnie," Ray was saying as I returned to the living room, "tell us what Billy was scared of."

"Well, I don't know. He wasn't real clear about it. He said bankers was on his ass."

"Bankers?" Uncle Ray stiffened. "What bankers?"

"He thought they wanted to take away his money."

"Money? What money?" Ray wanted to know.

"I don't know. I think he owed money to bankers. Maybe they was going to repossess it."

Back in the Toyota again, Crystal was driving, Calabash riding shotgun without adequate headroom, Jellyroll and I in the back. I was getting sick of riding in this Toyota, but Jellyroll still loved it.

"Artie," said Crystal, looking to me in the rearview mirror, "they just showed up. What could I do? I couldn't say, 'Look, let's go in the bedroom, because some CIA crazy bugged the rest of the place.' I mean, could I?"

"It's hard to know what to do. It's not like we've had a lot of experience."

"I *should* have, right?"

"No, it's all right." But I was too tired, too confused to make it sound convincing. Besides, Crystal knew it was not all right.

The Cross Bronx Expressway has to be one of the most depressing roads in North America. From the Cross Bronx Expressway, the entire city seems comprised of dirty prestressed-concrete walls, rusting bridge supports and abutments, careening truck traffic, and decaying infrastructure. Because of the budget cuts, the city has stopped picking up dead and abandoned automobiles, thinking, if at all, that eventually they'll erode away. Their stripped hulks lined the roadway. Some had been torched. Far below the elevated highway lay the South Bronx, dark and devastated like the footage of Berlin in 1945 you see on the Discovery Channel. Would we find Uncle Billy dead aboard the Zuzu?

We had to follow Ray's Lincoln because he had Arnie aboard. Ronnie Jax was driving like a lunatic, but then so was everybody else on the Cross Bronx. Crystal's Toyota sputtered and protested, but she managed to stay within sight. I wondered if Ray was intentionally trying to leave us in the dust.

There were too many unknowns. I brooded on them. I like things predictable. How long since things had been predictable? . . . Norm had said he lived on a boat in Pelham. From Pelham, he could be on City Island in ten minutes. Could he find the Zuzu? What would he do if he found Billy before we did? What would the rest of those assholes do if they found Billy? Tiny Archibald, for instance. We hadn't heard from him in—how long had it been? I tried to remember, but I couldn't. It seemed a career ago. How long had it been since Crystal and I had made love?

The pink Lincoln swerved around the curve at the City Island exit in the shadows of Co-op City, where more people resided in a single complex than in most villages and towns in this country. We sped through the darkness of Pelham Bay Park, careened around the traffic circle near the police shooting range, where two tons of lead a year get fired into the hillside, and the rain washes the lead into the bay. God knows the mutations that swim in its black depths. Then we crossed the bridge onto City Island itself. The main drag continued straight to the other end of the island, but we took a hard, squealing left at the foot of the bridge, around a bronze monument to something. Grubby rental boats were docked in the channel. Moonlight glimmered on the poisonous water, making it look tropical, pristine. To the north I could see the high chimney on Hart Island, a black mass in the darkness. For over a hundred years, Hart Island had been a potter's field. Now, every decade or so, prisoners from Riker's Island plow the decayed corpses into the earth to make room for more indigent dead, something New York will never lack for.

We pulled into a stony parking lot beside a rickety, paint-peeling bait-and-tackle shop, boat rentals available. It was dark and locked. So was the snack bar and the dive shop across the street. Crystal made a U-turn and parked the car near the Lincoln, but first she turned the car around to point us at the bridge, the way out. Altogether, there were seven of us. We got out of our cars.

A squat guy with long black hair cascading from under a Mets cap, big beer gut doing the same thing over the top of his sweatpants, came out of the shadows behind the bait shop. He stopped us as we approached the docks. "Sorry, private property," he said in a Long Island accent. He had huge forearms, just like—oh no!

Crystal must have been thinking the same thing—she clutched my hand.

Uncle Ray folded a bill into the man's T-shirt pocket. "Take a break, pal," Ray said without slowing down, and led us onto the wooden floating dock. It bobbed under our weight, causing us to walk with clumsy, high-kneed steps. I looked back over my shoulder at Norman Armbrister. He raised his hand and wiggled his fingers at me. Grinned.

Arnie stopped us at the *Zuzu*.

She looked homemade, jury-rigged, and raggedy-assed. Maybe thirty feet long, she was shaped vaguely like a lobster boat with a high upswung bow and low, open stern. A roof had been added, covering the steering wheel back almost to the stern, but the roof canted at a crazy angle because one of the support posts was too short. The cockpit was cluttered with gear.

"Ahoy," hailed Arnie from the dock in a small voice.

When I looked back toward the bait shop, Norm was gone, but I knew he'd be lurking somewhere in the shadows, his natural habitat.

Silence aboard the Zuzu . . .

Uncle Ray tapped Ronnie Jax on the arm, and Ronnie went aboard, over the cracked transom and into the cockpit. He went forward to the steering wheel, which was mounted on the extreme right side. Next to it was a hatchway that led down into the cabin, but the hatch was boarded up and locked. Uncle Ray asked Arnie for the key.

"Billy's got it."

"Break it," Ray said.

Ronnie Jax rummaged around in the fishing gear. He found an object with a long tapering point, like a fid or a big awl. He stuck the point through the padlock and twisted. Wood rended. Ronnie Jax shoved the hatch back. It was pitch-dark below. He struck his Zippo and held it into the darkness. From the dock, we could see nothing but the small flickering flame. He went below. Crystal stood with her fists clenched at her sides.

"Dark, boss," said Ronnie Jax as he climbed back out.

"Where's your battery switch, Arnie?" Crystal asked.

"Right behind the companionway steps."

Crystal went aboard. Lights came on below. I didn't hear her scream. There must have been no corpses aboard.

Ray called Ronnie back onto the dock and handed him another bill. "Go ask that asshole at the bait shop where

Billy went. If he can't tell you that, then ask him when he left. Give him the money first. If he don't tell you anything, take it back."

"I'll get this round," I said. Before anyone could reply, I bobbed up the dock. I went into the darkness beside the bait shop. There was a rancid-smelling dumpster back there, but that was all I could see.

"Hey, Norm," I hissed. I thought about Barry dead on the bench. I never doubted that Norm would do us all if it would serve his purposes or save his ass.

"Psst—"

He was behind me, at least his voice was behind me. Could he throw his voice? I saw movement from under the barnacled hull of a sailboat propped up on steel stands. He was motioning for me to join him over there.

"Watch the noggin," he said, pointing to the propeller at forehead level. I ducked under it. There was another, bigger sailboat on stands beside it. It was nearly pitch-dark between the two. "Who's the lardass with the pink Lincoln?"

"Crystal's uncle."

"No shortage of uncles. What business is this one in?"

"Pizza."

"You shouldn't be hanging out with pizza hoods."

"You bugged my apartment, didn't you?"

"What? No. Artie, you hurt my feelings. You are not a trusting individual. Here I've tried to be your friend. I've been here when you needed me, and now you accuse me of bugging your apartment."

"Then how'd you know Billy was here?"

"Because I never sleep."

There was no point in pursuing it. "Okay, where's Billy now?"

"I don't know. If I knew, you think I'd be hanging

around here in the dark, treading on, fish heads? I might ask you the same question about Uncle Billy."

"If Billy has the money, you can have it. Take it all and leave us out of it. That would be our last connection to this mess. You can have it."

"Why do you keep insulting me? I don't want the money. I'm no thief. Tran and I want to sail out of here, but I need the tape first. Or at least I need to know the disposition of the tape. I explained that to you once. You don't believe me. That hurts my feelings. Again."

"Tran's your wife."

"Right."

"Tran is a Vietnamese name, isn't it?"

"What, do you have something against the Vietnamese?"

"Absolutely not. I just wondered."

"She was a VC sapper. A killer. I tried to tell the Pentagon they couldn't ever defeat people like Tran, but they didn't listen. That's old soup. Let's talk about the present. Danny Barcelona got greased."

"What?"

"His body may or may not turn up."

"Who did it?"

"I'm not sure."

"Norm, what is Concom?"

"Shh—" hissed Norm, grabbing my arm.

Somebody was coming up the dock. Ronnie Jax. "Hey—" called Ronnie.

I looked back at Norm. Norm was gone.

I stepped out from under the sailboats.

Ronnie Jax stopped when he saw me. "What's goin' on?"

"Nothing. I can't find the guy."

"Hey, you, with the gut—" Ronnie called. No answer.

"He must have taken a break," I said.

"Yeah. What was you doing over there among the beached boats?"

"Taking a pee."

"I could use one myself."

The others were walking up the dock toward us.

"He was there, all right," said Uncle Ray. "His clothes are there, but he ain't. What'd the dock asshole say?"

"He's not around," I said.

"You guys go on home," Ray said to Crystal. "I'll get in touch with you. Something's funny here. Ronnie, I want you to stay till tomorrow. I'll send Leo out in the morning."

"Aww, boss, what the hell am I gonna do here all night?"

"Just what I tell you to do, unless you'd rather go back to drivin' the mozzarella truck."

"Aww, boss—"

"Take the cellular phone. Call if you see anything. But remember, any butthole with his own cellular can listen in." Uncle Ray headed for his Lincoln. "Leo, you drive."

"You got it, boss." Delighted it wasn't him assigned to stay, Leo leapt behind the wheel.

Uncle Ray hugged Crystal. "Don't worry, sweetie, we'll work this out. Ronnie, you get down on the boat. And stay awake. Arnie, you get in the back." Uncle Ray slid into the passenger seat. "I'll call you tomorrow," he said out the window as Leo drove the Lincoln away.

Crystal, Calabash, and I stood in the dark until the Lincoln crossed the bridge.

"That was Norm, wasn't it?" said Crystal.

"He told me somebody killed Danny Barcelona."

Crystal moaned.

"He didn't know who did it. At least he said he didn't." We waited awhile, but Norm didn't reappear. With Ronnie Jax around, we didn't wait. We went home and went to bed. We managed, but barely, to crawl out of our clothes first.

22.

THE PHONE RANG early next morning. Chet Bream didn't say hello; he just began speaking. His voice was thick and gurgly. "I've got it," he said.

"Got what, Chet?"

"The tape. I've got the tape! The whole story's gonna blow wide open now. This is Pulitzer material! . . . Only trouble is it'll have to be a posthumous Pulitzer." He giggled mirthlessly.

"Why?"

"Because they've killed me."

"How?"

"I want you to have it. Look, if you use it right this tape can save your lives. Please come, otherwise it's all pointless. If *they* get it, my death is useless!"

"I might, Chet. That's all I can—"

"Do you know where I am?"

"Yes—"

"Don't say it. I gave you a card, right? That day on the beach. Do you have it? Can you get it in front of you?"

I got it from my wallet. The address was 214 West Eighteenth Street.

"I moved," said Chet. "Here's where: add 'one-oh-two'

to the house number. . . . Got it? Now add 'two' to the street number. Got that?"

"Yes." Three-sixteen West Twentieth Street.

"Apartment One B. Come today. Tomorrow'll be too late."

I motioned for Crystal and Calabash to follow me into the bedroom. We sat in a row, me in the middle, on the edge of the bed. Thinking that looked cozy, Jellyroll hopped aboard. I told them exactly what Chet had said. Jellyroll placed his wet nose against the back of my neck to say, "Hey, remember me? I'm here, too."

"Chet thinks his phone is tapped?" asked Crystal.

"Or mine," I said.

"What the hell good do his precautions do us? So they won't know his address, all they got to do is follow you!"

I hadn't thought of that.

"Does he t'ink dey gave him de disease? Are we talkin' fooking germ warfare?"

We planned precautions. Crystal would leave first, catching a cab right in front of the building. She would go across town on the Ninety-sixth Street transverse, but when she got to Park or Lexington, she'd ask the driver to turn around, she'd forgotten something back on the West Side. She'd get out of the cab at her car, then drive it to the corner of Twenty-third and Tenth Avenue. There she'd wait for us.

Calabash would go next, by cab, to the IRT stop at Fourteenth Street. He'd catch the local uptown two stops and meet Crystal at the car.

Jellyroll and I—I was afraid to leave him alone, even though he made travel difficult—took another cab to Union Square. There we changed cabs, taking this one to Crystal's car. I had a little trouble getting the second one with Jellyroll along. Dogs-in-cabs is one of New York's ironies. No matter what a degenerate piece of rubble they're driving, when cabbies realize you mean to take this dog—the one you're plainly standing beside, the one attached to the leash in your hand—they often take personal offense, as if you'd just made rude noises about their sister's tits. Finally an aged Russian picked us up.

"Dogs is goot," he said to me in the mirror. "Dogs is goot, man is shit."

"Be careful. Don't do anything brave," said Crystal from the driver's seat as I got out. Crystal had taken routinely now to carrying one of Calabash's smaller guns in her purse. She drove away as planned.

Number 316 was a dilapidated four-story building in a block of well-maintained, expensive brownstones. The eighties gentrification—a word almost forgotten these days— had missed 316. It had the shape of its neighbors, but its facade was covered with sooty stucco. Cracks spider-webbed it. The window frames were rotted. Healthy locust trees flourished up and down the block. The two in front of 316 were dead and sere. A couple of winos sat stupefied on the stoop. Were they really winos? A half a block away, Calabash was pretending to be one himself, sucking on a bottle in a brown paper bag. Maybe these guys had the same ruse. Not wanting to do anything brave, I walked right past and down the block toward Calabash. I crossed the street and doubled back.

This summer day, sunny, not yet uncomfortably hot, was taking on an air of menace. The commonplace exuded death. A slight breeze from the direction of the river riffled the leaves of the locust trees, and I thought of cemeteries in autumn, desiccated leaves blowing across fresh graves. Crystal and I might be buried side by side, warm below while freezing rain killed the flowers above. I could skip this, I told myself. I could go back across the street and crawl into Calabash's pocket for him to carry me, when he felt like it, back to Crystal in the Toyota, but I didn't.

I crossed the street, headed straight for the winos on the stoop. They stank! Fifteen feet away I could smell them. There's no stench like the stench of the human body unwashed. That stink commonly clears entire subway cars during rush hour. You can't fake that. You can dress up like a wino, but you can't stink like a real one. The poor dissolute fuckers didn't even glance at me as I walked up their stoop.

The inside door was not locked. I went in. I waited, then peeked back at the winos. They hadn't moved. Dark stairs rose on my left. The banister was cracked, stiles missing. From apartment 1A I heard angry voices, a male and a female fighting in a foreign language. The hallway was narrow and shadowy, a film noir hallway down which I'd seen the stupid characters walk when another corpse was needed for suspense. If they'd killed Chet, they'd kill me too. And Crystal. And Jellyroll. I went stiff-legged down that hall to apartment 1B.

I knocked softly. Silence. A board creaked inside. Then Chet said, "Who?" from behind the door. It was made of cheap wood. I could have kicked a hole in it. There was enough adrenaline pumping through me to kick a hole in the old Berlin Wall. Chet was flipping dead bolts, about six of them. He peeked out through a crack. I recoiled a step at the sight of him and at the stink of shit that wafted through the crack.

His eyes blinked wetly from the bottom of two black craters. His skin seemed to have melted around the bones of his face. How long since I'd seen him on the beach at Fire Island? The change was shocking. His mouth hung open, and he gasped for breath. Each one whistled.

He opened the door wide enough for me to squeeze through, then he shut it again by leaning, almost falling, against it. On the beach, I remembered, his movements had been jerky, birdlike. Now he moved as if under water or something thicker, crank-case oil. Even his fingers, relocking the dead bolts, were emaciated and colorless. Chet wore a sad flannel bathrobe, blue socks without shoes.

"It's like cholera. . . . Cholera. You shit yourself to death. Did you bring your gas mask?" He tried to chuckle, but it didn't work. He began to cough dryly.

"Come on, man, we've got to get you to the hospital—"

He put his palm up. "Get real. They don't shoot you full of shit you can go to the doctor to get rid of. He'd want to take tests. I'd be dead before the results returned. I didn't think they'd do this to me, Artie. I really didn't think they would." He was sobbing, I think. Or maybe he was just breathing. I was beginning to panic with the shit stink and the fear. "Look, I got to sit down—" he said.

I half carried him to a ratty couch with the stuffing sticking out of the arms. "Where's your phone, Chet?"

"Why?"

"Why? Because I'm going to call an ambulance." The walls were bereft of everything, including telephones. The room was cluttered with dirty clothes. The phone was probably under them somewhere. I could see shit dried to a crust on a few garments.

Chet waved the forget-it gesture at me, then let his hand flop in his lap. "It's in the freezer."

"The freezer?"

"The tape. That's where I hid it. You can get it on your way out. But there's a few things you'll need to know. I can't say them twice. So listen . . . No, you tell me. What do you remember about the tape? Remember what I told you?"

"Johnny Barcelona, Tiny Archibald, Norman Armbrister, Trammell, and the Fifth Man are there."

"Not Johnny Barcelona. Danny Barcelona. What else?"

"There's a party going on around the pool. You can see the house in the background—why, Chet?"

"Table. What kind of table are they sitting around?"

"An aluminum one. With an umbrella over it."

"What color's the umbrella!"

"I don't remember."

"Green! It's a fucking great green umbrella!"

"Okay, Chet—"

"I felt a pinprick in my ass on the subway platform. Number Two train at the Times Square station. I thought it was a prank. Hell, I guess it was."

"Who did it?"

"I don't know. You want to hear a guess? Concom. That's the story here. Remember when it breaks. Concom's the story. My wife and kid . . . ex-wife, actually. I wrote them a letter." He gestured to his chest pocket, but he didn't have the energy to reach up there. "I'm sorry I don't have a stamp. Look, man, maybe you can do me a favor? I mean, besides mailing the letter."

"Sure, what can I do?"

"Hold me. Just hold me for a minute."

I did. I sat down beside him. I hugged him.

Then Chet died. His position on the couch didn't change. He didn't jerk or gasp—but I knew he had died. Life had sagged out of him. I looked in his eyes. Death had taken the place of life in his eyes. I'd never seen that happen in human eyes before, but I'd seen it in a dog's eyes. My childhood dog, a wild springer spaniel, got hit by a car. I ran to him. He lay on his side. He raised his head to look at me, then lowered it again. He was alive when he rested his head, but then he was dead. You didn't have to be a vet to tell. The lights went out in his eyes.

I sat there for a while holding Chet. Then I began to sob. It burst out. I wept loudly, the way I'd wept as a child

233

while I carried my dead dog out of the street. I hugged Chet and wept for a long time.

I'm not a naive person. I knew life was cheap here and everywhere else. Worse things than this were probably happening within two blocks of here even as Chet's lights went out. But the murder of Chet Bream, its means, it was so cold-hearted, so *personal*—something bad had to happen to these murderers. Maybe I'd see to it. When I stood up, Chet slouched sideways, but he didn't go all the way. He just listed there at forty-five degrees, head hanging.

I stopped crying. I paced, trying to decide what to do. For a short while, I forgot the stink. I took the letter out of Chet's pocket—there were four ChapStick tubes in there—and put it in mine. Then I took Tiny Archibald's phone number out of my wallet along with DiPietro's card—the Concom numbers—and I slid them into Chet's pocket. I wasn't sure what I was doing or what effect it would have, but I wanted to do something. I noticed the pathetic way Chet's stringy hair hung across his face.

I began to wonder if that was a bit too subtle. What else might I do, just a tad more blatant? . . . I looked around the kitchen, for what, I didn't know. I opened the cupboard under the sink and shoved cleaning fluids around. I spotted a can of spray paint. What color? I spun the can in my hand. Red. Can't beat red for blatancy.

I stepped up on the couch where Chet sat dead, and in two-foot letters, I sprayed:

CONCOM

When I stepped off the couch to survey it, Chet fell on over, burying his nose in the cushion. I stepped back up and put an exclamation point at the end. Then I began to wipe off my fingerprints with a greasy dish towel. I hear real cops chuckle sarcastically at the TV shows where actors get perfect prints every time, but why take a chance? What all did I touch? Not much. The inside of the door. Chet himself. Can you take prints off a corpse? I decided to take that chance.

I opened the freezer door with a spoon. There was a tape in there, all right, wrapped in aluminum foil. I stuck it inside my belt. God, I was thinking clearly, edges sharp, crisp. Did it take death and fear to cause that? I wiped the paint can and shoved it back under the sink. My fingers were red. I wiped them as best I could. I pocketed the dishcloth.

Farewell, Chet.

The winos hadn't budged.

Seldom does one inhale NYC air with delight at its purity. I did. It felt like Rocky Mountain air, babbling, crystalline brooks, John Denver clichés. I nearly ran the half block to Crystal double-parked at the corner.

"What!" She covered her mouth with her hand when she got a look at my face. I didn't know it was that bad.

"He died," I panted. "He's dead!"

"Ohh—" she moaned.

Jellyroll sniffed me thoroughly from the backseat. When he was done, he looked at me with sagging ears and closed mouth.

I jumped across the gap in the seats and began to kiss Crystal.

"Mmmf?"

I covered her face with my own.

"Artie, this isn't such a great time—"

"Kiss me!" I hissed in her ear. "DiPietro's coming around the corner!"

She threw her arms around my neck and kissed me. . . . Gee, it had been a long time. Almost instantly, a wave of desire broke across my body, enveloping me. No, call it lust, a wave of lust, flat-out, four-stroke lust. Crystal couldn't help but notice.

"What, you like danger?"

DiPietro went straight up the stoop past the wino statues and in the door. What was *he* doing here!—the question too obvious to ask aloud. We watched. Though double-parked, we weren't conspicuous, because we were in a line of double-parked cars. We slouched behind the dashboard, however. I told Jellyroll to lie down. "Good boy."

Who else was here? I poked my head back up and scratched my crown—that was the "alarm" sign to Calabash. He took a stroll past the stoop, glanced in, kept going. He stopped three doors away and pretended to drink.

How long did we wait like that? Fifteen minutes at most? DiPietro came back out. He was moving fast, glancing east and west, then rushing east. Calabash followed from a distance. I thought about doing the same from the other side of the street, but I didn't because I didn't want to seem to like danger.

We waited. Crystal took my hand while we did so, the tops of our heads peeking over the dashboard, until we saw Calabash round the corner, stepping fast. He went right past the car without looking at us, continued west to the corner, and rounded it. I assumed he was clearing his back. Apparently satisfied, he returned a short time later. I got in the back so he could sit up front, the only place he'd fit.

"Who was dot mon?"

I told him DiPietro was the phony cop from the beach.

"He went up de way and made a call on de pay telephone. He didn't talk long, but he seemed to do all de talkin'. Den he got in a cab and headed north."

Jellyroll, who can spot a mood a mile away, crawled into my lap and peered up into my eyes.

"Wot happen in dere?"

I told him about Chet's death. "I've got the tape." I had shoved it under Calabash's seat.

A panel truck pulled around the corner and stopped in front of Chet's death house. "Mack's Moving. Flatbush, Brooklyn" was painted on the side in big black letters. Three men, two white guys and a black guy, got out. They were all burly, barrel chested. I had never seen them before. They were pulling on gloves. The black guy pulled a stack of folded white sheets from the front seat, separated them, and tossed shares to the white guys. Without hesitating or speaking, the men hustled up the stoop and into Chet's building.

"What the hell?" said Crystal. "You don't think . . . ?"

The black guy came back out carrying an armchair covered with a sheet. The chair was shaped just like the one in Chet's apartment. He yanked open the big barn doors and shoved the chair into the back of the truck. A white guy, carrying the aluminum pipe-legged table, tripped on the top step of the stoop but regained his balance and threw the table into the truck. He hotfooted it up the steps and back for another load. Then for a while nobody came out. We waited, the truth dawning on us. I had read something like this in a George Smiley novel. Something had happened, something they didn't want found. They sent a truckload of guys to clean it up. They even had a name, something like the "House Cleaners."

The men came out with the couch on which Chet had died and piled it into the truck. The black guy followed with a pair of lamps. Next came poor Chet himself. At least I assumed it was poor Chet. He was in a trunk, like a steamer trunk or a large box. It too was covered with sheeting. It took two guys to carry it.

"Let's call the cops," said Crystal. "Let's call nine-one-

one without giving our names. These bastards shouldn't get away with this!"

When the movers went back into the building, we drove off in search of a phone—

"Dere's de one de phony cop used."

Crystal double-parked. I clambered out of the backseat and called 911. I must have waited through twenty rings before an operator answered. I gave her Chet's address, repeated it, and said, "A man named Chet Bream has been murdered in apartment 1B. Now—I mean *right* now—some people are trying to dispose of the body. They're posing as movers. 'Mack's Moving.' If you hurry, you can catch them in the act."

"What is your name, sir?"

"I'm not giving my name. Oh, and don't forget to perform an autopsy on Mr. Bream." I hung up.

We drove slowly around the block. We went around twice, each time looking down the street to be sure the van was still there. On the third lap, it wasn't. Neither were the cops. We went around twice more. Still no cops. After two more trips, we gave up.

Maybe it was the cutbacks.

23
.

VULNERABLE TO ATTACK from the blind spot astern, fighter pilots used to slew their airplanes from side to side in order to see the approaching enemy before he snuck into attack position. Fighter pilots used to call this maneuver "clearing their tail." That's what we were doing, clearing our tail. Crystal drove in intense, two-hands-on-the-wheel silence. Hunched into the passenger seat, Calabash reached a huge hand out the window and adjusted the sideview mirror. Jellyroll and I in the back watched the following traffic. When I'm engrossed in a thing, he insists on knowing what it is. He stood on his hind legs, his front legs braced on the seat back. His breath fogged the window.

We drove crosstown on Fourteenth Street. There was too much traffic to determine whether any of it was following us or just going our way. So Crystal threw the car into a hard left across the westbound traffic onto Irving Place. We headed north toward the elegant wrought-iron gate to Gramercy Park several blocks ahead.

A little white Japanese car, a Subaru or something, made the same left onto Irving Place. No other vehicle did so. Irving Place ends at the park—I could see the statue of

Edwin Booth as Hamlet—and traffic must turn right onto Twentieth Street, one-way eastbound. We could clear our tail by circling the park. I suggested that.

The white Subaru went right around with us. There were two men in the car, but I couldn't tell much more than that because by then the windows were pretty badly fogged. Dog breath is strong stuff. I told Jellyroll to sit, and that made him even more interested. He cocked his head at me. I told him he was a good dog.

"See the white car?" I asked.

"Hmm," said Calabash to the sideview mirror.

Crystal was looking in the rearview mirror as well. We turned onto Gramercy Park West. So did the little white car. Then it began to flash its lights at us at it moved up close behind us. Attack mode?

"Artie," said Calabash in his deadly calm voice.

"Yes, Calabash?"

"Move over behind me, 'cause I gonna shoot tru dat left-hand window."

I hunched my shoulders, pulled Jellyroll into my lap, and did as I was told. At the time, shooting through the window made perfect sense to me. It had come to that by then, the exchange of gunfire on a venerable residential street. I still could smell Chet's death on my hands. There was no reasoning with these assholes. You couldn't sit down with them, have a cup of coffee and work things out. You simply had to shoot them through their thick brows and worry later about the repercussions. Contrary to popular belief, you still can't hold a running gun battle on the streets of NYC and not suffer some legal repercussions.

"Wait!" shouted Crystal. "It's my Uncle Ray—"

Yes, I could see him now, in the passenger seat of the Subaru, and that was Ronnie Jax driving. The entire right side of the Subaru was mashed. What happened to his

Lincoln? Mafia cutbacks? Uncle Ray was motioning for us to pull over.

Crystal did so, stopping beside a fire hydrant. With my toe, I shoved the tape farther under Calabash's seat. Uncle Ray got his elbows out of the little car and used them to pry himself the rest of the way out. He waddled over to Crystal's car and hauled himself in with me. It felt like an air bag had just gone off back there. From my lap, Jellyroll sniffed him up and down. Uncle Ray was sweating profusely. It smelled faintly of marinara sauce. He wore no fancy three-piece suit now. A black-and-green running suit had taken its place. He must have ordered it from a tent store.

"They whacked Danny Barcelona," he panted. His eyes were wide. "I gotta back off. I'm sorry."

"What about Uncle Billy?" Crystal wanted to know.

"I ain't found him yet, but now I gotta quit looking. Fuckin' Danny—I used to know him—he let somebody make a movie of him doing business. They can't have that. A smoking gun. How can they have that? So they had him whacked."

"Who did?" I asked.

"The honchos. The heavies. The hot shits. And if they whacked Danny, they'd whack me if they even had a dream one night I knew something. So I can't know nothing. I'm sorry. Crystal, you need to get clear away from this. It wouldn't be a bad thing you were to get out of the country for a while. Take Billy."

"But Uncle Ray, I don't know where he is!"

"Listen, Crystal, I ain't trying to be a tough guy, but at this point, you got to think Billy's gone for good. Might never turn up. And you got to think about yourself." Jellyroll licked Ray's ear.

Double-parked, Ronnie was blocking traffic. Very dangerous. Obstructions make New York drivers crazy, even though there are obstructions everywhere. They began to honk long, hostile blasts. Ronnie Jax leaned out the driver's side. "Shuddup! I'm parkin' here!" He shook his fist at them. That annoyed me. They took the precaution of changing clothes and cars only to attract attention by starting a street altercation, the dumb fucks.

It seemed to annoy Uncle Ray, too. "Ronnie, you stupid gink, get outta the way!"

"But, boss—"

"Go around the block! Or you'll be back pickin' shit with the homing pigeons!"

Ronnie drove off.

"Crystal, if there's hard evidence out there that'll land them in the joint, they ain't gonna ask a lot of intelligent questions before they start whacking. You got to take me serious on this."

"I do, Uncle Ray."

". . . It'd be best if we didn't talk for a while."

"Okay," said Crystal without turning around.

"Do you forgive me on this?"

"Sure, Ray."

"You need money?"

"No, I'm fine."

"Here, take two grand." He handed the bills to Calabash. "Good luck, sweetie—" Uncle Ray couldn't extricate himself from the car. I gave him a shove from behind. Out, he turned around and thanked me.

No one followed us back uptown. At least, we didn't see anybody follow us uptown.

Crystal, Calabash, and Jellyroll lined up on the bed as I inserted the tape into the mouth of the machine. I couldn't remember my bedroom ever being so full of thick tension before. Malaise, yes, sexual longing and loneliness, certainly, but never a tension like this. We had in our hands—

more precisely, in my VCR—that which all the crazies wanted, the thing for which Chet had died young. I took a seat in the gallery, aimed the remote, and pressed the button. . . .

A snowy street in a small town. Homes bedecked with Christmas ornaments. A sign on a post: "You Are Now in Bedford Falls."

What?

The people in the homes, solid, simple, American homes, are praying:

"God, help George Bailey."

"He never thinks of himself, God, that's why George is in trouble tonight."

Then cut to the night sky, the firmament—Heaven—where God and Joseph are talking:

"Hello, Joseph, trouble?"

"Looks like we'll have to send someone down. A lot of people are asking for help for a man named George Bailey."

"Send for Clarence. He hasn't earned his wings yet."

"Hey," said Calabash, "I saw dis movie! *It's A Wonderful Life.*"

Crystal and I sat staring at these old, familiar images with our jaws hanging slack. Jellyroll wagged his tail at all the togetherness on the bed. George Bailey rescued his brother Harry, future war hero, from the icy pond. . . . For a dim instant, I thought Chet must have hidden the wrong tape in his freezer.

Then the light dawned. Suddenly I understood. Even before I could sort through the twisted logic of the thing, I understood. I was certain—

There never was any tape! It never existed.

"What is this," said Crystal, "some kind of sick joke?"

"No," I said.

"No?"

"Chet made it up."

"What do you mean, Chet made it up?

On the beach at Fire Island, Chet had told me that his story came to a dead end "but then he heard about the tape." He didn't *hear* about the tape. He invented it. He invented it to shake up the principals in the story, to dislodge them from deep cover, to blow them out into the open. And it worked. He'd started a war—trouble was, he had ended up one of its casualties. Even while I thought him utterly nuts, I admired him for his dedication.

"What are you talking about!" Crystal demanded.

I had drifted off, left her hanging.

"Chet was dying, and he knew it. He could barely talk, but he started coaching me on the contents of the tape. He told me how the assholes—Trammell, Tiny, Norm, Danny Barcelona, and the Fifth Man—were dressed, the time of day, even the color of the umbrella. Why did he waste his last breaths on that, if I could see for myself by watching the tape? Because I couldn't watch the tape—because there never was a tape." God and the angels watched while young George Bailey saved Mr. Gower, the distraught druggist, from ruin by not delivering those poison capsules.

"Look at it like this. Everything got started because the assholes thought there was a tape that'd incriminate them, a smoking gun, as Uncle Ray put it. Trammell decided to drown. Tiny Archibald kidnapped you as a way to get to Trammell, because he thought Trammell made the tape. Norm Armbrister showed up to help rescue you because he thought Tiny made the tape." The dance floor parted over the swimming pool. George and Mary went in first.

Crystal was staring off, thinking. "But wait a minute. He couldn't make up the meeting. There had to actually have been a meeting, right?"

"Yeah. Somehow Chet got wind of it. He said that the meeting took place during a garden party around Tiny's pool. Presumably, a lot of people attended. Chet must have learned about it from one of them. He said something about a guy whose body had to be identified by dental records—"

"Great."

Mary and George sang, "Buffalo gals, won't you come out tonight, come out tonight—"

"It doesn't make sense any other way. . . . Something else Chet said before he died—he said, 'If you use it right, this tape can save your lives.' "

"Right, it worked great for him."

"But his purposes were different from ours. He wanted to stir things up. We want to do the opposite. I think he meant that if they thought we had the tape, if they thought that harming us would cause the tape to go public, then they'd leave us alone."

"Yeah, when they hear we got our own copy of *It's a Wonderful Life*, they'll be paralyzed with fear."

"I love dot angel Clarence," said Calabash.

The phone rang. "Every time a bell rings, it means an angel gets his—"

"Hello?"

"Jesus, Artie, I just heard—" It was Shelly, Jellyroll's agent. "He actually *threw up*? Right there on the set, he barfed it right up—?"

"Shelly, can I get back to you—?"

"I just got a call from the Mr. Big butthole at R-r-ruff. He said Fleckton'll never work in this town again. He's a goner. Mr. Big said New and Improved R-r-uff's a goner, too. You know how he put it? He said, 'We're gonna have to eat this one.' I picture the dumb fucks sitting around this big boardroom table munching tons of kibble. Tell me, Artie, was it hilarious? When he hooped?"

"It was pretty hilarious." Poor Mr. Fleckton.

"They want to renegotiate. We're within our rights to

stick them with the rest of the contract. As Jellyroll's agent, I suggest that we've got them by the short ones, and we ought to run with it."

"Whatever you think, Shelly."

"You okay? You don't sound too good. Jellyroll's okay, right?"

"Everything's fine. I'll get back to you."

The phone rang again as soon as I hung up. "Hello."

"Can I speak to Crystal, please?"

"Uncle Billy? Is that you?"

Crystal leapt up beside me.

"This is Uncle Billy. Is this Artie?"

"Yes, Billy."

"Is Crystal there?"

I passed her the receiver.

He spoke for a while. Head bowed, Crystal listened. "Come on up, Billy." She hung up. "What could I do?" she asked me. "He was right around the corner."

"It's okay."

"There's probably a string of assholes following him. But I couldn't tell him to hang around on the street. Could I?"

"Of course not."

"I gonna go down and clear de way for him," said Calabash, sliding a gun into his waistband. I'd noticed that as time had passed, the guns Calabash stashed on his person had grown larger and larger. This one looked like a small bazooka.

I walked him to the door. "Be careful of yourself first, Calabash."

"Don't worry about dot."

When I returned to the bedroom, I found Crystal supine on the bed, her arm across her eyes.

"Are you all right?" I asked.

"I was trying to remember what it was like. When we'd just met. When we'd make love. They took that from us."

"I still love you."

"You do?"

I lay down beside her. I felt inopportunely aroused.

Calabash knocked his tap-tap-tappity-tap on the front door.

I got up to open it, and Calabash ushered Uncle Billy into the room. He was the picture of contrition, hands clasped in front, head down. I wanted to say something encouraging, but I couldn't think what.

"I hope you're not mad at me, Crystal."

"Don't worry, Uncle Billy, I'm not. I'm just glad to see you safe."

Uncle Billy, knees crackling, crouched laboriously to pet Jellyroll. I made coffee. We sat in the living room after Calabash and I dragged chairs in from the dining table.

"Where have you been, Uncle Billy?"

"I been hiding. People've been after me. That's why I decided to drown . . . like Timmy. But that didn't work out so good. I hid on Arnie Lovejoy's boat—remember Arnie?—but that didn't work out so good, either. People came. I'm tired of hiding, so I came here." He looked from one to the other of us and, finally, even to Jellyroll. Jellyroll licked his hand. I thought Billy was going to cry. "I never loved Timmy more'n I loved you, Crystal. I loved you both."

"I love you, too, Uncle Billy."

"He liked me to call him Timmy. He was like a son to me."

"Do you mind if I call him Trammell?"

"No."

How long had it been since I'd heard a measure of jazz?

"Uncle Billy, Trammell didn't really drown. He faked it. He stole money from thieves and had to disappear."

"No," said Billy categorically.

"No?"

"Timmy wouldn't do that to me. He wouldn't. I mean, he'd steal things. Timmy was not a good person, but he wouldn't go away like that and not tell me where he went. We was partners. No, not Timmy. Timmy just wouldn't."

"You were partners?"

"Yes, partners."

"In what?"

"Well, before Timmy drowned, he said I ought to have money for the Golden Hours and things like expenses. He put the money in a bank in Nassau, Bermuda. He said he knew he didn't treat you too good. He said when I died, I could give the money to you, and then maybe things'd be even. See, I told Timmy I knew he didn't treat you good as a husband, but it takes a man to be a good husband. Timmy wasn't a man. Timmy was still a boy. That was Timmy's problem. He did as best as boys can."

"Uncle Billy, do you mean to say you have their money now?" Crystal asked, as if speaking to a child.

"Their money? It's our money. Timmy gave it to us because he was sorry."

"Okay. But you have it?"

"Oh, yes. Well, no, I mean, I don't have it in my wallet or anything like that. It's in Bermuda. But I have the papers. I have the papers right here." Uncle Billy began searching himself, patting his pockets. He felt something inside his shirt and smiled at his success. He removed a green bankbook, much like a standard savings-account passbook. He handed it to Crystal.

Crystal opened it. Then she gasped. Her hand went to her mouth. Staring at Uncle Billy, she passed the little book to me.

I gasped, too. The book was stamped with twin rearing lions between which was printed "International Bank of the Bahamas" in fancy script. No transactions were noted, merely a balance in stark, naked figures: $34,888,000.27. I had to read it three times before I got it straight, before the *million* place became clear.

"That's a lot of money, Billy," Crystal squeaked.

"I know it. It's all yours." He was smiling now.

I flipped a page, and there it was:

Account: Crystal Spivey
Golden Hours Billards
254 Avenue X
Brooklyn, New York, USA

I handed the book back to Crystal. Absently, she passed it to Calabash. The sum knocked him back a half stride. Even Jellyroll didn't pull down that kind of jack.

I began to feel deeply frightened at the size of this monster. Trammell had stolen nearly thirty-five million bucks, yet nobody seemed to care. They only wanted the tape. I already knew those assholes were willing to kill. Mere money never impressed me as much as murder, but there was something about seeing that absurd figure next to Crystal's name. It felt like her death warrant.

"See, it's real easy," said Billy. "You just call a man at the bank and tell him your number and the password. You can change the number and the password anytime you want. The password used to be Barraclough, but I don't know why. So I changed it to Zuzu, like Arnie's boat. And I put it in your name."

Looking at the bankbook, Calabash said, "Dis is Nassau in de Bahamas. Dis ain't any Bermuda. Dis my home. We can take care o' t'ings in de Bahama Islands, me and Uncle Fergus and a bunch o' de hardboys." When Calabash speaks, people tend to listen. Was he taking over? I desperately hoped so. He put a hand the size of a welding glove on Uncle Billy's shoulder. "Say, Mister Billy, it time for you to go on a trip to my island. Nobody bother you dere. You can sit on de patio and watch de sea roll in and out."

"Bermuda?"

"No, not Bermuda. De Bahamas."

"Nobody'll bother me there?"

"Nobody. My own uncle take care o' dot."

Uncle Billy looked at Crystal. "Will you be coming?"

". . . Yes."

"You all be my guests."

"Gee," said Uncle Billy, "I always wanted to go to Bermuda."

"No, not Bermuda. De Bahamas. You like de Bahamas even better."

"How old is your uncle?"

"He about yer age."

"Does he like to fish?"

"Sure. Uncle Fergus love to fish."

"Gee, maybe we can fish together. . . . Can I go home and pack?"

"No, Uncle Billy," said Crystal, "I think the idea is you go right now. Can you do that?"

"Well, I didn't know what to do when I came here. I saw what they did to my house. I can't go there. So . . . yes. But I don't have any money."

"I'll take care of it," said Crystal with a quick glance at me.

It was all I could do not to giggle like a chucklehead.

So there it was, decided. Uncle Billy would leave for Poor Joe Cay. Calabash made a couple of phone calls to arrange for members of his family to meet Billy in Nassau, where they would catch a flight to the airport on Eleuthera. From there, they'd travel by boat to Poor Joe Cay.

Uncle Billy began to cry as the final arrangements fell into place. His Adam's apple bounced pathetically.

"I go down first," said Calabash. He stuffed a howitzer into his belt and went down to scout things out. Five minutes later, Billy and I went down. I didn't see Calabash on the street

I let the first cab go by just in case it was a setup. I let another go by and hailed the third. My street was nearly empty of pedestrians. A happy young couple strolled toward us, he carrying a bottle of wine in a bag, she a bouquet of flowers. I thought wanly about Crystal's fuchsia top and the old days of a week or so ago. I opened the cab door for Uncle Billy.

He paused before he got in, looked at me through wet eyes, then hugged me tightly. I watched the back of the old man's head disappear around the corner. It was dark now, ominous black clouds gathering to the southwest over the river.

I looked around for Calabash. But he was lurking somewhere in the darkness. Calabash can disappear behind a parking meter.

"Ach, Artie!"

I nearly jumped off the sidewalk. My heart pounded as I turned to face Mrs. Fishbein.

"I t'ought you vas a mugger. Waiting to pounce. Boof, boof on za brain—you're a turnip." Then she went into the building.

But if Mrs. Fishbein could sneak up on me, who else—? I spun around twice. There was a little old man, like the ghost of Mrs. Fishbein's husband, waddling up the street. As he got closer, I saw that he was a Hasidic Jew, in black coat, pants, hat, and earlocks.

I gave Mrs. Fishbein time to get into the elevator before I returned to the lobby. I had barely unlocked the street door when I heard a muffled squeal behind me—

It was the Hasidic man. His feet hung twelve inches off the pavement. He dangled from Calabash's enormous arms. They were wrapped around the Hasid's head. His hat fell off. I saw that the earlocks were attached to his hat, as opposed to his head. In the streetlight, I could see the top of the man's head. The hairless crown was ringed by a jagged, purple scar. I opened the door.

Calabash carried him past me toward the elevator and walked his face right into the wall beside the call button. "I gonna break your sneaky neck like a twig in a hurricane."

"Talk!" said Norm, muffled. "Talk first!"

Calabash dropped him, spun him around, and pinned his throat to the wall with one hand.

"Invite me up?" sputtered Norm.

Mercifully, the elevator arrived empty. Calabash heaved him in hard.

"If you keep doing that, I'm going to report you to B'nai B'rith."

That's what we needed, spook wit.

"So where's Uncle Billy off to in such haste?"

"The Klondike. There's been a big strike. He's a prospector at heart."

"Cold in the Klondike. Me, I prefer the lower latitudes. Say the Bahamas."

The elevator arrived at my floor. Calabash peeked out, found the hallway empty, and led us to my door.

"Evening, Crystal," said Norm congenially.

"Who are you supposed to be?" she said, looking him up and down.

"I'm Rebbe Armbrister. Calabash knocked off my hat. Without it, my disguise is incomplete."

"When are you going to get out of our lives?"

"Chet Bream is dead," said Norm. You could tell he threw it out to test our reaction.

"Did you kill him?" I said.

"No."

"Then your friends did it?"

"They're no friends of mine. Sure, we were associates in wartime. The Cold War. A great war, but it's over now, we just have to live with that. The police stopped two guys in a moving van. Turned out the van contained Chet Bream's body. Shots were exchanged. A policeman was critically wounded, and the two guys were killed. During this time, Chet remained in the van. Chances are the van was stolen and can't be traced to Concom, but the Concom folks are very nervous, and they're doing stupid things as a result."

"They killed Chet? Concom?"

"Sure. It's not Tiny's style. He's a businessman. Maybe Trammell, but I doubt it. I doubt the hoods did it. Germ warfare isn't their style, either. They did Danny Barcelona the way hoods do people—an honest bullet in the brain. That leaves Concom, in my opinion."

"How do you know about the germ warfare? How do you know they didn't shoot Chet in the brain?"

"I told you, I survive by knowing."

"Do you know that I have the tape?"

"Do you? Really?"

I repeated Chet's words to me about the details of the nonexistent tape. I didn't mention God or Joseph, George Bailey or Clarence. Norm seemed to believe me.

"Where is it now?"

"Bedford Falls."

"Upstate?"

"Bedford Falls, Pottersville. The fact is, it's everywhere." I tried to sound absolutely confident. I knew exactly what I was doing. I could pull this off. Hell, I had no doubts. I was up to this intrigue. Streams of sweat ran down the insides of my thighs.

"You mean, you've made arrangements?"

"Absolutely."

"You've taken precautions?"

"Of course. I've made copies. I won't say how many. I put one in my safe-deposit box. Safe-deposit boxes, as you probably know, are routinely opened in the event of the depositor's death. I've placed the other copies with friends. I told them that if anything happened to Crystal, Calabash, Jellyroll, or myself—even if one of us died from natural causes—then they are to take it directly to the cops and the *Times*. Oh, I've also included an essay telling the story and naming names, including yours."

Norm was thinking. He removed his Hasidic coat and dropped it over the back of a chair. "Mind if I sit?"

We sat around the table. Jellyroll circled several times and flopped under it. Silence.

Norm was thinking.... "I like it. Yes sir, I like it."

"What do you mean you like it?"

"I mean I *like* it. The intrinsic trouble with tapes is that tapes can be duplicated, just as you've done. Hell, say I took measures to acquire the tape from you—I won't, but just say—what would I have? A tape, not *the* tape. How could I ever know I had all the copies? I couldn't. No, the disposition of the tape is much more important than the actual possession of it. And I like that you have the tape, as opposed to another."

"Why?"

"Well, because I don't trust them any more than they trust me. I don't say I trust you, either, but your motives are simpler. You just don't want to end up like Chet Bream. That makes me feel secure, same way I felt back during the Cuban Missile Crisis. The tape won't come back to haunt me, because you can't do anything with it. You have to leave it in Pottersville. If you did anything with it, then its value as a life-insurance policy would plummet to nil, right? Is that how you're seeing it?"

"Of course."

"There's just one thing."

"Yeah?"

"The others need to know you have it."

"Why don't you just tell them?"

"I know you'll find this hard to understand, but they don't entirely trust me."

"Imagine that."

"Yes. So it would be best if you sent them a copy of the tape. Show them the policy as it were."

"I don't have one here, and I'm not about to go get a copy after all the trouble I went to hiding them."

"You'd never know who was following you?"

"Right."

"How do you feel about telling them you have it?"

"By phone?"

"It would be much better if you told them in person."

"Why?

"These are suspicious men."

"You can tell them I've seen the tape. How else would I know about its contents?"

"I'll be right there with you. I like it. I told you. So don't worry, they'll have to like it too. Look, this is the best way to get me—and them—out of your lives. I promise."

"Crystal stays here," I said. "Just me."

"And me," said Calabash, staring holes in Norm's forehead.

"Bullshit," said Crystal. "I'm in this, too. Don't try to be some Saturday morning TV hero. I hate that."

"God, don't you love strong women?" said Norm. "My wife Tran is like that, a strong woman. Defy her wishes on a thing, and she'll mortar your position. In fact, she did a couple times. It was in Quang Tri Province up near— Oh well, that's old soup, I guess. Nobody cares about the Nam now. Want me to set it up? A face-to-face? What say?"

"I say de same t'ing I said to you in de Posh van."

"What's that, Calabash?"

"Anything goes wrong—even if nothin' go wrong, if I don't like de look on any mon's face—you de first one I kill." He lifted his big gun out from under the table. He reached across the table and pressed the muzzle against Norm's forehead. When he pulled the gun away, a red ring remained.

24

IT WAS RAINING HARD, the first rain in weeks, as we crossed Central Park on the Ninety-sixth Street transverse. . . . Was this the stupidest trip I'd ever embarked upon? What were we going to do, exactly? Were we going to walk into that nest of snakes and say, "We got the tape, neh-neh-neh"? Norm was all for the idea, which made it even more dangerously stupid, but we were doing it. We were on the way.

He sat in the front seat with the cab driver, a Sikh in a purple turban. Crystal, Calabash, and I were crammed into the backseat, and though we didn't speak, it was clear they were as tense as I was. We were traveling at high speed. The windshield wipers were having no effect at all. Sheets of water seemed to be flowing under them. We were traveling blind at high speed. It began to dawn on me that we had as much to fear from the trip across town as from the Concom crazies at our destination.

Basically a roofless tunnel, the transverse cuts through the park deep below its surface. Black rock walls climb twenty feet on either side of the roadbed. There are no streetlights down here. There used to be, but not now, because of the cutbacks. It felt like we were speeding along the abyssal plain beneath the Atlantic Ocean. The Sikh accelerated.

I glanced sideways at Crystal's face. I missed her. We'd been in constant close proximity of late but not together in the sense of carefree lovers who only have eyes for each other. But that, I supposed, blasting through deep water, was romantic twaddle. Bank fraud, illegal weapons deals, generalized corruption in high places, murder—that was the stuff of reality. Out of the corner of my eye, I watched her elegant profile and felt deeply in love with it. She noticed me looking and took my hand in hers, but she didn't look back. She continued to peer straight ahead at the onrushing blackness broken only by hurtling head-lights passing us like tracer bullets.

"What de fook's de hurry?" Calabash wondered.

What did we have on our side against the conspiring crazies? A 1946 Frank Capra film about the intrinsic good-ness of mankind. Powerful stuff. The driver leaned over his wheel, pressed his nose against the windshield, and put the hammer down, I guess on the reasoning that since we couldn't see anything anyway, the faster we went, the less time we'd spend in harm's way. Then I realized that Norm was chatting casually with the driver in his *native tongue*. Norm must have subverted India at one time or another in his career, before he died.

"Hey, Norm," I said, "tell him to slow down."

"No, no, can't do that, at least not directly. That would be an affront."

Speaking of affronts, I considered borrowing Calabash's howitzer, placing the muzzle against Norm's medulla ob-longata, perhaps steadying the gun butt on the back of his seat, for at this speed, careening crazily, my hand would be unstable, and blowing out his brains. "Buffalo gals, won't you come out tonight, come out tonight?" Finally, we emerged and stopped at the light on Fifth Avenue.

Those of us in the backseat took the opportunity to breathe. Then we sped down Fifth, where at least it was bright and we could see the car that would kill us.

Number 919 Third Avenue had its entrance on Fifty-fourth Street. It was no different than dozens of other high-rise office buildings in midtown. Commercial real estate had sprouted like fungus on fallen tree trunks during the heedless expansion in the eighties, but now it was over. Several big buildings within sight of 919 stood incomplete, nothing but ruddy steel skeletons above the fifth or six floors. Real estate tapes call them "see-throughs."

Incongruously, a fact of Manhattan geology popped to mind. The reason there are high-rise office buildings in midtown and in the Wall Street area but nowhere else is that two great domes of solid granite bulge to the surface at those points. Only there can the island support such gargantuan weight. Anywhere else, high rises would sink to the size of duplexes. So what? Why'd I think of that? People ascending the gallows probably recall trash facts to deflect their minds from the unthinkable at hand. . . . Yeah, but we had the tape, goddamnit. They couldn't touch us with the tape. They wouldn't dare mess with George Bailey.

Norm paid the cab fare while Calabash, Crystal, and I hustled under the shelter of the cantilevered portico. Bleary-eyed contributors to the GNP were still straggling out of the revolving door. Most, regardless of sex, wore blue or gray pin-striped suits and carried leather briefcases bulging with yellow-paper homework. They looked up at the driving rain as if weather were a phenomenon unfamiliar to them, before they ran to waiting cars. If I had become a lawyer instead of the owner of a wealthy dog, I would have worked in a place like this, where you couldn't even end it all by hurling yourself from an upper story, because the windows don't open in high-rise office buildings.

Norm trotted up and stopped us before we entered the lobby. "See the security desk?" How could we miss it? It was a Kafkaesque structure, built high up against the towering black marble wall, from which uniformed guards stared down at passersby with indifferent looks on their faces. "They'll want us to sign in. Don't sign your real names."

I signed "Samuel Beckett." I didn't see what the others signed. On the guard's clipboard there was a column for time in. It was 9:15. I longed for the time when we'd sign out. The guards gave us guest badges to pin to our chests.

"Lighten up," said Norm as we ascended in the elevator at ear-popping velocity. "This'll be a piece of cake."

"If it ain't den I shoot you right tru de guest badge."

"I hear you, big guy," Norm chuckled.

The elevator, one in a bank of six, opened on the forty-ninth floor. There was a blank wall to our left. To our right, there was a glass wall. Affixed to the glass, brushed-aluminum letters a foot high said CONCOM INTERNATIONAL SECURITIES.

Beyond the glass door was an empty receptionist's desk. Norm stuck a pass card in the mouth of a slot beside the door. When a buzzer sounded, Norm pushed the door open.

The furnishings inside were as plush and as individualized as any you can order from an office-supply catalog. A long, narrow, naked hallway led away to our left and ended in a T, but before we followed Norm down its length, Calabash stopped him by grabbing a huge handful of the back of his windbreaker.

"Where we goin', Norm?"

I glanced at Calabash. His face was fixed and hard. It was a frightening face. His whole demeanor suggested sudden impact, disfiguring violence. At least that was in our favor.

"We're going down here, then to the left to a room. Don't worry about a thing, big guy."

"Don't tell me not to worry. What's dis room like?"

"You mean in terms of entrances and exits?"

"Of course."

"One door. No other way in or out. Unless you take the quick way down." Norm thought that was a hoot. "It's like a boardroom. You ever been in a boardroom before?"

"Fook no. Who's gonna be in dis boardroom?"

"Two or three people. Plus us."

"Who's gonna be outside?"

"I can't say for certain. They might have some security types hanging around, but they won't do anything untoward without orders, and since you have the tape, they won't get any untoward orders." Big grin. "Ready?"

We turned left at the T. That led to more of the same hallway. We walked to the end of it. We took another left. More hall. Was this it? Was Concom International nothing but a maze of narrow hallways? We made two more turns. No offices. The only break in the endless hall was a door to the women's rest room. I was completely disoriented, and the rest room reminded me I had to pee. Still the hall continued. Left, right, left. I was beginning to conclude that this was some kind of cruel hoax when the hall opened onto something like a room. There were more elevators on one side, a closed wooden door with a lever-type handle on the other. That door, apparently, was our destination. Without Norm, we'd never find our way out.

"I don't like de elevators here. Anybody could come right up after us." Calabash leaned against the wall near the door and said quietly to Crystal and me, "I gonna wait right here. When you go in, if you don't like somethin', give out a shout, den hit de floor, 'cause I gonna be comin' in to shoot everybody in de room. Includin' Norm."

"I heard you the last four times you threatened my life. Come on, I'm with you, big guy."

"Quit callin' me dat or I do it right now."

"Buffalo gals, won't you come out tonight, come out—" kept rattling around in my brain.

Norm opened the door and walked right in, barged in, more accurately, a bantam-rooster badass with a hole in his head leading us to—

Crystal went in next. I heard her gasp. I very nearly decided, fuck it, I'm going to shout for Calabash before I even see what's back there, but I didn't. I looked—

Two men sat side by side at the long teak table directly across from the door. Arms folded across his chest and a mean look on his face, DiPietro stood behind them.

Tiny Archibald sat at the table. His eyes were red, and tears tracked his face, puddled in the folds of his jowls. But because of the man who sat beside him, I noticed Tiny, and his tears, almost incidentally—

The man who sat beside him wore a black hood pulled down over his head. Through the eye holes I could see glasses with wood-colored frames. Crystal and I stood rooted in the doorway staring at the hooded man. He wore an expensive Italian suit over a powder-blue shirt, and a natty red tie. He could have passed for a respectable businessman, except that most respectable businessmen don't wear hoods over their heads. The front of it puffed out, then deflated with each breath.

Norm didn't bat an eye at the hooded man, either because he expected a hooded man at the conference table—it was that kind of conference—or because in Norm's circles, folks generally wore hoods. He sat down across the table from Tiny and the hooded man and motioned for us to join him. We took seats on his left. That left about twenty vacant seats around the table.

"Hey, thanks a lot for keeping the store open late," said Norm with his grin.

"Can we get on with it, Norman?" asked the hooded man. "You're a thorn under the saddle of progress."

"Yeah, well," said Norm, "who fucked up?" Norm glanced pointedly at DiPietro, then back to the hooded man. "Me? No indeed, not me. You and Mad Dog back there fucked up. Who drew civil authorities on our ass? Not Norm. Norm didn't go around shooting cops and alienating the civil authorities. However, that is your problem, it has nothing to do with me. I'm here to remove a mutual problem, and what do I get instead of thanks? I get called a thorn. . . . Hey, Tiny, what's the problem there? Buck up. Why does the big guy weep?"

"Haven't you heard?" asked the hooded man.

"No, I've been busy solving our mutual problem. Heard what?"

"Trammell's dead."

Crystal stiffened, but she didn't make a sound.

"He is?" said Norm. "Who did it?"

"Nobody did it. It was in the newspaper! Don't you read the papers? Does nobody read the newspapers?"

Crystal and I hadn't read the papers.

"If nobody reads the newspapers, why am I sweltering under this hood?"

"So what happened to him?" asked Norm, clearly surprised and suspicious.

"The fool drowned! He fell out of that boat and—drowned. The paper said his body had been in the water at least a week. It washed all the way to Sandy Hook. Partially decomposed, was how the paper put it."

Norm shook his head. "I'll be damned, he really drowned? Tch, tch." Norm chuckled at the irony. At least, that was the only thing I could see to chuckle at. Bruce had tried to tell us the truth—that too was ironic.

"Well," said Tiny Archibald in a petulantly teary voice, "I'm glad you find that so amusing!"

"Come on, Tiny," said the hooded man, "he was a fucking crook. How much did he steal from VisionClear? Ten million? Twenty million?"

"So what! You're a crook! I'm a crook! So's Norm!"

"I'm no crook," said Norm.

"He was like a son to me!" Tiny blubbered.

"Could we not get all mawkish here? We still have the question of the tape to deal with." The man adjusted his hood—it had pivoted when he'd turned his head, and the eye holes had gotten out of place.

"Trammell didn't make the tape," said Norm.

"No?" said the hooded man. "Who did?"

"Chet Bream—that journalist Mad Dog shot full of shit—he made the tape."

"Boy, you better quit calling me Mad Dog."

The hooded man held up his hand to quell any building internecine squabbles. "How do you know that, Norman?"

"Because Bream gave it to Mr. Deemer. What do you think we're all here for?"

"How do I know? You didn't exactly make that clear on the phone, Norman."

"You're the Fifth Man," I said in a voice I tried to pump up with false confidence.

"The Fifth Man? What are you talking about, the Fifth Man?"

"Your back is to the camera," I said. "You can see the other crooks—Danny Barcelona, Trammell Weems, Tiny Archibald, and Norm—"

"I'm not a crook."

"The five of you are sitting under a green umbrella near Tiny's pool." My forehead began to sweat. "A party's going on in the background. Every now and then, guests cross in front of the camera. That wasn't so shrewd, discussing money laundering in the middle of a lawn party." Was I pushing it too hard? A bead of sweat pooled in the inner corners of my glasses and threatened to run the length of the lenses, but I pressed on. "All we want, Crystal and I, is to be left alone. You leave us alone, and no one will ever see that tape. However, if anything happens to either of us, anything at all, then it goes straight to the newspapers, the cops, and every other law-enforcement organization in the country. I've already made copies of the tape and set up the machinery for that to happen if any harm comes to us."

"There you have it," said Norm. "Personally, I like it. Artie and Crystal will get out of the country while you clean up the mess you made. And you can rest assured that for reasons too obvious to mention, the tape won't ever see the light of day—if you can keep Mad Dog on a stout leash."

"You better tell him to quit that," said DiPietro in a cold killer's voice.

"Hey, you're an asshole. You could fuck up an ambush," Norm said. Then back at the hooded man, he said, "In my view that disposition of the tape serves everyone's best interests."

"Well, not in my goddamn view!" The hood puffed with each syllable. "And I don't want a business lesson from a cheap, washed-up little mercenary who had the top of his head blown off by his own goddamn wife! *I* don't like it! And that's who matters here. Concom! Not Tiny, not Trammell, who couldn't even stay on the boat, not some dumb dago hoodlum, not these two lovebirds, and not you! That tape is a smoking gun! Here we are fourth down and short yardage, and the best you and Tiny can do is bring me *Artie* and *Crystal*—who've already copied the tape!"

"I didn't bring them," said Tiny.

"No, you didn't, Tiny, you were too crippled with grief

for a juvenile delinquent to do squat!" The Fifth Man turned to me and said, "Hey, *Artie*, did you know these two were working together from the beginning?

". . . What?"

"What? I'll tell you what. It was all a setup. And it was all Norm's idea."

"What was?" said Crystal.

"What was? All of it was. Your kidnapping, for example."

"I don't understand," she said in a thick, fear-clogged voice.

"No? You don't? Allow me to elucidate. Your pal Norman figured out a way to ingratiate himself with you. He had Tiny kidnap you, so he could help Artie rescue you—"

"He poured gasoline all over me," said Tiny. "That wasn't part of the script."

"You see, Norman figured that your crazy old uncle must be connected to Trammell, and the best way to get to him was through you. So he pretended to be your friend."

We turned to stare at Norm.

Norm didn't look at us. He continued to stare coldly at the hooded man. Awareness, like a gob of something large and sticky, crawled up the back of my throat and began to make me sick.

"Anyway, the point is I can't let you live, not with the smoking gun out there. And I'm the boss, right, Norman?"

"Right, you're the boss." Norm pulled a gun from somewhere in the small of his back. It had a long, phallic silencer on the end. Norm pointed the gun at Crystal and me. "I'm sorry," he said. His eyes were flat and fishy. "If you shout for Calabash, I'm afraid I'll have to shoot you both."

"That's the spirit, Norman," said the hooded man. "And another thing, Norman. It's you who's going to get rid of these two and then clean up the mess. I mean, *entirely*, Norman, tape and all. Is that clear?"

"Yes, boss."

"Norman," I said, "you're a scummy dwarf."

Norm actually nodded, then he said, "There's still the question of their bodyguard out in the hall."

"What?" asked the Fifth Man. "Who?"

"Their bodyguard," said Norm. "Why don't you send Mad Dog here out to deal with him?"

"What," said DiPietro, "you don't think I can?"

"Sure, I think you can."

"Then do it," said the hooded man.

"No violence," squeaked Tiny. "We can't have violence in here! How can we cope with corpses in the home office?"

"Leave it to me, lardass." DiPietro marched around the table and out the door. He pulled it shut behind him with a pop. . . .

No . . . the door didn't pop.

Norm's gun popped, but I didn't exactly realize it then. Even after I saw the bullet pock the plaster portion of the wall beneath the plate-glass window, I didn't understand what had happened, not until the Fifth Man's hood puffed out sharply.

The bullet had gone clear through the center of the Fifth Man's chest and the back of his chair before it hit the wall. Maybe he never actually understood what had just happened to him. Maybe he was too dead. Somewhere, seemingly far in the distance, Tiny let out a thin squeal.

The Fifth Man sat upright for a while, as if nothing had happened. Blood had soaked the front of his shirt and was beginning to saturate his jacket when he sucked the mask to his face for the last time. Suddenly it, too, filled with blood. Only then did he flop face first onto the boardroom table. His forehead struck with a dull thud. Blood spattered, then pooled around his face and flowed off the edge of the table.

After that thud, the room was filled with a deep silence. It seemed to take days before the silence was broken—by Tiny whimpering. "Don't shoot me, Norm, don't shoot me, Norm, please don't shoot me."

"I shot him because he didn't like the tape disposition, Tiny. But I won't shoot you because you think it's a good disposition, don't you?"

"Aw, Norm, I think it's the best damn disposition I've ever heard of in thirty years in the business."

"That's good, Tiny."

Tiny Archibald began to weep. His jowls, like fallen breasts, trembled with his weeping. "But, Norm, what am I going to do with him dead in the main conference room!"

"Well, that's another reason I'm not going to shoot you— so there's somebody left to clean up the mess. But stand by, there might be another one to go with him." Norm put his ear near the door and called, "Oh, Calabash . . . Hey, big guy . . ."

"Don't call me dat."

Norm turned around and grinned at Crystal and me. "Poor Bernie never had a prayer."

Bernie? His name was Bernie DiPietro?

"Calabash," called Norm.

"Yes?"

"The man who just came out the door—"

"Yes?"

"Is he there?"

"He tripped and hurt his neck."

Norm opened the door, and we went out into the hall. The last I saw of that room: Tiny, weeping, was trying to wipe up about a quart of blood with a Kleenex. Out the window behind him, the lights of Queens flickered in the far distance as if from an airplane.

LUSH LIFE

Bernie lay on his back perpendicular to the elevator door. His head was bent over his chest in a way no living man's could bend. I could see only the top of his head.

"Well," said Norm, "I guess this is good-bye." Then he hugged us, actually hugged us, first one, then the next.

After he hugged Calabash, Calabash said, "I don't want none of us to ever see you ever again, Norman."

"But what if the wife and I want to stop by Poor Joe Cay as visitors on our way around the world?"

"Dot's different. We always welcome visitors. But visitors got to mind their p's and q's on de Cay."

"I hear you, big guy."

25
•

I T'S NOT CLEAR to me how long we've been here
now. Nearly six weeks, I believe. One day flows seamlessly
into the next without event; yet each is rich and deeply
textured. At night the sky is cloudless and crystalline, the
Milky Way arcing over the world with a brightness un-
dreamed of in Manhattan. The sky is still cloudless when I
awake at dawn. About nine in the morning, every morning,
cumulus clouds pile to towering heights in the north and
west over Young Brother and Old Brother cays. The cot-
tony billows transform themselves into spectacular thun-
derheads. Their bottoms, close down on the sea, flatten,
blacken, and sheets of rain obliterate the Brothers, but it
seldom rains on Poor Joe Cay. If nothing more than the
march of weather ever took place, that would be enough
for me. Crystal feels the same way, we've discussed it, and
I'm certain I speak for Jellyroll.

We've taken a simple three-room pink bungalow with a
white tile roof. (Sadly, the hut on the beach that Jellyroll
and I stayed in last year, that I'd hoped to share with Crystal, is gone, blown away by Hurricane Carmen.) Owned by
another one of Calabash's uncles, named Lightbourne, the

pink house perches on a scimitar-shaped spit of land, a fragment from an ancient coral reef that, like the rest of these islands, emerged from the sea during the last Ice Age. A hundred yards beyond the house, the scimitar's point dips back beneath the surface. Lightbourne is a dedicated gardener. The house is surrounded by poinciana, frangipani, jacaranda, bottlebrush, coral trees, pitch apple, African tulips, kapok, papaya, about eight different kinds of palms, and other things I've only seen on the Discovery Channel.

Uncle Billy stays at the little hotel called the Pink Conch on the other end of Poor Joe Cay. It is owned by Calabash's uncle Angus. Uncle Billy goes grouper fishing with the young guys from Poor Joe and the Brothers, whom Calabash refers to as "the hardboys." They stay out on the shallow banks for days at a time, living on their own bait. He looks like a pirate. The hardboys call him Crazy Billy, but he loves it. I don't think he'll ever go back to Sheepshead Bay. I think he's out of the billiards business.

Crystal's body has grown burnished and sinewy, a source of almost constant arousal for me. She's seldom fully clothed in the house and, having grown used to nudity, she's sometimes surprised to find me coveting her, leering at her from across the living room. We live in sunshine and sexual torpor. We discuss matrimony in our spare time.

Jellyroll is turning feral. He has taken up fishing. For hours on end he stands at the point staring motionlessly at the multihued fish going about their ancient business below. Then suddenly he strikes, spearing his head into the water, snapping and growling atavistically. He's never successful as a fisher. Since the water is gin-clear, the fish he seeks are often swimming eight feet or more beneath the surface. That's a hard concept for a dog to grasp, but he never tires of fishing. He often swallows too much salt-water, and he turns away from the sea to throw it back up. Then he goes right back to fishing. Does this constitute retirement? Before we fled, I called his agent, Shelly, at an hour I knew he wouldn't be in. I left a message saying hold all calls, we were taking a trip. I said I'd call later to explain. I haven't yet.

If nothing happens here on Poor Joe Cay, much has happened at home. We didn't search out knowledge of events at home. We stumbled upon it. An unappetizing British ex-patriate named Drake—Crystal and I call him Lord Haw-haw—who wears the same grubby clothes every day and who always goes barefoot despite or because of a savage case of hammertoes, has the *New York Post* delivered every day to the little seashell bar in the Pink Conch Hotel. We read the front-page headlines over his shoulder:

ATTORNEY GENERAL DECLARED MISSING

When Haw-haw finished the paper, we borrowed it from him. He tried to look down Crystal's top as we read:

Matilda Laxley, wife of U.S. Attorney General Gerald Laxley, told Washington police that her husband had failed to return from an August 18 meeting in New York. Justice Department officials refused to confirm or deny knowledge of his whereabouts.

Attorney General Laxley had fallen under increasing criticism over allegations of conflict of interest in connection with certain failed savings and loan institutions in California and Florida. The President affirmed his continued support of Mr. Laxley.

Naw, we said, couldn't be, not the attorney general of the United States, he couldn't have been the Fifth Man.

Another coincidence. They happen all the time to anyone over the age of six.

Lord Haw-haw made self-satisfied noises about American violence. "That kind of thing happens every day on the streets of New York."

"What kind of thing?" I said.

"Mayhem."

"It doesn't say he was killed. It says he's missing."

"Isn't that where you're from? New York?"

Crystal and I trudged home, shed our clothes, and went swimming. Jellyroll went fishing.

Several days later we made the mistake of returning to the bar for some conch fritters and a rum swizzle. Lord Haw-haw was (still?) there, muttering smugly about Dodge City, USA. I'm no patriot, but I didn't want to hear that from some odiferous Brit with deformed digits, so I ignored him. But Lord Haw-haw wouldn't leave it alone. He edged nearer, dragging his gin along the bar, and said, "Heard the latest?"

"What latest?"

He spread the front page out in front of us:

CONCOM LINKED TO GUN BATTLE

Crystal and I must have gone simultaneously ashen, because Lord haw-haw blinked and said, "You know about—?"

"Of course not."

Crystal yanked the paper away from him:

AUGUST 28. In a hastily called news conference, police disclosed some details of the mysterious gun battle on New York's Upper West Side that left one officer wounded and two men dead. Police refused to identify the dead men except to say that they were the operators of a moving van police stopped for a minor traffic violation. Shooting ensued.

Police returned fire, killing the two men. In the rear of the van police found the body of free-lance journalist Chester Bream. Police refused comment as to the cause of Mr. Bream's death.

However, an exclusive source close to the investigation has told the *Post* that the word CONCOM was scrawled in blood on the walls of Mr. Bream's apartment.

We rode our bicycles to the Pink Conch bar every day, because every day something new happened. But now we were much more casual about our visits. Lord Haw-haw had taken to watching us read his paper with his right eyebrow arched suspiciously. I pretended to be a crossword-puzzle fan. . . .

SENATE CALLS FOR CONCOM SPECIAL PROSECUTOR

MRS. LAXLEY FEARS FOUL PLAY

GERALD LAXLEY PRESUMED DEAD

REGINALD ARCHIBALD LINKED TO CONCOM

REGINALD ARCHIBALD VANISHES

PSYCHOLOGIST: NATION DEPRESSED BY CORRUPTION

And every day after we read we'd go home for a naked swim in the sunset.

Tomorrow we go get the money, almost thirty-five-million-dollars' worth. I'm not certain of the wisdom of that move. What if some other Chet Bream manages to follow the money? But I have a feeling that thirty-five million is chump change in this business. And besides, Uncle Fergus and Calabash, who have set things up in Nassau, feel confident about their arrangements. They've gathered six fishing boats at the town dock for tomorrow's predawn departure. We sail to Eleuthera, where two twin Otters will airlift us to Nassau. We need that many boats and planes to accommodate the small force of hardboys recruited to throw a cordon of muscle around Crystal as she enters the bank in downtown Nassau, where Fergus's friends in high places have assured him there will be no questions asked.

Crystal and I have discussed that money at some length and agree that we don't want it, that it would poison our lives. Besides, we don't need it. However, we also agree that we have to get it. We can't just leave it. Crystal, particularly, feels we have an obligation to try to do something good with it. I like that idea in principle, but I'm still scared of that much hot money. I want to go swimming and afterward position myself between Crystal's thighs and forget the whole thing. But I can't. We're going after the money.

What are we going to do with it? Certainly our hosts deserve a good chunk for their help, and there are many things that need doing here on Poor Joe. Beyond that, we've talked about setting up some kind of charitable trust. One thinks $34.8 million is big bucks until one starts thinking about something "good" to do with it. It goes fast.

Neither of us knows anything about the machinery of charitable trusts. Nor do we know anyone qualified or honest enough to run one. We certainly can't be directly involved, as I constantly stress. I think Crystal is getting sick of me constantly stressing that, but I'm frightened. We finally have what I wanted from the outset—a romantic relationship with nothing to fuck us up. Sure, we had to flee to a tiny island to have it, but that's cool. At least we have it now, and this is a lovely little island on which to have it.

We have to go home someday, though I know that will

depress Jellyroll and me deeply. This is not our home. We know we can't stay forever. If we tried, we'd end up like Lord Haw-haw. No, our relationship has to be able to travel, otherwise it's just a summertime thing.

However, right now, I can't wait for the Nassau trip to be over, to return to Poor Joe Cay, where—when Crystal is swimming in the sea—I'm the best pool player on the island. That can't be said of the island Manhattan.